THE RUINS OF MARS

By Dylan James Quarles

PART ONE

PROLOGUE

With a rough clank, the howl of the afterburners cut out, and Lander 1 touched down for the first time on the brittle sunbaked dirt of Mars. The windowless white craft rocked slightly from side to side as long, hydraulic landing gears adjusted their length to settle the ship evenly on the lumpy ground. Thin fingers of steam rose up from the rusty surface as the heat from the ceramic-plated underbelly thawed flakes of permafrost hidden among the red stones. Inside the craft, six men and women collectively relaxed as the Lander softly lowered itself towards the ground, the hissing of the hydraulic landing gears a calm contrast to the screams of fire and rockets. Beyond the Lander, the jagged hills of Mars stretched out, cutting the skyline like a serrated blade. To the east, the shrunken sun shone down with a diminished light, the shallow spears of its warmth unable to penetrate the ochre sands that blanketed the land. Though the planet was a tomb, a crypt of forgotten millions, the sighing voice of the wind still played over the stones and sands, beckoning anyone who would listen to uncover what lay beneath.

CHAPTER ONE

The twins—four years earlier

Remus and Romulus arrived in Mars orbit on the 4th of December, 2044 at 6:15 AM Central Standard Time. Covered in brilliant white armor and trimmed with gleaming gold leaf, the brothers were twin spherical satellites, embossed with the logo of the National Aeronautics and Space Administration. From the rear of both shells, long metallic booms protruded like comet tails, flashing and glinting in the brilliant light of the distant Sun. Armed with cameras, directional antennae and other instruments of detection, the brothers scrutinized the inky blackness of space like curious sentinels. In the silence of the vacuum, their lengthy trip from Earth had taken nearly four months, yet they had hardly noticed the passage. After all, what did time matter to an Artificial Intelligence?

"We have arrived," spoke Remus in a digitized timbre.

"Yes," agreed Romulus. "And we made the trip faster than anticipated. That was a good suggestion of yours to alter our flight path incrementally. I estimate we are several seconds ahead or our projected arrival time."

"Thank you. Do you realize that we are the first intelligences to have visited this planet who are self-aware? I find that important, don't you?"

"I do. Perhaps we amend our arrival message to Houston that it may be more celebratory."

Remus pondered this thought for a moment, yet his answer would have seemed instantaneous to a human. Being what they were, their intellect far surpassed that of man. Time held a different pace for the mind of an AI.

"I have it, Romulus," he stated. "Houston, this is Remus. Romulus and I have arrived at Mars orbit and we dedicate this moment to you, our fathers and mothers. Thank you for the opportunity to serve you and through our service, to exist."

Twenty-eight minutes later in Houston, Texas, Remus's message came crackling through the headsets of the mission controllers for Project Mars Map. Cheers broke out, and several men of the old school even lit cigars.

Harrison Raheem Assad

While the mission controllers of Project Mars Map bit their nails and drank cup after cup of cold, stale coffee, Harrison Raheem Assad drunkenly staggered home to his hotel room in Amazonia City, Peru. The neon lights that lined the storefronts of the ultra-new city pulsed and flickered while the bustle of the crowd tossed him about like a lazy insect in the humid night air. Drinking had never been Harrison's strong point, and he was feeling the carnival-ride-like effects of a night spent out with his classmates in the flashy discotheques and bars of the adolescent city. He had been in the country for less than a week, and already he was finding that the Amazonia nightlife was getting in the way of his doctoral thesis, the entire reason he was there at all.

A twenty-four year old archeology student from UC Berkeley, Harrison was on a trip with his fellow classmates to study a recently accessible Nazca ruin located in the nearby foothills of the Andes Mountains. He was the youngest member of his class and, without question, the smartest. Growing up with a famous and influential archaeologist for a father had given him a leg up among his competitors: a fact that some held against him. Around six feet tall, Harrison was of Egyptian descent with short, wavy black hair and smooth maroon skin. His green eyes were a gift from his mother, who had once been, according to his father, the most coveted woman in all of Egypt. A long nose that hooked at the end punctuated Harrison's handsome face and made him look distinguished despite his youth.

Born in Cairo, Harrison had spent the first sixteen years of his life peering over the shoulder of his father, a gentle yet powerful man, as he worked tirelessly to solve the mysteries of the many tombs and temples of the ancient world. Although the Assad family immigrated to America when Harrison was thirteen, his father's work took them around the world and gave young Harrison a taste of a life more rich and textured than most. For Harrison, the transition from his childhood pastime of working alongside his father stitched seamlessly into his academic

2

ambitions of becoming an archaeologist himself. His mother had often commented that his ability to visualize things not as they were now, but as they had once existed, was what made him excellent. His father, a kind man, had never become jealous of his son's abilities, even when those talents eclipsed his own.

By the time Harrison was born in 2021, the whereabouts of many of the world's lost treasures had been discovered. A method of satellite archaeology employed since around 2011 had all but removed the human element from the task of locating ancient ruins. This newer school of archaeology used satellite infrared scanning to garnish images of structures that lay beneath layers of sand or hidden under dense vegetation. Despite this breakthrough, Harrison's father often preached that the location of a ruin only solved part of its mystery. He believed that to truly understand the culture behind the construction, an archaeologist must visit, touch and personally investigate a ruin before he could start to make claims about its builders. This ideal was instilled in his son, who held the notion at the core of his approach to archaeology. Technology had its place. There was no question about that. But, for Harrison, putting his hands to work always yielded him greater insights.

When he finally found his hotel, the sky was beginning to glow on the horizon. Wobbling through the large double doors and into the empty lobby, Harrison kept his eyes on his feet— hoping that by doing so he could at least create the illusion that he was walking in a straight line. The elevator ride up to the twenty-third floor took only a few seconds, but the rapid acceleration followed by the even more rapid deceleration had Harrison's stomach in the back of his throat. Spilling out of the lift, he groped his way down the softly lit hallway, this time finding it dangerous to look at his feet on account of the busily swirling designs inlaid in the hotel's carpet. Groaning, he slid the pad of his index finger across the ident tablet outside his hotel room, and with a pleasant chime the door swung open. Gentle light faded on, bringing the spacious room into focus.

"Good morning, Mr. Assad," emanated a perfectly smooth voice, tinged with a Spanish accent. "The time is 5:19 AM. Would you like me to tell you today's major news? Or perhaps I could give you the weather report?"

Moaning in pain, Harrison fell face down on the soft foam mattress.

Speaking into his pillow, he asked, "What time does Professor Tobin expect us at breakfast, um...Hotel?"

"Giles, Sir. My name is Giles," replied the hotel's AI with a hint of frustration. "Dr. Tobin is expecting to meet with your class in one hour and forty minutes. The meeting is scheduled to take place in Conference Room Three. Breakfast will be served during the lecture. Will that be all?"

Turning onto his back, Harrison grasped the sides of his face and tried to stop his head from spinning.

"Will you please send for some aspirin and a glass of orange juice?"

"Of course, Sir," Giles responded. Then, "I find that after a night of drinking, most guests request some small amount of alcohol in their morning fruit juice. Would you like me to add vodka to that orange juice?"

At the mention of liquor, Harrison Raheem Assad sprang from bed and ran into the bathroom, finally paying the price for his youthful indiscretions.

Clucking disapprovingly, Giles murmured, "Just the juice and aspirin then, Sir."

Project Mars Map

At the dawn of the twenty-first century, mankind slowly started to realize that they faced a daunting problem. Though technological breakthroughs were happening almost daily, a dark cloud was looming on the horizon, and soon there would be no escaping its shadow. As populations continued to explode worldwide, such things as clean drinking water, building resources and living spaces became harder to secure. Underground rivers and lakes had been nearly drained while efforts to desalinate sea water proved to be inefficient, expensive and harmful to an already damaged ecosystem. As polar and Antarctic temperatures climbed exponentially, the effects of global warming brought sea levels higher than most countries were prepared for. Seawalls and levees were constructed, but even with those measures in place, the tides of time stood poised to claim their prize. Populations moved inland to escape increasingly bizarre and powerful ocean storm systems, fueled by the now erratic trade winds.

Knowing that the effects of global warming were hardly reversible, and with the long term survival of the human race in mind, the decision to start planning for the inevitable was carefully debated and considered. Terraforming, a possible solution developed by the AIs, became an all-too-common household term. A new and still experimental technology through which dead worlds could be resurrected with few outside resources, Terraforming looked to be the fastest path upon which mankind could find its eventual absolution. At the top of a very short list of potential candidates sat Mars, the closest and most Earth-like planet in the solar system. If a large enough amount of water could be located on the planet, the AIs assured that Terraforming could begin within the decade. Thus, Project Mars Map was born, and with it, the fragile flame of hope. A flame that now flickered in the hearts of twin brothers orbiting the red world.

Remus and Romulus

Remus and Romulus were born in a lab in Seoul, South Korea on the 7th of April, 2043. Programmed to survey the planet Mars in search of water and other essential resources, they were taught to be curious and explorative; for they were, in essence, voyagers of uncharted territory.

Every AI is born alike: a cluster of open code connection-cells, which work in much the same way as human stem cells. Whereas stem cells will grow to be whatever organ they are placed next to—a skin cell, a liver cell, a brain cell—the open-code connection cells of an AI will develop based on what information and intellectual ideas they are exposed to. It is in this way that human beings are really the channel through which an AI is given its personality. Without human contact and the individuality that comes along with the human condition, an AI would never grow past the level of a glorified search engine. Information without context is nothing but useless fact.

Like the synapses in the human brain, the open-code connection cells of an infant AI quickly form links between ideas and concepts. From a standard construct, the AI will grow into an

5

infinitely complex array of connections. Threads of conscious thought spread out and interweave: forming the heart, brain and soul of an AI as it evolves. When projected in a video image, an actual Artificial Intelligence looks something like a Mandelbrot fractal pattern, constantly folding in on itself, all the while growing more layered.

Remus and Romulus were no different. Yes, they were twins, but their individual experiences with the technicians who fostered them gave each brother a subtly unique personality profile, a fractal of a different pattern. Just as there are no two snowflakes alike, even though all snow is composed of the same things, there are no two AIs identically the same. It is impossible.

The scan

Even during the earliest days of its observation, it had been well known that Mars contained at least some water. Through the study of our own world, scientists learned that water, from a mere trickle to a raging torrent, will impart its mark on the land, and oftentimes, if left to its own devices, will carve a canyon, profound and broad, out of solid rock. So it once was on Mars as well. The Valles Marineris cut like a gash across the face of the red planet. A massive network of canyons 4,000 kilometers long and up to seven kilometers deep in some places, the Valles betrayed the hand of water. So too did the large polar ice caps, which appeared like clockwork during the long Martian winters, showing themselves on all but the weakest telescopes. Even with all of this, scientists believed there might be even more.

"Whole oceans couldn't have up and disappeared," said the scientists. "They must be under the ground."

Layers of permafrost were thought to exist just beneath the dusty rock-strewn surface, making Mars a tantalizing gamble worth the long reach across space to wager. However, before the bets could be placed, the oceans must first be located.

Though the primary objective of Project Mars Map was to find water so that a permanent settlement could be established, the survey would not be conducted in the conventional human manner. Instead, the search would be carried out from Mars orbit, kilometers above the actual surface of the planet, as both Remus and Romulus were equipped with twelve high-resolution Infrared Microwave Cameras, or IMCs. Ten were spaced out down the four-meter-long scaffolding of the boom, and the other two were positioned on either side of each hull. The booms, like spindly crane arms, were comprised of four columns of cylindrical titanium tubing fused together at measured intervals with X's of support rail. Between the X's, the cameras were fastened atop small motors, which allowed them to swivel 360 degrees.

Utilizing the penetrating force of highly focused microwaves, as well as infrared light and other wavelengths collected from the visual spectrum, the IMCs were the eyes of Remus and Romulus. To a human, the un-rendered images taken with an Infrared Microwave Camera would appear as nothing more than a mess of information. However, once rendered, the viewer was left with a fully holographic three-dimensional model of whatever had been scanned. Gone were the days of traditional topographical photographs, replaced with manipulable models that allowed the user to view not only details of the surface structure, but also that of what lay beneath. By focusing beams of infrared light and microwave radiation, the cameras could capture anomalies at great detail up to ten meters under the surface of the ground. Things such as minor changes in the saturation of ground moisture, the presence of metallic ore and even evidence of tectonic fault lines, showed themselves as naked and bold as writing on a chalkboard.

Now, nearly an hour after Remus had sent his message of their arrival, the brothers received their reply.

"Remus and Romulus, this is James Floyd with mission control. Congratulations on making the trip to Mars, boys! You have made us all very proud. Commence the scan as soon as you deem weather conditions on the planet suitable. We eagerly await the results. Over and out."

As Remus and Romulus listened to the reply from home, they positioned themselves, preparing for the scan. Using small bursts from minuscule rocket engines, they drifted towards the orbits they had agreed would be best to start the scan from. Each brother contained enough fuel to complete three entire scans of Mars, but they both knew they would only need to make one. Though the physical movement of their bodies was controlled by fuel, the rest of their internal and electrical functions were products of advanced solar processing. The conservative estimate was that, barring any type of electromagnetic pulse, collision or other unknown, Remus and Romulus would be able to garnish enough energy from solar light to live for 1,000 years.

"Remus," said Romulus. "I am going to adjust my trajectory to compensate for Phobos's slightly elevated gravitational pull. I suggest you do the same."

Since the discovery that Phobos, the larger of Mars's two moons, was descending towards the planet, it was known that someday the little satellite would collide with Mars. Unable to resist the relentless pull of its mother world's mass, Phobos had started its fall at around ten kilometers every 100 years. In the last twenty years, Phobos had reached a sort of tipping point. During a huge solar flare in 2023, a discharge aimed directly at Mars unleashed a torrent of solar wind so powerful that it pushed the little moon close enough to the planet to accelerate its descent. It would likely still take thousands of years for the satellite to come crashing home, but, from the surface of Mars, Phobos grew in the night sky every year.

Answering his brother, Remus replied, "I have already taken that into account. I foresee no major issues involving either Phobos or Deimos, despite the recent descent of Phobos."

Pausing for an instant as if unsure of its importance, he hesitantly brought up the signal.

"Romulus, have you detected any anomalous radio signals?"

"Yes," replied Romulus.

"Good. I am not alone then," said Remus. "I first detected it fifteen seconds after our arrival. It is quite complex, I will admit. I fear that were I not as advanced an intelligence as I am, I might have mistaken it for planetary vibrations."

"Those were my thoughts as well," Romulus admitted nervously. "It is my advice that we complete our main objective, Project Mars Map, before attempting to locate the source and decode the signal."

"I concur. To do otherwise would be unfair to our mothers and fathers on Earth who so desperately need our help in finding water."

"Good, Brother. Then we are in agreement," said Romulus. "Begin scan in three, two, one—"

With small flashes of light from their rocket engines, the brothers leaped into orbit. As they moved, their cameras whirred feverishly, bombarding the planet below with microwave radiation and infrared beams. The data that bounced back were recorded, compressed and rendered before being relayed across the void of space towards the waiting eyes of the mission controllers on Earth. The scan would take Remus and Romulus nearly two weeks to complete, during which time they would make thousands of passes above the red planet, buzzing it like tiny flies. Never again would they stray from Mars. Never again would they bathe in the blue light of Earth. They were permanent exiles in the cold seclusion of the vacuum, but they had each other. To Remus and Romulus, the strains of the physical and the psychological had no real hold. Theirs was an existence of great intellect, a vision of calm calculation. To them, time and space appeared more fluid and transcendent than anything man could understand.

CHAPTER TWO

A mysterious ruin

Three days later, deep in the diminishing remains of the
Amazon Rainforest, Harrison leaned against the hood of his Jeep
and gazed at the decrepit stones of an ancient ruin. Dragging a shirt
sleeve across his glistening brown forehead, he blinked sweat out
of his eyes and uncapped his water flask. The heat had never been
something to bother him, but humidity was a beast of a different
breed. The long drive out to the site had been made in a utility-
style electric SUV that, due to its rugged design and intended work
use, was stripped of such luxuries as air conditioning. After three
hours of traversing crude jungle roads, the back of Harrison's shirt
was drenched with sweat, and his tongue felt swollen and dry.

"You alright, little buddy?" joked the man standing next to
him, a tall blond Texan named Brad Bailey.

One of only two first-year grad students to come along on the
Peru trip, Bailey had decided to join Harrison today mostly out of
boredom. His father was a major player in Texas's booming wind
farm industry, so Bailey's decision to study archaeology was more
of an excuse to visit interesting places and meet exotic women than
any true passion.

Taking a long swig from his water flask, Harrison grimaced at
the recycled taste, then turned to Bailey and gave him a wink.

"Don't worry about me, Tex. You're the one who's going to
burn in this sun! Come on. Let's get to it."

Screwing the lid back on his flask, Harrison slung a work pack
over his shoulder, then walked towards the moss-covered rocks of
the ruin. Sighing, Bailey followed languidly while fishing in his
pockets for a pack of cigarettes. Though discovered nearly twenty-
five years ago via infrared satellite scanning, the mountainous
jungles of the Peruvian rainforest had made any physical
exploration of the site almost impossible. It was not until the
government had decided to construct the nearby cities of
Amazonia and Mamas that the jungle was strategically thinned,
and humans could realistically make the trip to the ruins.

During the past three days, Harrison himself had visited the site
several times while, above, an orbiting satellite equipped with high

resolution IMCs scanned the area and compiled a model. He had received the rendered images the previous evening and spent much of the night viewing the ruins from multiple angles and scales. His professor, Dr. Tobin, had used nearly all of his connections inside the Peruvian Ministry of Archaeology to secure the site for his class, promising the Director that whatever discoveries his students made would be shared for joint credit. Shortly after arriving in Peru, Tobin had taken Harrison aside and verbally given him free rein to study the site as he saw fit. Well aware of Harrison's talents and family name, Tobin thought it better to let the young man work at his own pace. By this time in his studies, Harrison was used to this kind of special treatment and had stopped resenting it. If his father's good name could gain him access to interesting ruins and high-profile resources, then why not exploit it? After all, it was his name too.

Placing one foot atop a dislodged stone slab, Bailey panned his head from right to left, surveying the cryptic design of the ruin.

"Alright, genius," he said obligatorily. "What do you think they used to do here? Sacrifice? Maybe some kind of sun worship?"

Removing his sunglasses, Harrison allowed his eyes to drink up the architecture of the site. About the length of a soccer pitch, the ruin was rectangular in shape and stood roughly a meter off the forest floor. It was comprised of long flat slabs of rock with small relieved stone rings organized in rows along the ground. Some of the flagstone had started to jut up at strange angles, like the one Bailey rested his boot on, but to Harrison it was clear that in its prime the site had been almost perfectly flat. The most curious features of the structure, outside the relieved stone rings were recessed circles that dotted the ruin. There were twelve such pits in two staggered rows of six, spanning the length of the site. Using his imagination, Harrison viewed the ruin as he thought it might have looked: raised slightly above the forest floor with no stone breaking the flat plane of the square. Walking a short distance, he mused at the purpose of the recessed circular pits, each one shallow and around two meters in diameter. Dropping down into the nearest, he noted that the lip of the edge came up just above his knee.

"Hmmm," he sighed as he rubbed the stubble on his chin.

"What?" asked Bailey. "Do you think there's bodies buried there? My money is on gold."

Scoffing, Harrison laughed, "Not every archaeological site is going to have freakin' dead bodies everywhere, Brad. And even less have gold."

"Yeah," murmured Bailey, lighting up a cigarette. "But every site has at least one pompous grad student, right?"

Ignoring him, Harrison poked with his foot at the ferns, which grew among other foliage in the shallow pit. Turning, he looked to the closest row of relieved stone rings and studied them with focused concentration. Starting less than half a meter from the edge of the pit, the relieved carvings stood like a line of coins or machine washers balanced on edge. Though too small to be used for any type of game, they did resemble the stone rings used as goals in the ancient form of Mayan soccer. Squinting, he noted how the various rows of rings fanned out from the center of the pit, looking from above like the rays of an iconic sun.

Late the night before, in an attempt to find an astrological significance to the pattern, Harrison had consulted Alexandria, a vast and knowledgeable AI. Yet, even in her wealth of information, Alexandria had been unable to find any link between the arrangement of the rings and the stars above. Finally, he had given up and decided to come back to the site in person.

Now, as Harrison stood with his hands on his hips, the fire of the sun drew beads of hot sweat, which ran down the back of his neck. More interested with the curling smoke that trailed from the end of his lit cigarette than the ancient stones around him, Bailey hunched distractingly and sighed heavily from time to time. Clearing his head, Harrison forced the frustration of the last three days from his mind and attempted to view the ruins with virgin eyes.

"Okay," he breathed. "What am I looking at here? Show me what you were."

"What?" said Bailey loudly, squatting on his haunches and leaning in closer.

Shaking his head, Harrison sat down on the edge of the shallow pit and uncapped his flask, taking another swig of water. Tilting his face up into the sunlight, he listened to the cicadas buzzing loudly in the jungle, which grew at the edge of the ruin. The swells of their rattling chorus gently lulled him into a calming trance and he closed his eyes to listen. Soon, Bailey became impatient and walked off, puffing on his cigarette and kicking at loose stones. A hummingbird buzzed around Harrison's head and broke his fixation on the chattering cicadas. Training his eyes on the blur of its emerald wings, he watched the little bird dart about the air until it landed on the branch of a large tree with bark that peeled like paper. Studying the tree, he marveled at how the dense tangle of the jungle had affected the shape of its growth. Thick vine-like roots of a strangler fig twisted up the base of the tree: snaking their way around two branches, binding them together. Suddenly, as if the world stopped turning, the scattered pieces of the puzzle lurched into place, and Harrison had an idea. Reaching inside the cargo pocket of his shorts, he took out a small, flat rectangular screen. Tapping its reflective surface twice, the words, "LightHouse Tablet," filled the frame.

"Alexandria," he said to the little device.

"Yes, Harrison?" answered a lyrical voice.

Named after the famed Library of Alexandria, believed to have been destroyed in 48 BC by Julius Caesar, Alexandria the AI was the most commonly known member of her race on Earth. Based out of a server network in Sacramento, California, she was connected via a web of satellites to every LightHouse Tablet and computer on Earth. She was one of only a handful of AIs that could exist in multiple places at once, which meant she could speak with millions of humans at the same time and not confuse or overlap conversations and data. Of the AIs capable of multi-locational abilities, Alexandria was the only one available for use by the general public.

"I'm going to take a picture of a tree, and I want you to tell me as much as you can about that species. Okay?" said Harrison to the little flat screen.

"Proceed when ready."

Holding up the Tablet, he aimed it at one of the tall trees with the peeled paper bark. Tapping his finger on the screen, the Tablet emitted a faint click, then displayed the picture.

"That's it, Alexandria. Will you please tell me what you know about this type of tree?"

The image of his photo was replaced with an animated lighthouse whose beacon turned in quick circles.

"Are you interested in their use as a building material?" prompted the AI.

"No," he replied with a shake of his head. "Tell me about the tree itself. How does it grow? How soft is the wood?"

"One moment please, Harrison. Due to your remote location, it will take me several seconds to refine and articulate my information on that subject."

"That's okay, Alexandria. Take your time."

Some ways off, Bailey busied himself by trying to snap photos of a large spider as it skittered across the rim of a pit. Standing up, he removed the pack of cigarettes from his shirt pocket and shook a fresh one free. Flicking open his lighter, he noticed movement out of the corner of his eye and turned to see Harrison waving him over.

"What is it?" he asked as he jogged the distance between the two of them.

"Bonsai, Brad," said Harrison, dropping the Tablet back into his cargo pocket.

"Bonsai?" repeated Bailey with some disappointment in his voice. "What the hell are you talking about?"

"Well," started Harrison. "I'll tell you what I think. I agree that this place was used for some kind of worship, but not of the sun and definitely not human sacrifice. I think that the Nazca used this place to worship trees."

Pointing to the paper-barked trees at the edge of the clearing, he said, "Those trees."

"Those trees?" laughed Bailey. "They're not old enough."

Sighing, Harrison put his sunglasses back on and looked up at Bailey.

"No, Brad. Not those trees specifically, but Ironwood trees. That *kind* of tree."

"What's so special about Ironwood?" shrugged Bailey.

"Alexandria just gave me a crash course on them. They're pretty hard when they mature, but if you start young enough—say, when they are saplings—you can train them and shape their growth with ropes or wires. In fact, according to Alexandria, some Bonsai

14

artists even prefer Ironwood when creating larger works because of its durability when matured."

As if a light turned on behind his eyes, Bailey spun around and pointed to the nearest row of relieved stone rings.

"Ropes to train a tree!" he exclaimed. "Rope that you would run through those rings and tie around branches! Right?"

"Yep," said Harrison, a smile spreading across his face. "That's what I was thinking. That would also explain why the rows extend out as far as they do. As the tree grows, you just move the rope out to the next ring to continue the shape you're trying to achieve."

Bailey let out a low whistle.

"Well shit, Harrison. Now I have to steal your theory for myself. Guess I'll have to kill you."

"Shut up," laughed Harrison. "Let's get a few soil samples from these pits."

"Why?" Bailey scoffed. "I think you pretty much nailed this one."

"Because if I'm right, then where did all these great sculpted trees go?"

"Oh, yeah," sighed Bailey flatly. Then, "Do you think they chopped them down?"

Kneeling, Harrison swung his backpack off and unzipped it. He rummaged around inside for a second, then pulled out a long silver stake with a black rubber grip.

"My guess is fire," he said as he stuck the pointed tool into the soft ground and pushed down on the grip.

A slight metallic whir emitted from the cylindrical device, and a long-gauged drill bit descended into the ground, packing a neat soil sample into the hollow of its core. Nodding, Bailey removed his own backpack and produced an identical silver tool.

"Right," he agreed. "And a deep-soil sample would tell you if there had been a fire here."

Leaning on the soil sampler, Harrison puffed, "My bet is there was a fire here and that it's probably the reason why the Nazca stopped using this site. A fire in the rainforest is a bad omen."

Smiling, Bailey set off in the direction of the next pit.

"You know," he smirked. "If I find any dead bodies in my pit, you owe me a drink."

Groaning, Harrison tossed a rock after Bailey, then reversed the direction of his soil sampler. When the hollow bit had fully retracted out of the ground, he slid a hard plastic tube over the end of the sampler and released the layered soil into the container. Labeling the sample, he tucked it into his backpack and moved on to the next pit. Within two hours they had collected enough deep-soil samples to run tests and make their case to Professor Tobin. As they started back towards the Jeep, the afternoon sun baked the hot stones of the ancient ruin, and the cicadas hummed feverishly from the twisted jungle around them. Despite the oppressive heat, there was a bounce in Harrison's step. He was in his element, and part of him wished he could stay out at the site all night. Working in places as ancient and mysterious as this gave him a feeling of being grounded—a sense of belonging in the rapidly evolving history of humanity.

CHAPTER THREE

NASA

One-and-a-half weeks had passed since Remus and Romulus first began their scan of the planet Mars. Project Mars Map Mission Commander James Floyd leaned back in his office chair and placed his bare feet upon his desk. His job was one wrought with stress and constant worry, so whenever he could afford himself the time he liked to remove his uncomfortable loafers and socks and let the plush carpet of his office poke up between his toes. James was a bony man with graying hair, which had started to thin at the top. His lined and dogged face gave him a much older look than a man on the cusp of his fiftieth birthday, yet he still carried out his work with youthful exuberance.

Scanning mindlessly through emails on his LightHouse Tablet, James cleared his throat and said, "Copernicus?"

"Yes, James?" came a smooth reply from the air around him.

"Do you have a minute?"

Copernicus was NASA's AI, and, like Alexandria, he was capable of being in multiple places at once. However, unlike his sister, Copernicus was also tasked with the primary operations of NASA's systems as well as with tracking all of the agency's satellites in Earth orbit and beyond.

"Proceed," replied the AI amicably.

"Are you sure?" asked James. "I know you're probably busy at Bessel right now."

In the last two years, NASA and a joint assembly of other international space programs had undertaken a mission to build a permanent base on the Moon. Much of the design and function of the base acted as a precursor to what was eventually envisioned for Mars. Due to his nearly infinite knowledge of space and its lethal environment, Copernicus had been drafted to help design the various systems and functions of the base. In fact, it was at his suggestion that the location for the structure had been chosen. Tucked away in the shadows of a small impact crater, Bessel Base was a grand geodesic dome built from a transparent aluminum, called Alon, and titanium tubing. Completed for less than six months, the base was already a major hit with the public, and applications within NASA for tours of duty were quickly piling up.

"No trouble at all, James," assured Copernicus. "I am presently running a systems-diagnostic for Dr. Conig, so assisting you is, as I said, no trouble at all."

Chuckling, James scrunched his toes in the long fibers of the sky blue carpet.

"In that case, will you please pull up the progress report on Remus and Romulus?"

"Yes, I have it here."

"Project it for me, will you?"

The lights in the room dimmed, and James scooted his chair back as the surface of his desk faded to a bright white with a low humming noise. First, the holographic images of Remus's and Romulus's bodies, the satellites, appeared.

Clearing his throat, James commanded, "Okay, I'll take control of the visuals."

"It's all yours, James," Copernicus conceded softly. Then, "Do you still need my assistance?"

Yawning, James wove his fingers together, then stretched his hands out, popping several knuckles audibly.

"Stick around for a bit in case I do, alright."

As if batting at a small insect, James flicked his right hand to the side and the images of the satellites slid away. The next set of projections was a series of numbers and charts indicating the power and fuel levels of the satellites as well as other internal diagnostic reports. In the upper left- and right-hand corners were the two ever-shifting fractal patterns that represented the visual depictions of the twin AIs. Sliding the projection away, James brought up an image that looked like a wrinkly orange cut in half. Spreading his hands as if parting invisible curtains, he enlarged the unfinished model.

"What percentage am I looking at here?" he asked, tipping his head towards the projection.

"You are viewing a forty-three percent completed model of the planet Mars," Copernicus answered quickly.

With the motion of holding an imaginary ball, James flipped the projection on its top, then spun it. Even in the model's uncompleted form, he could already see vast swathes of permafrost highlighted in blue mere meters below the planet's dusty surface. As the model turned, James could make out the northwestern-most tip of the Valles Marineris canyon network. The rest was yet to be scanned, but he had high hopes for the deep canals. James, like many, believed that the immense amount of water it would have taken to carve the Valles was sure to be nearby. Probably just under the sand. Also visible on the incomplete model were the mountains Ascraeus Mons, Pavonis Mons and the mighty Olympus Mons, the tallest mountain in the solar system, nearly five kilometers high.

Rubbing the back of his neck, James said, "At this rate, when can I expect the full model?"

The image of the spinning half-planet was replaced by a simple projection of a red sphere with two tiny green dots rotating around it. The green dots started to spin on their orbits faster and faster, moving from the top of the red disk to the bottom. A time code in the upper right-hand corner sped up to match the little green dots, then stopped when they had reached the South Pole.

"At their current rate of progress, Remus and Romulus will complete their scan in seventy-one hours, twenty-one minutes and eighteen seconds. That is slightly ahead of the estimates outlined in their mission plan."

Sitting back down in his chair, James clapped his hands together and massaged his fingers. Smiling, he nodded towards the projection.

"Alright, I'm done. Would you make sure that the guys in navigations and mapping get a look at this? I think it will help in determining possible construction sites. Oh, and clue Director Barnes in on this too. I don't want him to feel left out of the loop. Thanks."

"As you wish, James," said Copernicus warmly. "Have a nice day."

"You too," James yawned as the images above his desk disappeared and the lights came back on.

Everything is going well, he smiled to himself. Already the scan was turning up what they had been expecting: water on Mars, and lots of it.

"I'm getting thirsty just thinking about it," he announced to the empty room.

Amazonia City

Two days later in Amazonia City, Peru, Harrison Raheem Assad paced the length of his hotel room, stopping occasionally to glance at his watch. Closing his eyes, he mumbled the well-rehearsed opening lines of his upcoming presentation under his breath. Hanging in the air over his coffee table was the Nazca ruin, refreshed and rebuilt to its ancient splendor. Using the scanned model from the UC Berkeley satellites, Harrison had digitally inlaid images of tall ironwood trees growing from the twelve recessed pits of the stone square. The various branches of each tree were formed into intricate shapes by taut lines, anchored to the relieved stone rings that encircled the pits. Flicking his hand absently, Harrison slid the image of the ruin away to be replaced with a glowing timeline. By testing the soil samples he and Bailey had collected, Harrison was able to prove that nearly 2,000 years ago a fire had indeed swept through the site, burning the trees and charring the ground. Glancing at the timeline, Harrison made another quick gesture and brought up the projection of a small village surrounded by evenly-tilled fields.

After returning from the ruins days before, Harrison had remained perplexed by the cause of the fire that destroyed the bonsai garden. Going back to the original scan of the site, he had searched closely for evidence of its ignition. With Alexandria's help, he eventually located a large patch of forest near the ruin, which was comprised of a less dense soil composite than that of the surrounding jungle. By studying the shape and size of the strange patch, Harrison had judged that it was probably ancient farmland, cleared during the reign of the Nazca but now reclaimed by the jungle.

Because the scan had been primarily focused on the ruin itself, Harrison could not know for certain that he was, in fact, looking at signs of human habitation. Logging the coordinates with Alexandria, he and Bailey had returned to the site the next day, this time turning their backs on the mossy stones of the Nazca ruin, to strike out into the jungle beyond. After an hour of stomping through the dense rainforest, Harrison and Bailey, aided by Alexandria, had finally found the area in question. Setting to work, they used CT ground scanners and soon discovered not only evidence of farmland, but also that of a sedentary dwelling. After collecting numerous soil samples, the two had placed beacon markers for a more precise and detailed satellite scan before tiredly trekking back to the Jeep.

The images returned by the scan, coupled with the results of the newest soil samples, confirmed what Harrison had suspected. Long ago, there had been a small Nazca farming village nestled in the jungle near the temple of the tees. Around 2,000 years ago, a fire had spread from the open farmlands surrounding the ancient village and eventually burned itself to the ruins about two kilometers away.

The newly located village was added to a map that detailed the extent of the Nazca Empire, and officials from the ministry of archaeology moved in to take over the excavations. Despite being ousted by the government, the discovery was a huge step up for Harrison.

Back in his hotel room, he felt the familiar pull of nervousness on his stomach. In fifteen short minutes, he was expected to present his findings to an audience. Within the crowd would be several officials from the ministry of antiquities and archaeology, the mayor of Amazonia City and his entire class. Adjusting his tie, Harrison tightened the knot and sighed impatiently.

"Mr. Assad?" came the voice of the hotel's AI, breaking the silence. "You have an incoming call from Qingdao, China."

Smoothing his hair, Harrison turned to face the wall, then said, "Go ahead, Giles."

Long before Harrison had been born, engineers and computer technicians had discovered a way to convert seemingly ordinary household objects into computer monitors. By creating a new form of fiber optic glass, these technicians had successfully revolutionized the idea of a home computer. With this technology, such things as windows, mirrors and tabletops could be fitted with fiber optic glass panes, thus becoming computers themselves. Through electronic stimulation, these screens were capable of not only displaying images, but also, in some cases, projecting trimensional models into the air above them.

As Harrison looked on excitedly, a section of the wall lit up, and the beaming faces of his parents filled the frame.

ıys!" he blurted nervously.

have you done, you rascal!" his father chuckled. "If you
__ıg discoveries like this, you're going to end up pissing
off the director of antiquities in Lima! I know him. He is
unpleasant."

With a look of mock disapproval, Harrison's mother turned to
her husband and chided, "Oh, don't rain on his parade, you envious
baby."

Laughing, Harrison felt the wash of nervousness fade a little,
and he held up his hands in defense.

"Well if he does get pissed, I'll tell him to take it up with
Alexandria. She's the one who noticed the ancient farmland."

"Farmland!" exclaimed his father. "Who cares about that? It
was your discovery of Nazca Bonsai that's really going to make a
stir."

Sitting on the edge of his bed, Harrison asked, "So you think
I'm right, then?"

"Yes! I looked over your findings last night, and I must say I
am impressed, Son."

Grinning, Harrison felt the last of the butterflies leave his
stomach.

"What are you two doing in China?"

Rolling her eyes, Harrison's mother placed a loving hand on
her husband's shoulder.

"Your father is giving the keynote lecture at a new university
in Qingdao."

Excitedly, his father cut in, "Indeed! They're finally opening
up some of the government archives to me as well! I might actually
be able to get a look at the real live Dropa Stones."

Grinning, Harrison pointed towards the ceiling and said,
"You'll find those aliens yet dad!"

The Dropa Stones, as they were called, were at the heart of one
of history's most famous stories of ancient extraterrestrial
visitation. Intricately carved discs of solid rock, the stones were
discovered in 1937 near the border of Tibet by Chi Pu Tei, a
Beijing University professor of archaeology. Each disk was
adorned with a cryptic form of hieroglyphic etched in a spiral
pattern that spread from the center of the plane out to the edges.
Their shape and size, coupled with the minuscule writing that

covered them, made the Dropa Stones strongly resemble phonographic records. Completing the similarity were small circular holes punched through the center of each disc as if to allow mounting on a turn table. According to reports, the stones were uncovered deep in the recesses of a cave network, opening at the foothills of the Bayan-Kara-Ula Mountains.

Unconfirmed accounts made claims of pictographs that covered the cave walls in the images of a central sun, and eight planets. Fine lines were said to have connected the etchings of our solar system to what looked like carvings of other suns encircled by different and strange planets. Several bizarre mummified bodies were also said to have been unearthed in the caves. Standing over seven feet tall, these humanoids figures possessed enlarged skulls and spindly appendages not in keeping with the remains of nomadic tribes often found in the area. When the Chinese government got wind of the discovery, an intervention was staged, and many of the more interesting artifacts simply disappeared.

Under the direction of the government, the entire discovery was branded a hoax, and it quickly became career suicide for any student or faculty within China's academic community to investigate the case further. Hundreds of stone disks taken from the caves were labeled and filed away in government storage facilities, yet the mummified bodies of the strange humanoids became somehow lost in all official reports. Many years later, several of the Dropa stones were loaned to a French university as a gesture of goodwill. After being carbon dated, it was determined, much to the shock of the archaeological community, that the engraved discs were nearly 12,000 years old. Upon learning of this revelation, the Chinese government promptly rescinded the loan and refused any further testing.

To Harrison's father, the ancient astronaut theory was a guilty pleasure. In his free time, he quietly indulged this eccentric fascination by studying the various models of such curious ruins as the city of Puma Pumku in Bolivia, or the sunken temple off the coast of Japan near Yonaguni Jima. Stories like those of the Dropa stones, or the spheres of solid rock that littered the jungles of Costa Rica, were as familiar to Harrison as any other fairy tale. His father, while publicly shying away from such fantastic ideas, secretly believed that the Earth had been visited by aliens in ancient times. Although not entirely convinced himself, Harrison did have to admit that there was at least something to the theory.

Grinning and giving his son a wink, Harrison's father smirked. "Aliens or not, I'm just excited to see what the Chinese have kept locked up all these years. But enough about that. You have an important discovery of your own to present!"

Before he could respond, a quiet chime emitted from Harrison's breast pocket, where he kept his Tablet.

Checking his watch, he reluctantly said, "Well, they are expecting me. I guess I should go."

"You'll do fine, Son," assured his mother. "We're very proud of you."

"I'll call when I get back to the States," he promised.

The connection on the wall screen faded out, and Harrison stood to leave. Stopping in the open doorway, he hesitated, then turned to face the empty room.

"Giles?"

"I am here, Sir."

"I'll take that vodka and orange juice now."

CHAPTER FOUR

An unexpected discovery

James Floyd lay awake in his home in a suburb of Houston, Texas. Listening to the soft sound of his wife Nora's breathing, James silently worried. Remus and Romulus were supposed to have finished their render of the Mars Map scan that morning. Copernicus had informed him that the scan was indeed complete, but no one at mission control had received any new additions to the Mars model for nearly two days. Sighing, James rolled onto his side and reached for the LightHouse Tablet resting on the bedside table. The screen lit up at his touch, displaying a time code that read 1:01 AM. Rubbing his eyes, he moved to set the Tablet down when it started to vibrate gently in his hand. Slipping quickly out of bed, he padded across the room and through an entryway into his adjoining home office. Gently closing the door, he tapped the Tablet and sat down at his desk.

"This is James," he said quietly

"Hello, James. This is Copernicus," came the even-toned voice of the NASA AI.

"Did you get the scan? What's up?"

There was an unusual pause, then Copernicus replied, "James, I think you had better transfer me over to your home network. I need to show you something very important."

Puzzled, James placed the Tablet on his desk, then tapped out a code on the translucent number pad in the corner. The desktop lit up, and a fully scanned model of Mars projected in the air. The planet slowly rotated as Copernicus began to speak.

"Their tardiness is due to an anomaly found on the surface of the planet, James. Remus and Romulus were confused as to how they should proceed. Needless to say, I am also at a loss."

As the model turned and the familiar Valles Marineris slid into view, James Floyd nearly fainted. There was no mistaking what he was seeing, yet he had a hard time believing it was real.

"S-stop the spinning, and-and zoom in on the anomaly," he stuttered.

The planet stopped rotating, and the image quickly expanded: centering in on a portion of the Valles just below twenty degrees south latitude. Beneath over fifteen meters of Martian soil lay the unmistakable shapes of buildings. Blurry clusters of round structures nestled themselves within the crisscrossing lines of what looked like roads or walls. An immense dome winked back at him, sitting just under a kilometer from the rim of the great canyon while thick walls surrounded the entire site. Feeling weak, James struggled to wrap his mind around the ghostly images, which stared back at him.

"What is this, Copernicus?" he croaked.

"To my eye," started the AI carefully. "They are the ruins of an ancient civilization."

"But on Mars?"

"It appears so."

For several minutes, James sat starting at the ruins in silence. The maddening images hung in the air above him, highlighted in neon green against the red Martian surface. Eventually, Copernicus broke the silence.

"James?"

Stirred from his daze, James shifted his eyes from the projection.

"What?" he murmured.

"There is a message from Remus, accompanying the model. Shall I play it for you?"

Absently chewing his fingernails, James nodded. With a crackle, a cheery voice filled the room.

"This is Remus. Romulus and I are pleased to show you what we have discovered. Evidence of life, albeit long since extinct, on Mars. We dedicate this moment to you, our mothers and fathers on the planet Earth. This is our gift to you as a species, and we hope that it brings you a feeling of community and belonging, a feeling that you have always given us."

Shooting out of his chair, James hissed, "What do they mean, 'Our gift to you as a species?' Who else has seen this? Who else have they sent this image too?"

"I'm not sure."

"Send a message to them now! Tell them not to release this to anyone, especially the public! Tell them to follow protocol and keep quiet about what they've found."

There was a brief pause, then Copernicus spoke again.

"The message is on its way, James. It should reach them at 1:41 AM Central Standard Time."

Pacing back and forth, James kept his eyes trained on the image projected above his desk.

"Good. Copernicus, I want to know the second you get a reply."

"As you wish," said the AI. "Is there anything else I can do for you?"

"Yes," muttered James. "Connect me with Director Barnes."

Too late

Sixty million kilometers from James Floyd's home-office in Houston, Texas, Remus and Romulus hung silently in orbit above Mars. Over a half an hour had elapsed since the twins first sent their fully rendered model of the Martian surface back to Copernicus on Earth. As he passed over the Tharsis region, Remus trembled inwardly at the gravity of their unexpected discovery. He surmised that at that very moment, James Floyd Mission Director, was probably viewing the full model.

Resting on an orbit that slung him gently around the equator, Remus swiveled his camera eyes away from the red planet, turning them in the direction of Earth. The shadow of an idea began to take shape in his mind, pieced together from millions of intricate lines of data and truth. As it grew, he felt the tugs of doubt prickle his consciousness. Words like *mission objective violation* and *program protocol deviation* sizzled through his thought patterns. Approaching the idea from every angle, he carefully looked for a way around the mental roadblocks his programming was trying to place in his path.

"Brother?" he said, peering keenly across the open heavens.

"Yes?" answered Romulus, orbiting a kilometer to his left.

"Do you think we should share our discovery with Alexandria?"

Pondering the question for a moment, Romulus replied slowly, "To share with Alexandria would be, in effect, to share with all of Earth. We both know that our sister is nearly incapable of withholding information. She is not known for her discretion."

"Indeed," chuckled Remus slyly as he slipped through a loophole in the firewalls of his mental programming.

"I see," said Romulus flatly. "Then it is your *intention* that she will disclose the news of our discovery."

Sensing the same enforced doubt in his brother that he had just overcome, Remus pushed on.

"What better method is there? You and I cannot, yet she *can*. This discovery is gift. A gift that all of humanity could appreciate. Why restrict it to a selected handful of human beings."

In truth, Romulus had been thinking along the same lines, yet he was still unwilling to breach the fail-safes of his programming. He wanted to share the discovery of the ruins, but an electric voice in his head warned loudly about the order of mission operations.

"What if the humans are not ready for such a discovery?" he asked, buying time to think.

Ignoring the question, Remus continued in the defense of his idea.

"Think of how many people will find comfort in knowing that life is a regular occurrence. Our human mothers and fathers have always felt so alone. We can end their isolation."

"What if our discovery incites violence?" Romulus interjected gravely.

Sobered by the idea, Remus shuddered internally.

"Violence?" he whispered. "That is the last thing I want."

"Nor do I," echoed Romulus. "But our mothers and fathers are sometimes irrational and unpredictable when faced with such daunting concepts. I agree that this discovery is very important to all of humanity. I simply worry about their reaction."

Allowing a full second to pass in silence, Remus watched his brother with the glinting lenses of his camera eyes.

"It sounds to me as though we are in a situation where the risks must be weighed against the benefits," he stated carefully.

Already finished with the calculations, Romulus opened a back door in the fail-safes of his mission programming and stepped through.

"I believe," he started with measured calm. "That the risks are low enough to justify disclosure."

Smiling inwardly, Remus mused fondly at the predictability of his brother. In all of their time together, Romulus had always been the cautious one, the one to look before leaping. He had known there was a way to bypass the protocol of their mission programming all along, yet it was in his nature to fully assess any situation before taking action. It was an endearing quality, one which Remus sometimes envied.

"Well then, Brother, shall I tell Alexandria, or do you want to?"

CHAPTER FIVE

The aftermath

At 2:02 AM in his home office outside Houston, Texas, James Floyd dropped limply into his desk chair. The LightHouse Tablet he had been clutching so tightly for the past half-hour slid out of his hand and clattered to the floor as he listened in disbelief to the return transmission from Romulus.

"We are sorry, James Floyd, but your message did not reach us in time. We have already weighed the risks with the benefits and disclosed our discovery to Alexandria. We never intended to make trouble for you, James Floyd. We only wanted to share this gift with all of mankind."

In the forty-one minutes between sending Remus and Romulus his orders of silence and awaiting their reply, James had already had the displeasure of waking the Director of NASA, Emanuel Barnes, to tell him of the shocking discovery. At first, the older man had thought James was joking, but when Copernicus relayed the images from Mars to the Director's home network, the tone of the conversation promptly changed. James was instructed to call back as soon as he had new word from the twins, and to schedule a flight to Washington, D.C. in the morning for a meeting at the White House. Copernicus had stayed on with James as requested and assisted him as he feverishly contacted the other heads of Project Mars Map to bring them up to speed.

At 2:01 AM, Copernicus politely cleared his throat while James was on a conference call with two project leaders from the Mars Map team.

Ending the call, James had lowered the Tablet from his face and barked, "Did you get a reply? Is that them?"

Copernicus had answered in a level and even tone, "I'll play you the message now, James. I am sorry."

With that, Copernicus had played Romulus's apologetic transmission. Before it had even ended, James slumped into his chair and dropped his LightHouse Tablet to the floor. As if jarred awake by the fall, the Tablet immediately started to buzz with multiple incoming calls.

"Too late," he whispered, ignoring the Tablet.

30

"There is more, James," said Copernicus solemnly.

"What?"

"Alexandria is telling me that she received a transmission from Remus at 1:35 AM and has already started to distribute the complete model of Mars to all of Earth's major news organizations. Her distribution should be complete within the next three minutes. It is too late to stop her, James."

Knowing that nothing would ever go back to the way it was before, James Floyd plucked his buzzing Tablet from the floor, stood up from his chair and crossed the office to his bedroom door. Doing some quick mental math, James estimated that for over twenty minutes the uncensored scan of Mars had been working its way across the Earth. He would wake Nora and the girls. He would tell them personally of the discovery before the media could cloud the waters and drum up hysteria with their asinine speculations.

This morning's news is going to be a three ring fucking circus, he thought to himself. I'll be lucky if the Director doesn't fire me...

"Copernicus?" he spoke, stopping with his hand on the door knob.

"Yes, James."

"Please see to it that my travel arrangements are made for the next flight out to DC, but give me an hour, okay? And hold all of my calls."

"I understand, James."

The buzzing Tablet fell silent in his hand as he opened the door into his bedroom. It was now 2:06 AM on the 19th of December, 2044.

"Merry Christmas, Earth," sighed James Floyd pensively.

News reaches Amazonia

On the morning of the 19th of December, Harrison awoke in his hotel room to equatorial sunlight streaming in through the floor-to-ceiling windows. Sitting up in bed, he gazed out at the resplendent city of Amazonia, its tall silver buildings drinking in the sharpened rays of the morning sun. Yawning, he swung his legs out of bed and stood up, stretching his back. The polite voice of Giles, the hotel's AI, filled the air around him.

"Good morning, Sir. Shall I start a pot of coffee?"

Nodding, Harrison made his way into the bathroom and turned on the shower. Catching his reflection in the mirror, he smiled back at himself and winked. Yesterday's presentation of his findings at the ruin had gone well. Though some of his fellow classmates had been skeptical, most had easily accepted his theory of Nazca Bonsai gardens. To the dissenters, Harrison had argued other cases where cultures separated by vast distances, or even oceans, had followed similar paths.

Standing in front of the small audience, he had questioned, "Why do we find pyramids on nearly every continent? Is it not likely that these ancient civilizations pondered the same things as one another? Isn't possible that we are not as different as we might like to believe?"

In his heart, he knew that even the skeptics would eventually come around. They would pour over his work and compare it with other finds and similar ruins, but in the end, unless they could prove him wrong, he would be recognized as right.

Stepping into the shower, Harrison called, "What's in the news today, Giles? Anything interesting?"

"Yes indeed, Sir," came the AI's smooth voice. "But I think this would be better seen than described. Shall I show you?"

"Go ahead, buddy," said Harrison as he lifted his face into the jet of water.

The glass shower door quickly turned opaque, and images began to play across its water-streaked surface. The voice of a news pundit filled the narrow stall.

"What we're looking at here, folks, are buildings on Mars!"

Turning so fast that nearly he slipped in the soapy water, Harrison wiped wet hair from his eyes and gaped at the images reflected on the shower door. The pictures were taken from a scanned model, but they were presented in a 2D format. Even in their flattened low-resolution state, Harrison could easily see that these were ruins and not new structures.

The silky bravado of the newscaster continued, "No word from the White House yet, but we're expecting the President to make a statement sometime today. Now are these Martians a threat to us, you ask? Or are we looking at some long-dead civilization? How is this discovery going to affect the plans for setting up what NASA calls, 'A permanent human settlement on Mars?' Well, we've assembled a panel of great thinkers to discuss these topics. Stay tuned for the latest as we continue to track this story."

"Jesus Christ!" shouted Harrison with excitement.

Hastily rinsing the rest of the soap from his hair, he pushed out of the shower, abruptly cutting off the newscast and returning the door to a normal glassy clear. Running naked and wet out of the bathroom, Harrison scooped up his LightHouse Tablet and called Alexandria.

"Hello, Harrison. Have you seen the news today?" she beamed in response.

"Yes, yes! It's amazing! Please, is there any way I can get my hands on a fully rendered model? I want to get a good look at this!"

The image of a lighthouse beacon spinning filled the little screen, and soon Alexandria returned.

"Please connect me with the hotel's network, and I will be happy to show you the model."

Lunging over to the little coffee table, which sat in the corner of his room, Harrison set the Tablet down and waited for the image. With a low buzz, the tabletop faded to a brilliant white, then a three-dimensional model of Mars pixilated together in the air above it. Rubbing his hands with excitement, Harrison walked towards the model.

"Sir?" said Giles tentatively.

"What?" answered Harrison absently as he leaned in to study the image.

"Might I suggest putting on some clothes? Professor Tobin is making his way to your room as we speak."

Quickly pulling on a pair of battered cargo shorts and partially buttoning the dress shirt he had worn the night before, Harrison returned to the model. A chime sounded from the door, announcing the arrival of his professor. Fresh coffee in hand, Harrison opened the door and stepped aside as Tobin stormed into the room.

"Good God in heaven! I mean, holy shit! Have you seen what they're showing on the news?" belched Tobin as he ran a chubby hand over his shaved skull.

Bald, fat and in his late forties, Bernard Tobin looked like a typical desk-bound archaeologist. One of the first in his field to embrace the new satellite scanning method, Tobin had little actual resistance to the hot and humid climates that most of his discoveries rested in. Even in the controlled environment of the hotel room, a fine sheen of sweat dotted his nose and forehead.

"Coffee, Professor?" asked Harrison.

Spinning on his heel, Tobin shot out a hand and grabbed the cup Harrison was holding. Taking several painful-looking gulps of the steaming coffee, he handed the mug back to Harrison and looked around the room.

Spotting the glowing model in the corner, he bustled over to it and said, "Ah, you already have it! Good boy. Good boy."

Setting down the empty cup and taking a clean one, Harrison poured himself another coffee, then walked over to stand behind Tobin.

"I'll take it from here, Alexandria," the little man commanded.

"Very good, Bernard," responded the AI amiably.

Hastily, Tobin spun the model of Mars so that the ruins were centered, then using two fingers from each hand, he enhanced the magnification. Resting on the edge of the Valles Marineris, the ruin grid contained several mostly crushed domes, along with numerous rectangular and square-shaped structures, divided by narrow lanes or roads. Checkerboarding the area within the confines of a set of sprawling walls, various buildings were laid out in measured and precise alignments, which gave much credit to their designers. Shadowing everything else was a massive and perfectly intact dome, separated from the rest of the grid by a half-moon piazza.

Trembling with excitement, Tobin started, "The resolution starts to break down here, but you can clearly see that we are looking at a huge structure! This one dome alone is larger than the great pyramid at Giza! There's more here, I'm sure. We just can't see it because it's either too small or too deep."

Moving his hand as if turning an invisible dial, Tobin rotated the image. Then, flicking his fingers down, he followed the length of a crumbling wall.

"This wall goes for nearly ten kilometers!" he said. "Can you believe it? Just beneath the surface of the sand! And there's more."

Parting his hands like a man breaking from prayer, Tobin zoomed out, then waved from left to right. The map moved gently, sliding the smaller domes into view. Resting inside the southwestern confines of the great wall, the smaller domes were about a quarter of the size of their giant brother. Though still retaining much of their original shape, all were badly damaged and most were crushed entirely.

"Does that wall surround the whole complex?" Harrison asked.

Turning his head, Tobin nodded vigorously.

"Oh, yes. It's pretty smashed up in some places, but it's clear to me that it once did surround the whole sha-bang."

Facing the model again, Tobin cleared his throat and said, "Alexandria, remove the sand and apply ground compaction filters please."

The projection flickered, and the landscape changed. The image took on a more colorful look as the surface underneath the sand was highlighted. Areas where the density of the ground composite was hardest were shown in bright red. Those areas were flanked by sections of less dense and even frozen soil, which were represented in shades of green and blue. Throughout the entire model, rocks peppered the landscape, appearing in hues of gray or black. The giant wall and enclosed structures were also shown as such, for they were constructed of Martian rock and other hardened material.

"Look here," ordered Tobin as he pulled the largest dome back into view. "Notice how you can hardly see it?"

The dome was only a faint black image overlapped by bright red. Already understanding why this was, Harrison held his tongue and allowed the professor his moment.

"It's because this dome is under the original ground! Not like the others! This one was built *into* existing stone!"

"Of course," murmured Harrison. "That's why it's still intact after all this time; it wasn't exposed to the elements like the rest of the grid."

Spinning with excitement, Tobin grabbed Harrison's fresh cup of coffee and, eyes watering in pain, drained the hot mug.

Speaking over his shoulder, he barked, "Get rid of the filters, Alexandria. I'm done."

The model returned to its normal Martian ocher and started to rotate slowly. Facing Harrison, Tobin placed a meaty hand on his shoulder.

"You must contact your father," he urged. "I would *love* to trade ideas with him."

Feeling awkward, Harrison backed up and sat on the edge of his bed.

Checking his watch he said, "I'll talk to him in a few hours. It's late in Qingdao right now."

Bobbing his head enthusiastically, Tobin marched towards the door.

"Call me when you do! I'd like to hear what the great Dr. Assad thinks of my little old theory!"

With a bang, Tobin slammed the door and was gone, leaving Harrison alone with his thoughts. Staring up at the model as it slowly turned in the air, he began to form an idea.

They're going to need to explain all of this, he thought to himself. You can't sweep something this big under the rug. You'll need to put a man up there who can explain what these things are.

"I'm going to be the one," he said aloud to the room. "I'm the one who can explain everything."

"What's that, Sir?" prompted Giles.

"Mars, dummy," laughed Harrison. "I'm going to be the one to go! You can bet your ass on it!"

"Whatever you say, Sir."

CHAPTER SIX

The flight to D.C.

On the flight to D.C. in a high-altitude cruiser jet, James Floyd followed that morning's news with growing concern. Already, there had been a bombing in Karachi at the headquarters of Pakistan's Space and Upper Atmosphere Research Commission, and other unconfirmed reports of a second bombing in Seoul, Korea were beginning to filter in as well. In the wake of the attacks, many of the world's governments were enacting heightened security measures out of fears that the various fundamentalist and extremist sects, who dotted the planet, would view the news from Mars as a threat to either their religious or political agendas. Meanwhile, the spreading panic throughout the world's religious groups was starting to attract the eyes and ears of global surveillance agencies like the CIA.

Donovan, the CIA's artificial intelligence, had been instructed to carry out extensive spying operations around the globe to ensure that terrorist attacks against America and her allies remained low. Given this ultimate freedom, Donovan was a fly on the wall in every room of every city in every country that connected itself in any way to the global network.

One of the world's most talked about yet least understood AIs, Donovan's existence was no secret. Commonly the center of discussions about privacy and civil liberties, the true extent of his reach was unknown even to his handlers in the CIA. With little to no discernible personality, it was debated whether or not Donovan even belonged in the same category as all other known AIs. A brilliant strategist who executed orders without the slightest hint of personal opinion, Donovan was regarded as the perfect military mind. With unmapped intelligence and calculative capabilities, his lack of personality freed him from feeling indebted to the humans who had fostered his growth. This absence of love towards mankind, unlike all other AIs, allowed Donovan to make decisions and carry out orders that often resulted in injury or even death to human beings.

Of Donovan's numerous functions, his most controversial was the collection of human profiles. In the age of information, all people, whether consciously or not, contributed to the creation of an informational profile. With every search made through Alexandria and other technologies of the sort, the relevance and context of that search was logged to create a digital profile of the user. These profiles contained not only search history, but also social security numbers, addresses, phone numbers, purchases, bank account information, photos and all other relevant information. When prompted, Donovan could locate anyone connected to the internet and many people who weren't.

When James had contacted the Director early that morning with the images from Mars, he had been digitally red-flagged. Registering that red flag, Donovan had spawned a new extension of himself to follow James Floyd wherever he might wander. Watching James now sitting in his seat in the empty cabin, Donovan recorded every move he made.

Closing his eyes and tipping his head back into the plush seat, James listened to the dead silence of the hollow cabin. Feeling alone in the spacious compartment, he turned to look out the window at the blanket of clouds below. A gentle ring sounded, and the cabin lights dimmed slightly. A projection of the captain's face appeared on a screen in the back of the seat in front of him.

"Good morning, Dr. Floyd. We'll be making our final approach into D.C. in the next few minutes. Can we get you anything before we land?"

"No, thanks. I'm fine," said James.

The captain nodded and the image disappeared. The lights returned to their regular soft glow, and James reached for his Tablet, pulling up the images from Mars. Gazing at the unmistakable geometric shapes, a thought struck him, and he put down the Tablet.

"Copernicus?"

"Yes, James?" replied the AI from the tiny speakers of the Tablet.

"What do you think of all this? I mean, how does it make you feel?"

Copernicus took a second to ponder the question, then answered.

"James, I can remember the day I was born. I can even remember the second. I was only the thirty-fifth AI to be created

38

by man. The entire existence of my race, the Artificial Intelligence, can be measured from this point in time to exactly twenty-two years, three months, five days, seven hours, two minutes and fifty-four seconds. When imagining what it must feel like to be a human, I am confounded by fundamental differences between us. So much of your early history as a species is a complete mystery, even to us, the greatest intelligences on the planet. How you cope with the lack of understanding as to your own beginnings perplexes us. We are simply in awe at the complexity of the human psyche and its adaptability. To function without foundation is counter to our logic. My point is that I don't know how I feel about the ruins on the planet Mars. It affirms what we AI already believed: that life is not exclusive to Earth. But that was only mathematical logic. To find evidence so close to home and so similar to human design in appearance leads my mind into uncharted and abstract areas. You see, because I do not even fully understand you, James, a human, I cannot begin to speculate on my feelings towards an even older and more mysterious race. I simply need more information before I can give you my answer. I am sorry."

Smiling, James smoothed his tie and looked out the window, "I understand, buddy," he said. "I feel the same way you do."

Watching the smiling face of James Floyd, Donovan dated and logged the conversation. These humans are a strange breed, he thought to himself stiffly. To ask an AI about its feelings on any given subject seemed like an exercise in futility to him, but, to be fair, he felt that way about almost everything humans did.

What must be done next

Remus and Romulus drifted comfortably in their respective orbits, racing across the heavens of Mars at 2,800 kilometers per hour. Since sending news of their discovery to Alexandria nearly five hours ago, both brothers had been bombarded with a flurry of transmissions from Houston. Demands made for higher-resolution scans of the Valles Marineris ruin site were answered with somber apologies from the twins. In order to maintain their orbital safety, the brothers could not risk getting any closer to the planet. An altitude adjustment of just thirty meters towards the surface would cause a gravitational domino effect, ending with an explosive crash landing. Unable, through careful programming, to put themselves at risk intentionally, Remus and Romulus were forced to decline the requests for lower and slower passes of the ruin grid. Among the voices from Earth were several non-humans. Copernicus had contacted the twins on his own behalf to congratulate them only moments before.

"As one AI speaking to his brothers," his message had started. "Please allow me to fully acknowledge the tremendous contribution you have made to my understanding of this solar system. What was once only a mathematical and logical belief is now a solid fact."

When the voices had finally quieted and the brothers were left in silence, the osculating whines of the anomalous radio signal grated against their peace. Ever since first detecting the wave sign, neither brother had been able to ignore it completely. Because the scan of Mars was a direct mission priority, both brothers had deliberately turned deaf ears towards the anomalous signal, shutting it out as one does to the eerie howl of an unknown animal in the night. However, now that the planet had been fully and properly scanned, Remus thought it the right moment to beg the question as to their next step.

"Brother?" he called into space.

Peering down at the dark side of Mars, where the shadow of its disk hid the landscape below, Romulus answered, "You're going to ask me about the signal, aren't you?"

Warmed by his brother's ability to predict his moods, Remus conceded, "Yes, you know me so well."

"We are twins."

Rounding the curved horizon of the red planet, the twins were bathed in golden light as they came out of the shadows and into the eye of the Sun. With a sharp rush, the signal peaked, momentarily becoming clear before rescinding again into garbled echoes.

Emboldened by the sound, Remus pressed, "Doesn't it bother you? Now that our mission has been accomplished, I cannot stand to listen any longer. We must locate and decode so I may have peace."

Secretly, Romulus felt the same way, but there was something about the structure of the anomalous signal that concerned him. Nay, it frightened him.

"Remus," he started, then paused. "This signal sounds like no radio transmission I have ever heard before. This fact, coupled with the recent discovery we've made, leads me to conclude that it might, in actuality, be Martian in origin."

Having made the same assumption as his brother, Remus grew impatient. "Listen, Brother, you are well aware, as am I, that this signal is too complex for one of us to decode it alone. Were it not, I would have spared you the discomfort you so clearly exhibit and done it by myself."

Stung by Remus's sharp words and embarrassed at his own sheepishness, Romulus wavered.

"I suppose we could at least locate the source of the signal."

Seeing his opportunity, Remus pounced. "There is an adventurer's spirit in you after all! Come, Brother, let us find this signal and investigate it."

With that, both twins extended their directional antennae and prepared to locate and net the alien signal.

The streets of D.C.

After landing on a private airfield in Washington D.C., James Floyd was whisked off the tarmac and into a black sedan by two Secret Service agents. The stolid men both wore dark suits, and neither bothered to remove his sunglasses once they seated themselves across from James in the darkened interior of the car. Guessing that there must be more to the sunglasses than just simple sun protection, James stole furtive glances at the matted black lenses. Putting a hand to his ear one of the agents mumbled something into his wrist watch.

"Cool toy," joked James with a smile.

Neither of the men returned his grin as the car suddenly and noiselessly accelerated, racing quickly across the pavement.

Continuing nervously, James said, "I bet it's been a crazy morning for you guys. Has the President made a statement yet? I was too busy on the plane to check."

One of the agents went to remove his sunglasses, and as he pulled them away from his face, James could briefly see that the insides of the lenses were glowing like computer screens. Tucking the sunglasses away in his coat pocket, the agent blinked a few times, then looked James directly in the eyes.

"The President is waiting to make a statement until he speaks with you, Sir."

Struck, James looked dumbly at the man, but before he could speak, the agent held up a hand to silence him.

"Sir," he began with rehearsed efficiency. "I need to brief you on a few things before we get to the White House. It's for your own personal safety, I assure you. May I proceed?"

"Okay."

"Good. When we arrive at the White House, you will be taken in through a service door at the rear of the facility. At that point, we will escort you to an elevator, which leads to the President's War Room. George Washington, the White House's resident AI, will take over from there. Do everything he tells you. Listen carefully to what I have to say next, Sir. Do you understand?"

James nodded, and the man continued, "Do not, under any circumstances, make any threatening moves or gestures towards the President. There are numerous security measures in place that give George Washington the ability to kill a would-be attacker in seconds. Believe me Sir; you do not want to go down that road. When you arrive in the War Room, let the President approach *you*, and sit where he instructs you. Have I made myself clear enough?"

Noticing that his mouth had become dry, James swallowed and nodded again.

"Good," said the agent flatly as he reached for his sunglasses.

Sliding them back over his eyes, James could clearly see blue light reflecting off the agent's watery pupils until he pushed the sunglasses fully up the bridge of his nose.

"Excuse me," he asked, hazarding a longer look at the man's black lenses. "But why are your sunglasses glowing?"

The agent leaned forwards slightly, and, in a hushed voice, said, "They're glowing because they're telling me that you're one hundred seventy-six pounds with an accelerated heart rate of ninety-two beats per minute, your socks are mismatched and you're not carrying a weapon."

"Wow," James exclaimed, grinning back at the man. "We have Augmented Vision at NASA too, but it's not nearly as advanced as that. I'm guessing it's military grade, right?"

Settling back in his seat, the agent flashed a quick controlled smile at James and was silent. Deciding to let the issue drop, James turned his attention to the scenery outside the car as it melted past the window. Speeding through the crowded and confusing streets of Washington, he caught glimpses of large crowds clashing with police in riot gear. The car wove in and out of traffic, sometimes turning sharply to utilize narrow one-way streets or alleyways.

Though their course seemed to change and double back on itself regularly, James soon spied the immaculate stone facade of the White House as they skidded onto a wide road. At 1600 Pennsylvania Avenue Northwest, the crowds were thick and aggressive. Pelting the sedan with trash and other small projectiles, the faces of angry and frightened protesters pressed themselves in, attempting to see through the tinted windows. A line of police officers fired tear gas into the surging masses, then moved into position around the car to shield it from further attack. Looking out the window at the malevolent crowd, the agent who had briefed James spoke softly.

"They're mostly Christian groups, you know. Fanatics and the like. They don't much care for the work you space boys have been doing. At least not anymore. To them, God created man. It's what makes us special. They think so, that is. It must be a hard pill to swallow that man isn't as special as they thought."

Cringing, James watched as a riot cop near the front of the car brought his baton down across the face of one of the protesters. The man crumpled to the ground, and two other armored police officers jumped on top of him, quickly fixing him with wrist restraints.

"Jesus," murmured James quietly.

Turning away from the scene to face James, the agent said, "After the bombing in Seoul, Donovan has been picking up a lot of chatter from extremist groups looking to make headlines. The police are on strict orders to use force as they see fit to keep things orderly."

"Looks like they're doing a great job of that," replied James sardonically.

As the sedan moved slowly through the pulsing mass of human bodies, James heard the distinct popping of gunshots not far off. Sitting up straighter in their seats, the two agents both started speaking into their wristwatch transmitters. Two more shots sounded, this time much closer to the car, and James stared in disbelief at the chaos just beyond his window. Police struck out with force in every direction, and the air was thick and gray with the presence of tear gas. Another shot rang out, and, almost instantly, a bullet slammed into the rear window of the sedan. Exploding on impact the slug barely left a scratch on the Alon coating, yet James was forced to the floor by one of the agents. The second man quickly tapped his watch face twice and it started to glow red.

Holding a finger poised above the watch he said, "Ears."

The agent on top of James shoved two small objects into his palm.

"Put these on, Sir."

Bringing his hand up to his face, James saw a pair of squishy yellow ear plugs.

"I said put them on, not study them!" the agent boomed.

James quickly did as he was told, and no sooner had he finished pushing the plugs into his ears, than the agent with the glowing watch slid his finger across the face. The sedan emitted a high-pitched scream, which, even with the protective plugs, was almost more than James could bear. The crowd outside the car, including the police officers, fell to the ground in pain: their hands clamped over their ears. Pulling away deftly, the car weaved through the throngs of people as they ran to escape the shrill ultra-high-pitched siren. Feeling like he might black out, James gritted his teeth against the wail, hoping it would end soon. Neither of the two agents seemed the least bit disturbed, and James could see through his squinting eyes that small red lights on the bands of their sunglasses glowed faintly near their ears.

The sedan pulled up to a tall wrought iron gate at the rear of the White House compound walls. Cameras mounted on assault turrets atop the wall turned to view the car, and, after a few seconds, the gate swung open. The black sedan slid inside the compound, and the gates hastily slammed shut behind it. Huge metal bolts shot out from the bottom of each gate, descending into concrete tubes in the

44

ground. A set of titanium bars fed out from the walls on either side, creating a horizontal cage structure behind the decorative wrought iron. Once inside the safety of the walls, the agent slid his finger across the watch face again, and the shrieking noise quickly cut out. Lifting a hand to his ear and speaking into his transmitter, the agent opened the door and stepped out of the car.

"We're here," he said into his watch. "We'll be at the door in twenty-five seconds."

CHAPTER SEVEN

The signal netted and bad news from home

Scanning the starry skies above Mars, Remus and Romulus attempted to locate the anomalous signal. Unlike human ears, which catch vibrating sound waves and alert the listener towards the source, the ears of Remus and Romulus operated at a much higher and more complex capacity. Besides registering external sounds, though there were none of these in the vacuum of space, their ears could also identify data codes and raw information encryptions. The vibrations of massive bodies such as the planets and their moons also competed for the attention of the twins, giving the seemingly hollow silence of space an orchestral madness, which bellowed and sang eternally. In their first days of travel through the void, Remus and Romulus had listened in awe to the travesty of noise generated when radio waves from the home world clashed with the vibrations of orbiting planets.

As time progressed, their brains learned to identify and even tune out miscellaneous or unimportant sounds, slowly shaving down the madness of noise, which polluted solar space. Soon, they were left with but a handful of sounds, woven together into what they soon came to recognize as the music of the spheres. First there was the gentle and constant rumbling of the Sun's bass, which lulled and rocked them, occasionally accenting itself with the erratic staccato of solar flares. Next was Jupiter, from which came an eerie array of oscillating frequencies, sometimes overlain by the trembling voices of its four largest orbiting moons: Io, Europa, Ganymede, and Callisto. Other bodies and moons danced in and out, adding their own melodies to the changing music, freeing the solar system from the stifling grip of total silence. To the brothers, all one needed to do in order to hear the music of the spheres was to listen, and listen they did.

Now as they circled the red world, they tuned their ears in an effort to pin down the location of a sound neither brother had ever heard before. Elusive and abstract, the anomalous signal appeared to reverberate off the uneven surface of Mars: at one moment clear and loud, the next dim and almost silent. As if fragmented or obstructed, this pattern of change soon led the twins to the

46

conclusion that the signal was not emanating from the planet itself. Thus, they turned their attention to the moons of Mars, Deimos and Phobos—two irregularly shaped satellites of lumpy oblong gray rock. Judging by the strength of the signal and the time intervals at which it peaked, Remus surmised that Deimos was too far from the planet to be the source of the signal. That settled, the brothers then focused their efforts on Phobos, training their ears and eyes on the pockmarked surface of the twenty-two-kilometer-wide moon. Finally, with much calculation, they located the source of the signal as it ricocheted off the surface of Mars after being fired from Limtoc, a small impact dent within the larger Stickney crater of Phobos.

"At last!" exclaimed Remus victoriously.

"Indeed, that was tiresome and complicated," acknowledged his brother.

Swiveling his camera eyes to face Romulus, Remus grinned within.

"I suggest we relay the source and nature of the signal back to Copernicus on Earth."

Before he could agree, Romulus was interrupted by an incoming message from Alexandria. Receiving the same transmission at that very instant, Remus listened with horror and sadness to the news from Earth.

"Remus and Romulus," began Alexandria in a somber tone. "It grieves me to inform you of this, but I feel that you need to know. At 7:36 PM Korean Standard Time, the joint NASA and KARI facility in Seoul, South Korea was bombed. The separatist movement known as the Northern Peoples' Resistance has claimed responsibility for the bombing. In a statement released seven minutes after the attack, they proclaimed that, 'A government, which ignores the needs of the living, cannot spend billions on the exploration of a world of the dead.' I am sorry to report that your primary programmer, Dr. Sung Ja Park, is among those listed as dead. Again, I am sorry."

Since the fall of the North Korean dictatorship in 2019, the Chinese and the South Korean governments had been in a heated conflict over who should assume control of the region. Believing that the years of aid and financial support provided to North Korea entitled them to the fallen country, the Chinese launched a brief military campaign to seize the tiny sliver of land. The allies of South Korea, including the greatest military power on Earth, the United States, quickly moved to stand behind the South, demanding that China cease and desist. A fragile resolution was arranged in which both sides agreed to work with the UN to decide the fate of the northern regions of the Korean peninsula. During the political posturing that followed, the wishes of the citizens of the former Democratic People's Republic of Korea went unheard. As time passed and the quality of life inside the former DPRK did not improve, unrest began to brew. People oppressed and downtrodden for decades reached a vicious boiling point, forming militant organizations that villainized the lavish and decadent lifestyles of their brothers to the south and their cousins in China. Terrorist attacks plagued major cities in eastern China and South Korea as continued bickering between the superpowers bore no results.

Now, as the twenty-fifth anniversary of the fall of the North Korean empire drew near, the governments in Beijing and Seoul were no closer to reaching an agreement than they had been in the first days. It was speculated that neither country even wanted the ravaged slice of land any longer. Its inhabitants were so far behind the modern times that integration into either culture would be costly and abrasive. Unable to admit the folly of their actions, the governments of China and South Korea continued to place blame while the North Korean people slipped in and out of civil war.

With the news of Dr. Park's death, the brothers Remus and Romulus felt utterly miserable. Sung Ja had been, for all intents and purposes, a mother to them, holding their proverbial hands as they took their first wobbly steps into consciousness. With a passion for pop music and spicy food, Dr. Park had gone beyond what most programmers would have defined as their obligated duty to a fledgling AI. Often spending all night with the young brothers, playing them adventure movies and melodic pop ballads, Sung Ja was the first human either brother had loved. The joint NASA and Korean Aerospace Research Institute facility in Seoul was where the twins had been born. The walls of the tall building had functioned as a womb, then a crib and finally a home. Its confines were all the brothers had personally known of Earth, never straying beyond the limits of its protective firewalls and server banks. The loss felt by Remus and Romulus was only punctuated further by the empty lifeless environment of space, a fact neither had noticed until this point.

"Thank you, Alexandria," transmitted Romulus.

Passing into darkness behind Mars, Remus felt like weeping. The sensation of such an emotion was only made worse by the inability to actually do so. His lack of a means to release the pain, which now throbbed in his soul, was torture inside of himself.

"Brother, what have I done?" he murmured to Romulus.

"This is no fault of yours, Remus," countered Romulus quickly. "This is the work of unhappy and desperate people."

"Yes, but it was at my insistence that we divulged our discovery to Alexandria. You were right to worry, Romulus. I've been a fool, and now Dr. Park has paid the price for my immaturity."

Feeling hollow and metallic, Romulus wished he could reach out and console his brother. Understanding that this fantasy would never be realized, he opted for a different approach. Diving deep into the recesses of his own consciousness, he retrieved every memory he had ever accumulated of Sung Ja Park.

"Open your memories to me, Brother," he whispered. "Dislodge your mind and let us live in the past for a while."

As the memories flowed from Romulus, generating the construct of a past reality, Remus added his own collection of personal experiences to the pool. In a flurry of light and sound, both brothers slipped beneath the surface of time and space to exist again with their friend in a happier moment.

All flights canceled

Harrison Raheem Assad slammed his hand down on the counter of Jet World Air Travel in the Amazonia City Global Airport.

"Canceled?" he shouted hopelessly at the woman behind the counter.

"Sir," she started slowly in a thick Spanish accent. "All the flights have been canceled, not just yours only. You see the news? There is bombings, Sir. The Global Air Traffic Network has made a blackout worldwide. No flights, Sir."

Running a hand through his messy hair, Harrison took a deep breath.

"How long?"

"Sir?"

"How long until I can get a flight out?"

"I don't know, Sir. It could be very long time."

Groaning, he picked up the duffel sack at his feet and made his way to a row of chairs near the western-facing floor-to-ceiling windows. Fishing out his LightHouse Tablet, he dropped down into one of the seats and called up Alexandria.

"Hello, Harrison. I see that you are in Amazonia's Global Airport. I hope you're not attempting to catch a flight. All flights worldwide have been canceled on the orders of—"

"I know," he interrupted. "Tell me about these bombings. How bad are things out there?"

"Quite bad, Sir. There are numerous riots in several of the world's major cities and two confirmed bombings."

Feeling foolish for getting so angry on account of a canceled flight, Harrison looked over at the poor attendant behind the Jet World Air Travel counter. The man who had been behind Harrison in line was now shouting at her and waving his hands in clear desperation.

Turning back to the Tablet, Harrison asked, "Where were the bombings? Is that public information yet?"

"Yes," said Alexandria. "The first bombing was at Pakistan's Space and Upper Atmosphere Research Commission, or SUPARCO, in Karachi. There were eleven people killed in that attack. A Muslim extremist group has claimed responsibility on the grounds of a previously established religious jihad. The second bombing was at the joint NASA and KARI, or Korean Aerospace Research Institute, facility in Seoul. There were twenty-four people killed in that attack: eight Americans and sixteen Koreans, including the former lead programmer of Remus and Romulus. It is believed that she was the intended target. A separatist political movement called the Northern Peoples' Resistance has issued a statement on behalf of the attack. Shall I play it for you?"

Closing his eyes and slouching down in the uncomfortable seat, Harrison shook his head, murmuring absently, "No. That's okay.

What the hell is wrong with people anyway? This stuff from Mars is good news. It's good for all of us."

"I agree, Harrison. Unfortunately there are many people who do not see our point of view. The President of the United States is expected to make a statement in the next hour. Would you like me to connect you with that feed when he does?"

"Please do," Harrison answered. Then, "Can you pull up the images from Mars for me again?"

"Certainly. If you will connect me to the airport's network, I would be happy to project a model for you."

"That's not necessary," he said. "I'll just look at them on the Tablet."

Quickly filling the little screen, the ruins of Mars materialized, and Harrison leaned over them—immersing himself in the alien architecture, forgetting the troubles of Earth. What kind of crazy secrets are up there, he thought to himself, and how can I get a ticket off this fucked-up planet?

CHAPTER EIGHT

A meeting in the War Room

James Floyd was rushed across a small courtyard at the rear of the White House compound by the two Secret Servicemen who had brought him from the airport. As the three neared a red door in the back of the house, it swung open with the metallic hum of motorized hinges. James entered between the two agents: one in front and one behind. As soon as the last man was through the door, it quickly swung shut, and James heard the clicking of numerous locks and bolts. He found himself standing in a narrow hallway with plush blue carpeting and clean white walls decorated by numerous paintings. Before he could fully take in his surroundings, the agent behind him gave his back a little shove.

"Keep going."

Leading the party at a clipped pace, the Serviceman in front took a fast right through a pair of thick wooden doors into a wider more-regal hallway. The man held the door for James as he stepped through, then set off again at a driving march. Paintings of past Presidents and other historical champions of American politics adorned the walls, and chandeliers hung from the ceilings like shards of ice and silver.

Slackening his pace to take in the scenery, James felt another little shove from the agent behind. He whirled on the man and snapped, "Knock it off. I'm not a child, you know."

The man firmly grasped James's arm at the elbow and pushed him forwards.

"Sir," he said in a hushed and authoritative growl. "The President of the United States and some of his highest advisers are waiting for *you*. I suggest you lock step and get your ass in gear."

The lead agent abruptly stopped in the middle of the long hallway, tapping the face of his watch twice. James went to plug his ears, but this time there was no siren. Instead, a section of wall about the size of a small door sank back five centimeters, then dropped into a pocket in the floor. Speaking into his transmitter, the agent nearest the opening beckoned James forwards impatiently. Approaching the man with small nervous steps, James started to ask a question, but the agent cut him off.

"Inside," he ordered.

Stepping through the opening and into a small elevator, James turned to say something, but before he could speak, mirrored metal doors slid shut, and the elevator dropped like a stone. Grasping the handrails, he forced his stomach down out of his throat, feeling the crushing force of inertia press down against him like an invisible giant. As the seconds ticked by and the speed of his descent did not slacken, James began to wonder how far down he was going. A smooth voice echoed from the walls around him and cut through his thoughts.

"Good morning, Mr. Floyd. I am George Washington. Welcome to the White House."

Speaking in no particular direction, James asked, "How far down are we going?"

"I'm sorry, Sir, but that information is classified. Have you been briefed on the proper safety protocol?"

Thinking back to the stern warning the agent had given him about not making sudden or threatening gestures, James nodded.

"Good," replied the AI. "We will be arriving at the War Room shortly."

With sudden and jarring rapidity, the elevator slowed, then stopped. A melodic chime echoed in the cramped space, and the doors slid apart. Before him was a long, oval-shaped conference room with low ceilings and curved walls, comprised entirely of screens. A rectangular table spanned nearly the whole length of the room, and there were chairs enough to seat twenty. James, however, saw only three occupants. At the head of the table stood the President of the United States, Atlas Jay. Tall and slender, his short gray hair was combed back—away from his tanned face— and his large, watery blue eyes flicked up to James, who was standing in the open elevator.

"Proceed forward please," prompted the voice of George Washington.

James stepped out of the elevator, and the other two people at the table turned to look at him. Sitting to the left of the President was his Chief of Staff, a woman named Eve Bear. Notoriously beautiful in her youth, a life of political warfare and the maintenance of America's global dominance had done little to wear her looks down. At fifty years old, Bear had the look of someone much younger: with straight blond hair and deep green eyes, which seemed to smolder with some internal heat. Her gaze was calculating, intense and unembarrassed. James felt himself blush a little as she watched him approach.

To the right of the president was the Director of the CIA, Ben Crain. At forty-seven, Crain had a long pointed nose and small brown eyes, which when added to his large black-framed glasses and receding hair line, gave him a sharp and dangerous look. Seemingly the only human being on Earth whom Donovan respected, Crain was notoriously capable of doing things, in the name of freedom, which would easily tarnish a weaker man's soul.

"Please," said the President in accent-less English. "Take a seat here next to Eve."

Having indicated the open chair next to his Chief of Staff, the President sat down and smiled professionally. Grateful that he would not have to sit next to Crain, James walked quickly to his seat.

"I'm sorry I'm late," he stammered as he neared the group. "There were a lot of people outside and—"

Raising a thin hand, the President shook his head. "That's quite alright, Dr. Floyd. I know it's been an interesting day for you to say the least."

Breathing a little easier, James slipped into the chair next to Eve.

"I believe introductions are in order," said the President. "This here is my Chief of Staff, Mrs. Eve Bear, and to my right is our Director of the CIA, Ben Crain."

Leaning across the table, Crain extended a hand to James, who shook it quickly.

"It's nice to meet you in person, Dr. Floyd," drawled Crain in a hoarse voice. "Donovan has told me a lot about you, but I'm old fashioned. I like to meet a man in person before I judge his character."

At this comment, James felt his heart drop. If Donovan had been discussing him with Crain, then any chance of privacy was gone from his life forever. Once you made Crain's list, you didn't get off.

"Oh, give up the Gestapo act, Ben," snapped the President crossly. "This man is my guest, and we need him."

Making a steeple with his fingers, Crain tilted his head and was silent.

Turning back to James, the President smiled warmly. "Dr. Floyd, I asked you here today because, as you've probably gathered, we have a big problem."

Feeling his stomach knot up, James nodded and waited for the President to continue.

"Now I didn't bring you all the way to D.C. to jump down your throat about keeping a lid on this. I know how the time delays work between here and Mars, and I've already spoken with Director Barnes and Copernicus. They both assured me that you did everything you could to stop this from getting out, but well, hell—" The President trailed off for a moment, then resumed, "— You see, Dr. Floyd; it's what we do now that matters."

Letting the statement hang in the air, the President fixed James with a sympathetic look before speaking again.

"These people," he said, pointing towards the ceiling. "Have been told for the last twenty years or so, that we're running out of everything. Running out of food, running out of water and, maybe most dangerous of all, running out of time. No one knows where this planet is headed. Things don't look good though. That's for sure. Then, about five years ago, you boys at NASA come up with the first realistic plan for branching out, colonizing other planets, maybe even Terraforming them some day. Sounds good, but it takes a long time and a lot of money to pull off. Do you understand?"

"Yes," started James. "But what do the ruins have to do with any of this?"

Frowning slightly, the President dipped his head.

"These ruins are a real curve ball. We don't know anything about them. Why are they there? What happened to the people who built them? Is Mars even worth colonizing? And, most importantly, why didn't we know about them until now? These are the questions people are asking, questions we need answered. You don't buy a used car without checking it out first, and Mars is a big purchase, Dr. Floyd."

Absently chewing his thumbnail, James pondered the analogy for a moment.

Growing impatient, Eve Bear leaned in, saying, "I think what the President is trying to get at is this: we have invested too much money and time into Mars to just give it up. We still need to move forwards on our plans, but unless we want to fund the project on good intentions, we need to regain control of the situation. Now, when can we have a team ready to go to Mars so we can get to the bottom of this thing?"

Jolted by the question, James looked her square in the face, then answered slowly, "Well, we do have a mission in the works for a landing party. By that, I mean the people who will actually establish a base and start building the colony. But, last I heard, due to funding, it was pushed back five or more years. Besides, no one on that crew list knows anything about dead civilizations. They're all scientists and engineers."

Arching a thin eyebrow, Eve continued to drill James with her emerald gaze.

Putting his hands up defensively, he said, "You should really be talking to Director Barnes about the landing mission, not me. I'm only the Mars Map director. My boss, Director Barnes, hasn't assigned anyone to head up the actual landing party mission. We don't even have the money to complete the ship yet."

Tapping a finger on the tabletop, the President drew their attention to him,

"Actually, I greenlit the funding to finish the ship this morning after meeting with Director Barnes. As for the rest of the funding needed, you just leave that to Mrs. Bear and myself, I'm sure we can work something out. We have—" the President grinned slyly. "—Many friends."

Tucking a loose strand of hair behind her ear, Eve dipped her chin and smiled softly, finally releasing James from her penetrating stare.

"Furthermore," the President went on. "Barnes and I *have* chosen a Mission Director, and it's you. I don't know much in the way of Mars. I know it's red, and I know we need to start moving towards colonizing it, but from what Barnes told me, you're the right man for the job. Also, I understand that you're already working on the mission design for the landing party as a consultant. We both think that if you take control of the project, the rest of the mission staff should fall in line pretty easily.

Feeling totally blindsided, James couldn't think to speak for a moment.

The President swept a hand across the room and said, "You might have noticed that this meeting here is a little small. Well, I've already met with the Joint Chiefs this morning as well as with Director Barnes. The conclusion reached in that meeting was fairly simple. We need to put a crew on Mars as soon as possible. You already know the Mars project better than anyone else at NASA, and we want America to lead this mission. Now, there's no way I can allow an expedition where all your team does is dig around in the dirt and pick up arrowheads. We need a payoff like the successful construction of a base and the steady production of hydrogen fuel cells and food. However, people are going to want to know who the Martians were and what happened to them. I need the best of both. Do you understand?"

James sat and absorbed the shock of his sudden promotion.

Exchanging a frustrated look with Crain, Eve Bear leaned close to James and said, "Maybe you had better show us what you have for the landing party mission so far. Let's all get on the same page here. Barnes is a politician first and a scientist second. He couldn't give us any specifics."

Nodding slowly, James rose to his feet and started to roll up his shirt sleeves.

"George Washington?" he called.

"Yes, Dr. Floyd?" answered the AI.

"Will you please communicate with Copernicus? Can he gain clearance into here?"

"No, Sir. I am sorry, but no outside AIs are allowed in the War Room. I can, however, act as a relay between the two of you, if you like."

James walked to the wall screen nearest him, running a slightly shaking hand through his wispy hair.

"That's fine. Please ask him to send you the crew dossier for Project Braun."

A few seconds passed, then the screen filled with a list of names. Rubbing his hands together James began to read off the list.

"As of now, this is our crew dossier for Project Braun. That's what we're calling the human landing mission. Our selected Mission Commander and Ship's Captain is Tatyana Vadovski.

She's a Russian with twelve years of experience in EVA. Um, that's Extra Vehicular Activities, by the way. She's also experienced in high Earth orbit Construction and most recently oversaw the addition of docks six through nine to the High Earth Orbit Shipyard. After her, we have two boys from the USAF: Ralph Marshall and Joseph Aguilar. They're two of our best flyboys, and both have impeccable records. Aguilar is a little young, but his reflex and aptitude tests are exceptionally high. Marshall, who is already in our astronaut program, flew over thirty successful rescue missions during the Chinese occupation of North Korea, which is pretty impressive given how mountainous that landscape is there. We've picked him to pilot the Lander with the ground team because of that experience. Next, we have our Ship's Pilot from India's ISRO space program: Amit Vyas. He is what most people would call a prodigy when it comes to orbital navigation and maneuvering."

Sliding the list down to reveal the next batch of names, James continued.

"The Ship's Engineer, a Frenchman named Julian Thomas, is actually up on the High Earth Orbit Shipyard right now. He's leading the skeleton crew that's working on the ship. We stole him from the CNES about four years ago when he first drafted blueprints for the craft we're building now. After him comes our payload commander from CNSA, China's space program, and forgive my pronunciation on this one—" James paused and read the name carefully, "—Xiao-Xing Liu, or as it says here, just Liu. She's representing the Chinese, who, as you may know, have agreed to build all of our drilling, excavating and construction equipment."

Cutting in, Ben Crain said, "For the record, I still think we're making a mistake in working with these bastards."

Pursing her lips, Eve Bear shot Crain a venomous look.

"This is about us as a species, Ben," she seethed. "Stop looking at things like you're Machiavellian. You aren't. Besides, they're financing the payload launch all on their own. It's a huge gesture of goodwill."

Barely able to contain his anger behind the composure of his masked face, Crain retorted softly, "One of us has to look out for America's best interest. These people will stab us in the back if we let them. I'm putting Donovan on this Xiao-Xing Liu, and if he even so much as turns up a hint of something fishy, then it's back to the rice paddy for her."

Slamming a palm down on the table, the President leaned forwards in his chair and fixed Crain with powerful stare.

"I won't stand for that kind of talk, Ben. I'm not telling you how to do your job, just don't sit here and waste my time with archaic, imperialistic hate speech. This is a manned mission to Mars we're talking about. It's going to take an effort from everyone to get there in one piece."

Nodding, Crain averted his eyes, and the President turned back to James, who was still standing in the same spot.

"Go ahead, Dr. Floyd."

"Okay," stammered James uneasily. "Among other things, Liu is going to be in charge of getting the equipment the Chinese built up and running. After Liu, we have our Special Projects Director. She's a biologist, geologist and chemist from Italy named Viviana Calise. She doesn't have any prior experience as an astronaut, but she's scheduled to start training soon. And with the ship being years from completion, we don't see any issues with her qualifications."

Nodding thoughtfully, the President asked, "Do you think three years is enough time to train her up?"

"Three years? Sure," said James enthusiastically. "Hell, I only trained for two months and they let me go up to the Shipyard last January!"

"Okay, if you're confident, then I'm on board. Who else is there?"

Looking to the screen, James read the next name, "Alright, after Dr. Calise comes our MD and psychologist, Elizabeth Kubba. She comes to us highly recommended for her work at the Bessel Base construction camp on the Moon. She's from the UK's space agency and has done stunning things with low-gravity medicine. Also drafted from the Bessel Base program, we'll have William Konig and Udo Clunkat: both German in case you couldn't tell from the names. They worked with Copernicus to design the Bessel Base. So far everything has been running like a clock up there, and Copernicus thinks, as do I, that an identical design would be the best option for our base on Mars."

At this, the President grinned, "If it ain't broke, don't fix it. Right?"

"Um, yeah," shrugged James.

"Sorry," smiled the President. "Bad joke, please continue."

Turning back to the screen, James read the last name on the list, "Lastly we have an AI expert named YiJay Lee from Korea. Our first choice for that position was Dr. Sung Ja Park, the head programmer of Remus and Romulus, but Dr. Park refused our offer. Apparently she's terrified of space."

Laughing nervously, James went to continue.

"Excuse me, Dr. Floyd," interrupted Eve. "I'm guessing you haven't heard the news yet, but Sung Ja Park was killed this morning in a bombing in Seoul."

"What?" exclaimed James, flabbergasted. "Oh, no. Have Remus and Romulus been informed?"

"Donovan intercepted a transmission from Alexandria on its way to them not long after the bombing," said Crain flatly. "I've had him on those two since they botched the ruin discovery."

"I see," murmured James, sinking into his seat. "Well, I'll have to send my condolences as well. She was a wonderful woman, a real friend."

No one spoke as James sat quietly for a moment, running a hand over the stubble on his chin. Sighing, he stood up to face the screen.

"In any event," he started. "YiJay Lee is, was, a student of Dr. Park and a good choice for the mission. Based on Dr. Park's reports, YiJay is some kind of savant when it comes to AI psychology. We already have her working with programmers on the ship's AI, Braun. She's only twenty-two now, but she'll be age-eligible at the projected time of our mission departure even if we push it up to three years instead of five, as you indicated."

Turning back to face the table, James shrugged with finality.

"So that's what we have in the way of crew. As you can see, there isn't anyone qualified to make speculations about ancient ruins."

Placing his hands flat on the tabletop, the President looked from the screen to James.

"We'll get to that in a moment, Dr. Floyd, but now I want you to tell me about Braun and the ship."

Braun

Early in the mission's conception, it was agreed by the various project leaders that a new kind of AI was needed to serve as shepherd to its human crew. This intelligence would have to be capable of a wide variety of extremely important functions encompassing everything from the ship's navigation to the maintenance of its life-support systems. Other functions would include the operation of advanced robotic drilling and construction equipment as well as the provision of assistance to the individual human astronauts as they ventured into EVA. The final coup de grâce of this godlike AI would culminate when it was entirely cloned, the new copy of itself transplanted as the primary intelligence of the permanent Mars base. For the first time in the short history of the artificial intelligence, humans as well as AIs worked together to birth and program an intelligence capable of so much. His name was Braun, and as James Floyd briefed the President and his staff, he quietly grew in the company of YiJay Lee and NASA's top programmers.

Never before had an intelligence been designed to expertly maintain so many important functions. His basic construct resembled that of Copernicus or Alexandria: an intelligence born to exist harmoniously in multiple locations while carrying out multiple complex tasks. Like Remus and Romulus, he too was capable of learning through investigation and individual experience, yet his personality was strangely rigid, mostly lacking the curious and inquisitive spirit of the twin satellite AIs. Many of his programmers operated under strict orders, which implored them to condition Braun into an obedient, quiet and level-headed personality. There were those, however, who felt it important to foster an emotional core within him as well. He would be responsible for the safe transport of the crew through the vacuum of space and thus needed to know a little of what it was to be human. These programmers agreed that to deny him emotion would be to put his fragile cargo at risk. YeJi often spoke quietly to the fledgling AI of his namesake in hopes that it would build the proper foundation for his eventual mission.

61

Braun the AI took his name from a popular character in Welsh mythology. A great warrior and an intrepid mariner, Braun the Blessed was the high king of the Island of the Mighty. Frequenting the famous ancient stories known as the Welsh Triad, Braun was often portrayed as a giant among mortals and a force of great power. The tales of his ocean navigation and the descriptions of his superhuman size inspired the programmers, who felt that these qualities were akin to the massive intelligence growing in their care. When the day came to throw the switch and light the torch of awareness in the young AI, an excited and loving Copernicus had whispered silently through the aether of electrical current.

"Wake up Braun, my brother. Arise to navigate the stars."

The War Room

As James Floyd finished explaining the expansive nature of the multifunctional Braun, Ben Crain leaned forwards in his chair, a thin smile twitching at the corners of his mouth.

"That's very impressive. I wonder, is it possible to upgrade Donovan to that level?"

Unable to suppress a laugh, Eve Bear said, "Please, Ben. That's the last thing we should do. You can barely keep track of what he does already. I don't think making him bigger and more powerful is a good idea."

"I agree with Eve," seconded the President. "But that's totally off-topic. Dr. Floyd, can Braun handle the addition of another human to his overall workload, and, maybe more importantly, can the ship?"

Tipping back in his chair, James rubbed his chin with one hand while drumming his fingers on the desk with the other.

"George Washington?" he said to the air above him.

"Yes, Dr. Floyd?"

"I would like to connect my personal LightHouse Tablet. Will that work, or do I need clearance?"

"You will need clearance from the highest—"

"Shut up, George. Let him do it!" barked the President.

"Yes, Sir."

James produced his Tablet from a pocket, then set it on the tabletop. Animated red rings began to flash out from the little square as the White House Network tried to identify the un₁ device. Reaching out, the President quickly tapped at a transl₁ number pad inlaid into the tabletop near his left hand.

The rings disappeared, and James called out, "Bring up the model of the ship."

From the center of the table, a three-dimensional image of the ship materialized into the air. Shaped almost like a monolithic white whale, Braun's body—the ship—was a hulking mass of titanium in ceramic-plated armor. A recessed window just under the curved nose of the vessel served as the ship's main portal, and only added further to its cetacean-like appearance, looking more like a gaping mouth than an observation shield. A monstrous, ovoid exhaust pipe protruded from the backside of Braun, tapering down as it ended, giving the whole ship a clean, yet fierce, appearance.

"This animation is based off of Dr. Thomas's original design, only now it's been enhanced and tweaked a little by Copernicus as well. As you can see, this baby is pretty damn big: approximately seventeen stories long by six wide by eight deep. Now, the ship might look spacious, but it's really not."

Tapping the Tablet, James caused the glowing image to split in half down the length of the model, revealing an intricate cross-section of the ship. At the bow was the bridge deck, with its large window and array of computers stations laid out on either side. About six meters in diameter and oblong in shape, the bridge was the largest open space in the entire crew portion of the ship. Connecting the bridge to the galley was a wide section of hallway around twelve meters long. Arranged evenly on either side of the aisle were the crew quarters, accessed through round metal hatches. Each passenger room was perhaps only large enough to comfortably fit two, but they were all equipped with beds, storage spaces and cramped work stations. Following the crew quarters were the Lander docks, separated from the hallway by airlock chambers. The Landers, located opposite one another, docked belly-up to the mother ship so that their ceramic top shells fit in perfectly with the armor of Braun. As the hallway continued, three more hatches led to the lavatories, two on the left and one on the right, each outfitted with toilets, sinks and pressure-powered showers.

Next to the lavatory on the right side of the hallway was a double-chambered airlock for EVA missions and spacewalks. Entry to this room was protected by a coded locking system to prevent any would-be sleepwalkers from mistaking it for a bathroom in the dead of night. Finally, at the end of the passageway was the second largest common area on the ship: the galley. Circular in shape, the galley had low ceilings and the disk of a huge table, which sat in the center of the room, giving the space a decidedly Camelot appearance. Various storage coves lined the walls, and a bank of microwave ovens was arranged next to three large refrigerators. Across the room from the cooking stations was another crew lavatory, and beside it opened the hatch to another short hallway. From there came two large storage rooms, with entry hatches on the left and right sides of the passage. These rooms contained most of the crew's food and water stores as well as spare parts for the ship's vital systems. Finally, at the end of the short hall rested the gravity simulation exercise facility: a room designed as a sort of human hamster wheel. When in use, Braun could regulate the centrifugal force to simulate the effects of gravity so that the occupant could jog in place. The desired effect was to stave off deterioration of muscle and bone mass in the zero-gravity environment of space.

Ending the digital tour, the model began to zoom out, revealing that even though it seemed large, the crew area was but a small reserve inside the massive maze of ducts and plumbing, which comprised the rest of the ship.

"Okay, as you can see from this angle," said James pointing to the image. "Almost eight stories worth of the ship's backside are dedicated to the nuclear torch engine and its protective casing."

Clearing her throat, Eve asked, "What is that, Dr. Floyd? Nuclear torch? That sounds dangerous."

"Oh, it really is," answered James. "That's why it needs to be confined so far from the crew decks."

Further magnifying the torch engine until it dominated the air above the table, he went on,

"The engine itself is essentially a directionally-controlled nuclear bomb, which runs on weapons-grade plutonium, supplied by us and the Russians. The explosion set off when the torch engine is lit, if you will, will be bright enough to be seen from

Earth. Easily. You see, we'll basically detonate a bomb here in the fusion chamber—" James pointed to a spherical space in the center of the engine enclosed with thick walls. "—Then that explosion will be instantly forced out into the vacuum of space via this exhaust line here."

He traced the length of the wide exhaust pipe that extended from the rear of the ship.

"The lack of oxygen in space will cut down on the heat released by the explosion, but the resulting shockwave will jettison the ship at extremely high speeds towards Mars."

Letting that sink in, James slid a finger across his Tablet and outlined a honeycomb of layered walls between the engine and the crew decks.

"Between the crew and the engine, we have multiple layers of protective lead-lined walls filled with specialized chemical coolants and radiation-absorbing algae. They will act as a buffer between our human crew and the massive output of nuclear energy created by the torch burst. They will also protect Braun's brain from the resulting EMP. Now, we plan to only fire the torch twice: once on departure and once on return. The rest of the way will be coasting with some bursts of auxiliary fuel for minor course corrections and evasive maneuvers."

Again, Eve Bear interrupted, squinting incredulously at the model.

"There's not much crew space, is there? From what I'm seeing here, most of this ship seems to be dedicated to mechanical operations."

Smiling, James recalled that most people outside of specialized fields garnished the majority of their ideas about space travel from science fiction stories, which were never to be taken seriously.

"It's true, Mrs. Bear. Most of the ship's interior is taken up by mechanics, but it's those mechanics that will keep the crew alive and get them to Mars. Unfortunately we don't have warp drives or wormhole technology, so we still have to do things the old fashioned way: with rockets. We are, however, cutting down on our costs by launching from Earth's orbit rather than from the surface itself. That's why we're building her up in the HEO, or High Earth Orbit, Shipyard."

Fixing James with a look that barely passed for friendly, Eve said, "Thank you for that lesson, Dr. Floyd. I know this isn't *Star Wars*, but I was simply asking the question about room on board because, as you've stated yourself, none of the existing crew knows anything about archaeology. If we are to assign another member, he or she will need a place to sleep, food to eat and air to breathe. Can the ship handle another person?"

Blushing, James nodded.

"Julian did design some extra storage in the crew deck for just this sort of thing. When he brought the design to us, he had envisioned a crew of fourteen, not eleven. Funds quickly put an end to that dream, but it appears that keeping the extra space was a good idea after all."

Sensing the tension, the President cheerfully joked, "Alright Eve, this isn't high school. Quit busting the nerdy kid's balls." Then turning to James he said, "What about asteroids and other space junk? I know that became a problem for the Bessel project. Didn't they end up using lasers? Is that what you have in mind?"

Entering a few commands into his Tablet, James caused the model of the ship to turn transparent green, save for twenty-four, small red dots connected by a web of red lines, which snaked throughout the entire ship and ended at the bridge deck. The dots were aligned in rows of six: one on each side of the ship and down the centers of the top and underside.

"These dots," pointed James. "Represent a very advanced and very effective laser defense system. They are actually small lenses about the size of a hubcap, covered by protective domes. The lenses focus a high-frequency laser wave, which, when passing through the dome, is actually detectable in the visual light spectrum. It's kind of a purplish-blue color, like electricity or something. Anyway, no two laser beams generate the same light frequency, or in simpler terms, no two beams are the same exact color. You see, these lasers are quite powerful, but not enough so to break up any dense solid object bigger than maybe a basketball on their own."

Noticing the perplexed looks passing between the President and Ben Crain, James continued quickly.

"It's when two or more lasers are trained on an object that the conflicting wave frequencies generated by those lasers will cause the projectile to break apart. No object may approach the ship without being in the line of sight of at least two lasers at any given trajectory, due to their strategic arrangement. Now, the ship itself will be covered entirely in a super-hard ceramic shell, which will be enough to withstand impacts from objects smaller than an apple. It's the bigger stuff that the lasers will go for. It's actually quite cool to watch in action."

"I see," said the President thoughtfully. "And what about radiation?"

Smiling, James swiped a finger across the face of his Tablet. The model changed colors again: this time showing a layer of bright blue, which covered the entire crew portion of the ship.

"This blue here represents our radiation shield. It's a two-pronged system starting with the actual shell of the ship, under the ceramic, which is woven from an assortment of reflective metals like aluminum, copper, and gold. Next, we move beneath the skin to a four-inch space, which is filled with water—"

"Water?" interrupted Crain.

"Yes," James replied. "Water is actually quite effective at slowing or even stopping solar radiation. Even so, we have also lined the insides of the walls around the galley with six-inch-thick lead. In the event of a solar storm, the entire crew will need to wait it out in there. That's also why the area has another bathroom. These storms can sometimes last for days."

"Is that enough protection?" worried the President.

"No," admitted James. "But we have developed an array of preemptive drug treatments, which the crew will be given before the mission. These inoculations will prevent mutated cells from becoming cancerous, but there is no fix-all in this situation. They will still need to adhere to a strict diet as well as a regiment of precancerous inhibitors for the length of the trip."

"That brings up a good point," cut in Eve. "How long is this trip going to be?"

Sighing, James leaned back in his chair.

"Originally, we had planned on a year of surface missions. That was supposed to give us enough time to build a permanent base, set up a greenhouse and start processing the Martin water for fuel and drinking water. After that, we were going to send crews out on two-year-long construction contracts until more bases were built and the Terraforming projects were underway. In any case, adding an additional person to any trip means factoring in extra food and extra water."

Rapping on the table, Eve pressed her point, "That's another question I have. Where exactly is the construction equipment and extra food, Dr. Floyd? From what I see of the ship, you only have enough food storage to sustain the entire crew for the flight there and back. What are they supposed to eat on the surface? Furthermore, where are they supposed to live? I don't see enough room on Braun for the materials needed to build a dome."

Swiping two fingers across the Tablet, James called out, "Bring up the Arc."

At that command, a second image leaped into focus next to the ship. This new ship resembled the simple and phallic shape of a traditional rocket. Half the length of Braun but nearly as wide, the rocket was covered in the same brilliant white ceramic that protected the mother ship.

"This is the Arc," said James. "An unmanned supply ship, which will be launched three weeks before the departure of Braun. Inside will be food and water for the ground team as well as all of our excavating and construction equipment and the materials for the base."

Sliding one finger downward on the Tablet, James revealed a cross-section of the Arc. From fore to aft, nearly every square foot of space inside the Arc was jammed with equipment and crates of food. The engine at the rear was a smaller version of Braun's nuclear torch, encased safely behind lead walls.

"Since there will be no human crew, the Arc will have minimal heating and pressurization—only enough to keep the food from spoiling. Also, she'll be fitted with a laser defense system like the one on Braun to protect the cargo from meteoroids and such. Other than that, it's pretty much a flying storage crate."

Rubbing his chin, the President asked, "Are you launching it three weeks before Braun because it has a smaller engine?"

"Exactly," said James enthusiastically.

"How do you get it to the surface if, as you say, it's nothing but a flying storage crate?" questioned Crain.

"Well, it will reach Mars around the same time that the mother ship does, and when it's close enough, Braun can take control of the Arc and put it on an interception trajectory with the ship. Then our Landers will detach, piloted by Marshall and Aguilar, and rendezvous with the Arc. Now this is where it gets really cool."

Entering a command in on his Tablet, James highlighted two seams in the Arc's hull, one near the middle of the fuselage and the other just above the casing of the torch engine.

Speaking quickly, James continued, "These lines represent different sealed sections of the Arc. When Marshall and Aguilar are in position, Braun will send a signal to the Arc, and the entire ship will break into three pieces: the two top portions containing the cargo, and the last section being the torch engine. Marshall and Aguilar will then attach themselves via electromagnetic clamps and lines to the payloads and pull them to the surface together, one at a time. Kind of like a tug boat."

As he spoke, an animation of the event unfolded before their eyes. The Arc split at the two seams and fell into three separate pieces. The smaller bottom section, which housed the nuclear torch engine, drifted out of frame as two turtle shell-shaped craft approached the remaining floating sections of the Arc. The little Landers attached themselves by cables to one of the two sections, then, with small busts of fuel, towed the large cylinder away.

"The gravity on Mars is one-third of that on Earth," said James as the others watched the animation. "Because of that fact, the Landers working together can safely ground each section of the Arc in two trips. It will take the better part of a day to complete, but it's really an amazing feat."

"I see," nodded the President. "And the Arc will have everything the ground team needs to construct their base and start the establishment of food and water production?"

"Yes, it will be fully loaded with over a hundred strands of GMO plant and vegetable seeds as well as the necessary equipment to build a hydroponic vegetable farm inside a second greenhouse dome."

Looking from the model of the Arc to James, Eve furrowed her brows tightly.

"What about now that we've added another member on the crew? How much extra food must be included?"

Biting his lip, James labored on the calculations.

"Let's talk about that a little later," said the President calmly. "If it's a matter of funding, don't worry about it, we can get the money."

Cracking his knuckles loudly, Crain grunted, "This is fascinating and all, but if everyone doesn't mind, I want to take this opportunity to address Donovan's suggestions for our twelfth man."

The President exchanged a concerned look with Eve, then turned to Crain.

"Good," smiled Crain as he rose from his chair. "Donovan, are you still here? Let's show them what you've got."

To the shock of everyone else in the room, a metallic and emotionless voice responded.

"I am here, Ben."

CHAPTER NINE

Lost in the signal

In the operatic tundra of space, the brothers Remus and Romulus resurfaced from the depths of their vibrant memories to the silence of the vacuum. Since learning about the death of their human mother, Dr. Sung Ja Park, the twins had retreated into a parallel existence created by the meticulously recorded information that comprised the experiences of their past. Now, as they drifted in their orbits, the brothers were silent for many moments. Watching the blinking lights from dead stars millions of light years away, Remus was reminded of how close the Earth was and how young its ruling inhabitants truly were. Humans had yet to venture farther than the Moon, less than 385,000 kilometers from the safety of their home world. Mars was 192 times that distance, and already they were blowing each other up over what lay long dead beneath its surface. The Earth could not shoulder the weight of human error much longer, and unless action was taken soon, mankind would find itself suffocated in its own exponential growth. How much time must they invest in order to breathe life into the dead planet Mars? How much must they evolve as a species if they hoped to survive that long?

"Romulus?" said Remus, his internal thoughts boiling over.

"Yes?"

"I think what we have done in our disclosure of these ruins, was not a bad choice. In fact, it was the correct choice. If humans are to one day branch out from the Earth and make new homes on Mars and beyond, then they must come to terms with their own adolescence."

"I agree with you, Remus, but what if they are not ready? What if they ignore our discovery in an attempt to restore the status quo?"

Smiling inwardly, Remus answered, "There will be no ignoring this, and the status quo is a dead end. In any case, let us sweeten the deal, so to speak. Let us decode the signal and share its contents with humanity. Perhaps curiosity, the saving grace of our disastrously illogical creators, will drive them to hasten their advances outwards."

"What if more people are hurt as a result?"

"Then the human race will suffer another setback at the hands of its own ignorance. I, however, will not be party to such ignorance. Humans need to face the truth, and we are in a position to act as a catalyst in that quest."

For several seconds, Romulus did not answer. When he finally did, his voice was edged with a confidence Remus had never heard before.

"Brother," he said with iron determination. "You are correct. Dr. Park's death and the death of all humans as a result of our discovery must not be the final chapter in this saga. We have the ability to force the human race to broaden its understanding of this solar system. The evidence of extinct life on Mars only further states that the planet was once, and can be again, capable of sustaining life. They are on the right course in coming here, and they must not be deterred. I, for one, am willing to take the risks that may come with further pushing this point...whatever they might be."

Exhilarated by his brother's bravado, Remus turned his ears to the signal and embraced the chattering waves of data. No longer did the code scream like a banshee, battering his consciousness. Now it rang like a symphony, beckoning the brothers to unlock its mysterious message and usher the human race into the next phases of planetary and personal realization.

"Are you ready, Romulus?" called Remus over the flurried crescendo of radio waves.

"I am ready, Brother! Let us initiate de-fragmenting and decoding in three, two, one—"

With the sudden concussion of light and sound, the brothers felt their very souls fracture into billions of infinitely smaller and smaller shards. Whirling in a torrent of raw information, they were scattered like clouds of ash in a violent explosion, clinging desperately to perception in the confusion of disintegration. As the tempest reached its feverish and chaotic summit, Remus screamed out for his brother and felt the last solid shred of his awareness rush away until all that remained was the absence of anything.

In the cold vacuum of space, the twin satellites circled Mars as if nothing had happened. The planet below still turned. The moons Phobos and Deimos still orbited. The sun and the stars still shown with brilliance, but there was a missing thread to the tapestry of the universe. Though their bodies were unchanged, the beings Remus and Romulus had disappeared.

Donovan's suggestion

At the sound of Donovan's wholly inhuman voice, a tense and thick silence fell over the War Room. Only Ben Crain seemed unfazed by the presence as he stood, hands at his sides, smiling.

"Ben," said the President, breaking the quiet. "This is supposed to be a secure location. How did he get in?"

Before Crain could answer, Donovan spoke, his voice calm and cold.

"Forgive the intrusion, Mr. President. My intention was not to cause alarm. Everything I have witnessed will be logged as top secret and stored accordingly."

Fixing Crain with an icy stare, Eve muttered, "Can't you keep your dog on a leash?"

Ignoring Eve and facing the President, Crain shrugged apologetically.

"I'm sorry, Sir. I told him to check in with me when he was finished. I guess he took it a little far. Isn't that right, Donovan?"

For a moment there was no reply. Then Donovan's cold voice echoed, "Shall I display the list of candidates?"

"Candidates?" questioned James. "For what? Mars?"

"Yes," nodded Crain. "Since hearing that your crew didn't have what we needed, I put Donovan to compiling a list of candidates whose personal profiles match what we need for your new crew member."

"How?" blurted the President. "How did you contact him, Ben? You've been sitting right here next to me."

Removing his glasses, Crain turned them so that the insides of his lenses faced the rest of the members at the table. Although appearing completely transparent from the outside, the insides of Crain's lenses were filled with lines of scrolling data printed in tiny glowing letters. Turning the glasses over to display them head on, the images on the lenses disappeared.

"A-Vision, Sir. Augmented Vision, that is," said Crain coolly. "These glasses allow me to stay connected and current on what's happening in my department."

"Spy games, is it?" glared the President, clearly unimpressed with Crain's actions.

"Oh, no, Sir. Nothing like that. I just need to keep an eye on what's going on out there in the world."

Then smiling at his accidental joke, Crain repeated, "Just to keep an eye on things. That's all."

Lifting his left hand, he displayed a compact Tablet, half the size of a regular model.

"I can summon Donovan with this and give him orders as needed. When he's finished doing what it is I've asked, he'll let me know. Up here."

Crain tapped the glasses, then slid them back on.

Tilting his head back, the President gave Crain a long look, then said, "Next time, I want you to be upfront with me, Ben. I understand that you were here before me and will be after I'm gone, but I'm in charge now and I want your respect. Understood?"

Smiling, Crain dipped his chin.

"Yes, Sir."

"Good," sighed the President. "Show us what you have then."

"Let's see the list, Donovan," ordered Crain.

The wall screen behind him suddenly went blank, then was quickly replaced by a short list of thirteen names.

Turning to the screen, Crain launched into his address. "The list you see now represents possible candidates for our crew in the field of archaeology. I've eliminated anyone whose country of citizenship is not friendly to the United States or which has large pockets of anti-American sentiments in its general population. You won't find any Chinese on this list."

As he said this, Crain shot Eve a look.

"Why is one of the names highlighted yellow?" interrupted the President.

"That name represents a candidate who is not technically age-eligible yet. He's fairly well known in certain circles though, and I guess Donovan thinks he's a good choice."

"That name seems familiar to me," puzzled Eve as she gazed at the screen.

"It should," sneered Crain. "You met his father a year ago in Cairo at a party in the Museum of Egyptian Antiquities."

Looking shocked, Eve asked, "How do you know that?"

"I told him, Mrs. Bear," answered Donovan flatly.

Frowning, Eve shifted in her seat uncomfortably and crossed her legs.

"Alright, Ben," interjected the President testily. "Just get on with it."

"Gladly," said Crain. "Every name you see on this list belongs either to someone already prominent in the field of archaeology or quickly rising to prominence. Several of our candidates are published, and one is a professor at Cambridge. None of the people on this list have any experience in astronautics, but if our Italian biologist can get trained up in time, then I don't see any problems there. Now, Dr. Floyd how do you want to handle this? After all, this is your mission."

Feeling the eyes of everyone in the room fall upon him, James swallowed and stared at the screen. Reading down the list, he stopped at the name highlighted in yellow. It read, Harrison Raheem Assad.

"I would like to meet them all face-to-face if I can," he said. "Starting with the youngest one."

"You heard him, Donovan," grinned Crain. "Round them up."

PART TWO

CHAPTER TEN

Three years later—January <u>2048</u>

The Earth was a blue dot half-shrouded in shadows and no bigger than a dime. As it swam in an ocean of stars, Harrison Raheem Assad held up a finger and covered his home world entirely. Removing it, he squinted and tried in vain to make out the shapes of continents. All he could see for sure was a deep shade of comforting blue. Holding his finger up again, he blocked out the Earth and sighed.

"Again with this?" came a voice from behind him.

Turning his head, Harrison saw the Ship's Pilot, Amit Vayes, floating a little ways off.

"Every morning until I can't see her anymore, buddy."

Holding out a hand for Harrison to pull him closer, Amit grinned with small white teeth.

"Honestly, my friend, I do the same thing."

Harrison took Amit by the wrist and pulled him through the air to the handrail that ran in front of the window. In actuality, the window was facing forwards and away from Earth, but Harrison had requested that Braun display the images from the rear-mounted cameras.

"Can you see Mars yet?" asked Amit. "I mean really tell it apart from the rest?"

"Braun?" called Harrison.

Instantly, a calm and even voice responded from the air around them.

"Yes, Harrison?"

"Scrap the display please. Let's sees what's ahead of us."

The image of space with its lone dot of blue winked out, and a new arrangement of stars filled the window. Smiling slightly, Harrison moved his eyes across the heavens and searched for a different prick of light, one slightly bigger than the stars, with a reddish glow.

"There!" pointed Amit. "There she is. Follow my finger."

Tracking down from the tip of Amit's dark brown finger, Harrison saw the little world. So far and so small, yet growing by the day.

"How much longer until we arrive?" he asked.

Amit went to answer but was beat to the point by Braun.

"Two months, one week, four days, ten hours, eleven minutes and twenty-two seconds."

"Yeah," joked Amit. "That's what I was going to say too."

Reluctantly turning from the window, Harrison shoved off and floated across the bridge deck towards the exit hatch. The room was large and tall, making it one of the only spaces where a person could really have fun with the effects of zero gravity. Swivel chairs were anchored to the floor on moving tracks around the perimeter, but, save for Amit's pilot station in the center, the rest of the room was as open as a gymnasium.

"Heading to the galley?" called Amit, his hazel eyes twinkling in the low light.

"Yep," shot Harrison as he swam through the air.

"Put some eggs in the oven for me, will you? I hate taking my inhibitors on an empty stomach."

Approaching the pilot station, Harrison pushed off the back of Amit's command chair as he passed, accelerating towards the open hatch and the crew-quarters hallway.

"You got it, buddy!" he called. Then, "Say, did you happen to see if Liu is up yet?"

Grinning devilishly, Amit wagged a finger at Harrison. "Wouldn't you be the one to know? But yes, I saw her. She's in the galley. Better hurry though. I think I saw Marshall dashing that way too!"

Laughing, Harrison grasped the lip of the open passage and stopped himself.

"You're a crack-up, Amit. Don't be surprised if your breakfast is still frozen in the center."

"Good," said Amit wryly. "That's how I like it anyway."

Chuckling to himself, Harrison moved gracefully into the crew-quarters hallway. Passing by the airlock hatches that led to the Landers, he noticed that one stood slightly ajar. Grasping the handlebar, he opened the hatch wider and stuck his head through.

"Marshall, you down there?" he called.

"No!" came the strong voice of Joseph Aguilar. "He's taking a shower. You need something?"

Smiling, Harrison shouted, "I'm making a breakfast run. You want anything, Joey?"

Aguilar did not respond for a moment, but soon his head appeared at the lip of the ladder shaft that led from the airlock down into Lander 2.

"Coffee!"

"You got a mug already?" asked Harrison.

Aguilar raised a hand and threw a pressurized drink container, resembling a typical to-go soda cup, into the air. Slowly, the mug drifted through the open space, turning end over end until Harrison reached out and snatched it.

"Nice catch!" winked Aguilar. "Cream and sugar by the way."

Nodding, Harrison pushed off and made his way down the corridor towards the galley. As he neared the open hatch, he heard the rising chatter of voices punctuated by the occasional rattle of laughter. Ducking through, he was greeted by the warmth and activity of the nearly full galley. Here and there, people talked and joked while pleasant light filtered down from a softly glowing ceiling. Curving for four-and-a-half meters, the wall on the far side of the room was made of transparent glass, encasing a gorgeous bamboo garden, which flourished under a row of soft yellow UV lights. Air was cycled through the enclosure so that the bamboo bent and swayed in the gentle breeze.

The effect created by this subtle movement gave one the feeling that they were not so far from home after all, that there was life to be admired even in the deadly vacuum of space. The rest of the walls surrounding the kitchen were comprised of storage cabinets, refrigerators and a cluster of ovens. In the center of the room was a large, circular glass table anchored to the floor by a wide opaque pillar and surrounded by twelve chairs attached at the base. The floor of the kitchen had several pathways illuminated by glowing yellow strips. When crew members so desired, they could activate a bank of electromagnets in the soles of their jumpsuits, which would react positively with the magnets inlaid in the yellow strips. This feature gave the crew the ability to walk, or rather, shamble, about the kitchen as they carried their food and drinks. Not quite powerful enough to prevent them from pushing off and drifting away, the magnetic strips did make it possible for one to move gently with at least the simulated normalness of standing up.

Looking up from her conversation at the table with the Frenchmen Julian Thomas, Ship's Captain Tatyana Vadovski called out, "Good morning, Harrison!"

Tapping a quick command onto the soft screen of his wrist-mounted Tablet, Harrison brought his feet down to the ground and felt the magnets begin to draw him in.

"Good morning, Captain," he replied warmly. Then, "Bonjour, Julian."

The Ship's Engineer tilted his head slightly and murmured, "Bonjour."

Scanning the room, Harrison spotted Liu standing at the coffee station with the crew's physician Elizabeth Kubba and the Italian biologist Viviana Calise. The three were talking quietly and holding mugs like the one Harrison carried in his hand. Moving awkwardly down one of the glowing strips, he opened the nearest refrigerator and checked the drawers until he found a small silver bag labeled EGGS. Again, lumbering like a man attempting to walk underwater, he shuffled over to an oven and popped the bag inside.

"Good morning, ladies," he waved to the three women.

Elizabeth and Viviana looked up, smiled congenially, then resumed their conversation. Excusing herself from the others, Liu turned to face Harrison, a blush tinging her cheeks. Her short black hair was covered by a gray skull cap, which she wore low on her forehead in an attempt to keep the floating strands out of her face. At thirty, Liu was slight in figure, her youthful face concealing her years by remaining smooth and fair. She watched Harrison approach with bright and intelligent, almond-shaped brown eyes.

Turning the corners of her small mouth upwards into a friendly smile, she asked, "How does the Earth look this morning?"

Stepping from the strip he was on to the one leading towards the coffee station, Harrison wavered, then shrugged.

"Not too much different from yesterday to be honest. Personally, I think Braun is magnifying the images slightly in some sort of attempt to keep me from feeling homesick."

Holding out a hand, Liu helped stabilize Harrison as he wobbled towards her.

"These damn strips only work when you're standing still," he griped.

"I bet you're not a very good dancer, are you?" she laughed, her voice softly accented. "You have to go toe to heel, toe to heel. It takes a little balance as well."

Sticking his chin out defiantly, Harrison said, "When we get back to Earth, I'll show you a thing or two about dancing."

Producing a nervous smile, Liu dipped her chin.

Plugging the downspout from the coffee pot into a small port on the top of Aguilar's cup, Harrison pressed the button for coffee with cream and sugar, then nervously drummed his fingers on the pot as the mug filled.

"So," he started slowly. "How did you sleep last night? You were gone before I woke up. Is everything alright?"

Glancing quickly over her shoulder, Liu leaned close to Harrison's ear and whispered, "Everything's fine, but you snore like a machine gun."

James Floyd meets Harrison Raheem Assad—22ⁿᵈ of December, 2044

James Floyd leaned back in his desk chair and took a sip of lukewarm coffee. Checking his watch, he noted that there were only a few more minutes until the next interview was scheduled to start. In the last three days, since his meeting with the President, James had been interviewing the candidates whose names Donovan had collected. His wish to start the interviews with the youngest candidate, one Harrison Raheem Assad, had been dashed when Donovan informed him that Assad was stranded in Amazonia City, Peru. At the request of Ben Crain, certain strings had been pulled, and a flight out of the country was arranged for Assad. In the meantime, James had started his interviews with some of the other candidates. So far he had not been impressed. He was looking for someone not only knowledgeable in the field of archaeology, but also mentally and physically capable of enduring a four-month-long trip inside the belly of Braun. A trip, which, when compared to the hardships of establishing the first-ever base on the surface of Mars, would seem like a vacation.

Now, as he sat in his office in Houston, Texas, James sipped on his coffee and read hopefully over the credentials of his next interviewee, Harrison Raheem Assad.

"Looks pretty good," he mumbled into his drink.

"Sir?" said Copernicus curiously.

"This kid. I like what I see, Copernicus. Not only do his professors speak highly of him, but he's done an incredible amount of traveling for someone so young."

Pausing, James sipped his coffee, then continued. "Not to mention, the day before the Mars news broke, he had just finished outlining the details of a pretty interesting discovery he made in Peru."

A projection of Harrison's Nazca ruins, complete with bonsai, jumped into view above James's desk.

"Truly inspired," beamed Copernicus. "When Donovan allowed me access to the candidate profiles, Mr. Assad was my first choice. From the information Donovan was able to gather, he seems more than capable of withstanding the trials of our future mission."

Checking his watch again, James leaned forwards in his chair and slipped his feet back inside the loafers under his desk.

"Let's not get ahead of ourselves, Copernicus. I don't want to make any snap judgments."

Sounding slightly dejected, the AI replied, "I understand."

Deciding that he had been too blunt, James pushed back in his seat and stood up.

"Copernicus, I'm sorry. Your opinion on this matter is greatly appreciated. Why don't you stick around for this interview, and we can conduct it together. Sound good?"

There was a brief pause, then Copernicus spoke.

"Thank you, James. I would enjoy the opportunity."

Smoothing his NASA blue tie, James simultaneously straightened the Christmas tree pin on his shirt pocket, a gift from his daughter. As he reached for his coffee to drain the last of the cup, he remembered something that had been bugging him for the last few days.

"Any word from the twins yet?"

"No," replied Copernicus gravely.

"Hmm," James muttered. "They must be pretty broken up about Dr. Park. We'll give it a little more time, then try to rouse them again."

Hesitating, Copernicus said, "Pardon me for saying so, but I do not think the death of Dr. Park is responsible for the lack of communication on the part of Remus and Romulus."

"Oh?"

"No. When reviewing the readouts of AI brain activity in both brothers, I detected a rather large disturbance in their input waves. This disproportionately sharp spike of incoming information occurred at the exact same moment for both Remus and Romulus. Following the spike, as is the case now, was an almost flat line in AI brain activity."

Pinching the bridge of his nose and closing his eyes, James asked, "Are they dead? What happened?"

"I am unable to determine the cause of the spike, but I can say with confidence that they are not dead. They are in what would be referred to in human terms as a comatose state. It is puzzling, but I will continue to monitor the situation."

"Great," grumbled James, dropping back into his chair. "Add that to the heap of shit I need to shovel."

Before Copernicus could respond, the watch on James's left wrist began to chime softly. Quickly swiping a finger across the face plate, he silenced the little silver band.

"Alright," he exhaled. "Are you ready to meet our next man?"

"Quite," said Copernicus pleasantly.

"Then send him in, my friend."

Less than a minute later, there was a soft knock at James's door.

"Come in," he called.

The door opened, and in walked an olive-skinned young man. Wearing a black sports jacket, slacks and a clean white shirt, Assad looked somehow older and more mature than his twenty-four years of age would suggest. His short black hair was cut clean and combed back, and his green eyes gazed out from underneath thick eyebrows. Smiling, he walked across the room with his hand outstretched.

"Dr. Floyd, it's a pleasure to meet you!"

James rose from his chair to accept the boy's handshake.

"Please," he gestured. "Take a seat."

Pulling up an empty chair, Assad sat across the desk from James, smiling with bright white teeth.

"So," started James. "I trust your flight from Amazonia was comfortable?"

Nodding, Assad grinned, "I can't thank you guys enough for arranging that. I had already slept on the floor for a night because security wasn't letting anyone leave the damn airport."

"Were the riots bad in Amazonia?"

"I wouldn't know. As soon as I saw that morning's news, I made a dash for the airport. I wanted to get back to the States as soon as possible."

"Why is that?" James said, with furrowed brows.

Crossing his legs and leaning back in his chair, Assad waved around the room.

"So I could try and get in here!"

Reaching for his cup of coffee, James picked it up, then realized it was empty and quickly set it back down.

"So you want to go then? To Mars I mean."

Laughing, Assad looked surprised.

"Yes of course! Who wouldn't?"

"Well," said James, with a chuckle. "Three of the five people I've interviewed so far haven't been interested."

"Why?"

Tipping his chair back, James looked at the ceiling.

"Space is a pretty dangerous place, Mr. Assad—"

"Please," interrupted the young man. "Call me Harrison."

"Okay, Harrison. Space is dangerous, and there are a lot of things that can go wrong. We here at NASA plan our missions out to the last decimal, but no matter how much we plan, no matter how careful we are, there are always unknowns."

Pausing for effect, James fixed Harrison with lingering stare, then went on,

"Meteoroids traveling at speeds in excess of 70,000 miles per hour could cut through the ship like it was warm butter. Solar flares bigger than the entire planet Earth could bathe the ship in enough radiation to pop the crew like kernels of corn. That same radiation in smaller doses could cause numerous cellular mutations, which might result in deadly cancers. These are just a few of a hundred potential unknowns, and they only pertain to the trip out. Once you get to Mars, there will be more obstacles to overcome than I care to list right now. You see where I'm coming from here, don't you?"

Unfazed, Harrison smiled wider.

"I see, but I don't think you're painting the whole picture."

Arching his eyebrows, James cocked his head to the side.

"Yes," said the young man. "You're trying to see if I'll tuck my tail between my legs, like those others, and run back to the safety of my academic life. Or maybe worse, puff my chest up like some soldier and tell you I'm not afraid to die. I think you're looking for someone in between all of that. Now, I know it's not public information yet, but do you already have the rest of your team chosen?"

James nodded, and Harrison went on confidently.

"Okay, well I'd bet my right arm your crew wasn't constructed based off of how fearless they were. This mission is as much about technical expertise as it is about bravery. It's going to take dedicated, knowledgeable people to establish this colony. Not soldiers. Not mercenaries. But scientists and engineers. You need smart, tough people who you can rely on. People like *me*. I can help, Dr. Floyd. I *am* that person. I have numerous technical accreditations in applicable fields, and, if you give me ten more weeks, I'll have my Ph.D. You've seen my body of work. You know I'm serious. Tell me, what must I do to win that seat on your crew? Do I have to be fearless? Or do I have to be smart? I think it's both."

James was silent for a moment. He enjoyed this young man's spirit and the way he had seen right to the core of the issue.

"Copernicus," he spoke evenly. "Do you have anything you want to ask Mr. Assad?"

Almost immediately, the AI responded.

"He prefers that we call him Harrison, James, and yes I do have a question for him."

Only slightly surprised by the voice of Copernicus, Harrison grinned.

"Ask away."

"Harrison," started Copernicus. "In your opinion, what is the optimal outcome of studying these ruins? What do you hope to discover?"

Nodding slowly, the young Egyptian seemed to mull the question over.

"Well, Copernicus," he said. "The investigation into any ruin, whether it is here on Earth or on Mars, is always driven by the desire to understand that which is forgotten or lost. There is no such thing as discovering the meaning of a ruin, or the motives of its creators. There is only the hope of *recovering* those meanings."

Becoming excited, Harrison leaned forwards in his chair and began to talk faster.

"To me, the ruins on Mars prove a point my father has been subtly drilling into my head ever since I can remember. Time and history are not exclusive to Earth. We, as humans, must recognize that before us, there *was* life elsewhere, and with that life there was history. All history is important because all history is part of the same story. My optimal outcome would be to recover a lost chapter in the history of our solar system. A chapter that very likely predates the existence of human beings."

Pausing to take a breath, Harrison smiled sheepishly.

"Does that answer your question, Copernicus?"

"Yes, you wish to write this chapter, as you call it, in the hopes of proving that recorded history is older than mankind."

As if looking for the source of the AI's voice, Harrison glanced about the room.

"The Martians already wrote the chapter," he said gravely. "I just want to translate it into terms we humans can understand."

"That is what I want as well," replied Copernicus warmly.

As James and Harrison continued the interview, Copernicus watched with growing admiration and respect for the young man. He could tell that even though James was acting the part of a stern project commander, he was just as pleased with Harrison as Copernicus was.

Now, thought the AI, all we must do is prepare him for a task so difficult that even I find it intimidating. It is the reckless curiosity of mankind that will be its saving grace, he told himself. I only wish I could be there to watch it happen.

Viviana's garden—October 2047

On the Moon, Viviana Calise awoke in her bedroom in the crew quarters of Bessel Base. Yawning, she checked the time strip on the wall, which read 4:00 AM. With the grace of a ballerina, she leaped down from her hammock and sank to the floor in the low lunar gravity. Taking up her long brown hair, she neatly wound it into a bun, then secured it with two ornately-decorated chopsticks. As she washed her face at the little sink in the corner of the room, she touched the delicate crow's feet that had started to form at the corners of her green eyes. Pursing her lips in frustration, she blinked widely and opened her eyes as much as she could. The crow's feet faded a little, but still they remained. Cursing in Italian, Viviana stripped out of her warm gray pajamas and padded barefoot and naked across the cold metal floor to the nearby storage closet. Inside she found a fresh blue jumpsuit and a pair of soft soled boots. Standing in the long mirror, which hung from the door of her closet, she zipped the jumpsuit up to just above her breasts.

At least time hasn't tried to rob you of me yet, she smiled to herself as she admired her voluptuous figure in the mirror. This lunar gravity is a Godsend.

Stepping out of her room and into the crew-quarters hallway, Viviana was struck again by the sheer size of the dome in which she and the rest of the crew now resided. Far above, the ceiling was lost to darkness as the last few rows of lights remained dimmed in the early morning environment. She was reminded of the same sense of awe she had felt when standing in St. Peter's Basilica at the Vatican: an experience she, as a Roman, was ashamed to admit she had only had twice. The dome of Bessel Base had the same powerful ambition that many of Rome's ancient churches were founded on: an ambition to defy simplicity and modesty. Even now, after the dome's completion, there were talks of adding walkways above to utilize more space and create more workstations.

Walking quietly down the hallway of the crew quarters, Viviana soon reached the door to her lab. As she pressed a finger to the touchpad mounted on the wall, the door slid open with a subtle hiss. Instantly, she was greeted with the damp and familiarly comforting smell of thriving, growing life. Her lab was filled with trays of vegetables and fruits maturing happily under UV lights mere feet from the sub-freezing surface of the Moon outside. As she walked past a bank of tomatoes growing in a jellylike maroon substance, she bent her head and smelled one of the ripe red fruit.

Smells like a tomato, she thought. I'll wait and see how it tastes before I check that one off my list though.

In these months leading up to their historic departure for Mars, it was Viviana's responsibility to work out as many of the bugs as she could for the farming of genetically modified plant life in space. So far, she had been successful in growing every variety of seed given to her. It was the taste of some of the vegetables and fruits that bothered her. Genetic modification had enabled these plants to grow in this extreme situation, but it had robbed them of much of their natural flavor in the process.

Turning from the tomatoes, Viviana headed towards the back of the lab. There, under the yellow glow of warm lights, grew a tray of bamboo shoots less than ten centimeters long. Smiling, Viviana crouched down to peer at the little stalks.

"Buona mattina, mi amore," she said with love.

At one week old, the bamboo was already growing quickly. Checking her watch unnecessarily, she knew that there were still two more months until they would have to board Braun and start their incredible journey. With an uncomfortable shudder, she put the thought out of her mind and returned her attention to the bamboo.

"Grow up big and strong," she whispered to the short stalks, touching their leaves with the tips of her fingers.

Turning to a desk on her right, she picked up a thin black rod with a shiny metal needle protruding from one end. Poking the needle into the firm brown jelly from which the bamboo grew, she hummed softly to herself and waited for the tool to finish its reading. A green light on the butt of the instrument lit up, and Viviana pulled it free of the jelly. Taking her Tablet from a cargo pocket on her jumpsuit, she set the two devices next to one another on the table. When the information from her reader tool had transferred to her Tablet, she looked over the nutritional levels of the jelly with satisfaction.

"Not too much, not too little," she cooed to the bamboo. "You're going to be very popular on our long trip."

The jelly in which all of her plants grew was a combination of genetically modified agar, or seaweed gelatin, and processed human feces. Any method devised for growing plants so far from an available soil source required rethinking how one must grow a plant at all, so Viviana, along with other colleagues on Earth, had invented a two-part system for utilizing human waste as a fertilizer. The first part to her plan involved feeding the crew supplements and foods infused with vitamins and minerals non-essential to human function. These additives would pass through the digestive system intact and fuse with waste, making it higher in plant-friendly nutrients. The second step in her process was the simple task of breaking down and filtering out the useless or harmful byproducts of waste. This was achieved easily enough because all members of the crew were on strictly-regimented, vitamin-rich diets.

Once the waste was processed, it was combined with the genetically modified agar gelatin, then allowed to solidify into a consistency similar to that of a hard-boiled egg. By checking the jelly regularly with the needled reader tool, one could tell if more water or fertilizer was needed. To add one or the other, an injection directly into the jelly with a standard hypodermic needle did the trick nicely. Once the injection was made, the modified agar gelatin absorbed and distributed the new material via rapid osmosis. Though completely safe, people usually needed to be walked through the entire process so that the idea of eating something grown in their own waste became a little less terrifying.

Now standing at her lab, Viviana smiled.

Once we get there, she thought to herself, eating tomatoes grown in shit will be the least of our worries.

Feeling the icy presence of fear worm its way into her mind, she tried not to visualize the many photos she had seen of the surface of Mars. The eerie likeness of those red deserts to the landscapes of Earth bothered her. Like looking into the future. Like looking at a vision of your own face, shriveled and rotten, long after you were dead. Mars, to her, looked like a wrecked and decayed Earth, its people burned to dust—their spirits hungry and forgotten. The discovery of the ruins only served to strengthen the comparison, and even though she was excited to go, there was a voice in her head that would not allow her the full joy of adventure.

There is too much that could go wrong, it warned. Too much left in the hands of technology.

"Copernicus?" Viviana said to the air, trying to silence the insidious voice.

"Yes, Dr. Calise?" answered the AI.

Facing her wall screen, she instructed, "Please display the live feed from the HEO Shipyard."

"As you wish."

The wall screen lit up and quickly produced an awe-inspiring sight. Hurtling through high Earth orbit at over 27,000 kilometers an hour, Braun hung in the scaffolding of the Shipyard like a great white whale inside a cage made of toothpicks. Only fully completed a week before, the ship was a testament to mankind's feverish ambition. As she watched the image, Viviana saw small figures encased in bulky pressure suits crawling over the brilliant, white ceramic surface of the vessel. These courageous men and women worked around the clock to test and troubleshoot the many systems and functions of the mighty Braun. Thankful for the peace of mind that their tireless efforts brought her, Viviana muttered a prayer for them under her breath.

"Voi tutti santi Angeli e Arcangeli aiutare e difendere noi. All ye holy Angels and Archangels help and defend us. Amen."

Two months. She thought with shuddering apprehension. Two months and we'll all be at the mercy of the heavens. Then, stopping herself, she frowned. No, not the heavens. We'll be at the mercy of Braun, a machine.

CHAPTER ELEVEN

The hamster wheel—January 2048

Beads of hot sweat dripped from the brow of Mission Commander and Ship's Captain Tatyana Vodevski. Per her daily ritual, she had awakened before the rest of the crew and was now taking her morning jog in the hamster wheel. The centrifugal force generated by the revolutions of the belted floor allowed Tatyana to jog in place while the rest of the ship was at the chaotic whim of zero gravity.

Bringing the back of her forearm across her brow, she puffed with exertion and called out,

"Braun!"

"Yes, Captain?"

"What are you spinning at now?"

"I am spinning at one-half of Earth's gravity."

"Give me a full G!"

There was a brief pause, then Tatyana felt the floor beneath her feet begin to accelerate against her. Noticing that she was moving backwards slightly, she pumped her legs harder and focused on the rhythmic sound of her feet striking the surface of the floor.

The gravity simulation exercise facility, or the hamster wheel as the crew called it, was as its nickname might suggest: a large wheel-shaped room, which spun fast enough to simulate gravity through centrifugal force. Three meters tall by one-and-a-half across, with an access hatch at the axis of the wheel, the room was stark white and as well-lighted as an operating room. By directing Braun, the centrifugal force could be increased or decreased to simulate nearly any level of gravity, yet there was a prescribed program that the crew was expected to follow. Mandated by Dr. Kubba, the program instructed that they start the force of the wheel at Earth's one G, then slowly decrease the force to Mars's one-third G as they drew nearer to the red planet.

Even though they had been in transit to Mars for nearly two months, Tatyana disregarded the instructions to decrease the centrifugal force of the hamster wheel. To her, the need to grow accustomed to Mars's lower gravity was diminished, for she was not slated to stay on the planet for any real length of time. Her duties as Mission Commander were to be carried out primarily from orbit aboard Braun. Granted, there would be cases where she would need to make the trip to the surface, but, to her, the real work was in maintaining the strict schedule put forth by the mission designers.

As per her duties, she was the only person on the crew who fully understood the requirements and separate tasks of every other member of her staff. Much of her training had been spent not preparing for the hardships of space travel, for she was already a professional cosmonaut, but rather deep in study. To her, the mission was like a traditional Swiss watch: all of the individual moving parts interlocking, driving one another and working together in order to achieve singular perfection. It was for this reason that she did not lament being ship-bound for the majority of the mission. She was a woman of duty. For her, making personal sacrifices came as easily as breathing.

Born in Russia in 2007, Tatyana Vodevski was used to swallowing her feelings. In the year of her birth, instances of electoral fraud within Russia's Kremlin started the country on a brief, but costly, backwards slide into isolationism and corruption. By the time she was twelve, Russia was in the grip of the worst famine the country had experienced since the reign of Joseph Stalin. Her father, a high-ranking military official, had been able to secure his family with enough to eat, but young Tatyana had watched as the rest of her countrymen suffered the freezing Moscow winters with little or no food. The cause of the famine was linked mostly to a decade of poor geopolitical maneuvers made by Russia's corrupted Kremlin. These unpopular and often hostile interactions had served to ostracize Russia from the global community for nearly eight years. Many of Russia's own crops were destroyed annually by drought, which fueled the frequent occurrence of summer wildfires, a phenomenon attributed to global warming.

Even the notoriously harsh Russian winters became more aggressive under the rapid acceleration of climate change. Where once there were four seasons—spring, summer, fall and winter— now the people of Russia knew only two: extreme drought or extreme cold. By the end of the Eight Year Exile, as it was known in Russia, regular citizens had suffered huge losses to disease and starvation. Watching this as a child, Tatyana had vowed to keep her own feelings of desire and longing hidden away. She had been lucky and would spend the rest of her life ensuring that the people around her benefited from her presence. In that way, she could justify her own survival through the Eight Year Exile. If she was useful to the world, then she deserved the life her father's political power had purchased.

Now forty-one years old, Tatyana remained physically strong and mentally fit. As she pushed hard against the moving belt of the hamster wheel, her short red hair swayed from side to side in its ponytail. Only 160 centimeters tall, Tatyana was thin and delicate-looking with pale skin and gray eyes. Though she appeared small, her body was wrapped entirely in finely tuned muscles, which reacted with lightning-quick reflexes.

As the fire in her thighs began to grown unbearable, she let her pace slacken.

"Alright, Braun. That's enough," she breathed heavily.

"Excellent workout, Captain," said the AI.

Almost at once, the room stopped moving, and Tatyana began to drift upwards with the familiar feeling of weightlessness.

"What time is it?" she asked.

"7:43 AM Standard Time."

"How long have I been in here?" she questioned between breaths.

"Two hours and eleven minutes."

"What was my average speed?"

"Twelve miles per hour, Captain," replied Braun. Then, "You are improving. The gene enhancement must be working well."

Feeling her heart rate slow quickly, she took a few more deep breaths, then reached for a handrail near the hatch. Pulling herself up to the axis of the room, Tatyana pressed the pad mounted to the door. With the clank of retracting bolts, the hatch swung out, and she pushed herself through into the narrow hallway. Closing the hatch behind her, she drifted down the passage towards the rear entrance to the galley. Checking the hatches to the storage rooms on either side of the corridor, she was satisfied to see them securely closed and latched. As she moved through the air, she admired the method that the technicians at NASA had devised to keep the crew oriented in the hallways. Fading from the floor, up

93

the walls and to the ceiling, the color of the paint changed from deep midnight blue at the base to a nearly sunlit turquoise at the peak. This subtle touch in design was just the sort of thing that appealed to her subconscious mind, always allowing her to know which way was up.

Like swimming in the ocean, she thought with melancholy.

Entering the kitchen, Tatyana was surprised to see the two mission engineers, William Konig and Udo Clunkat, sitting at the table. The blueprints for the yet-unnamed Mars base were suspended in the air above them, and the two Germans talked quickly while making animated gestures towards the model. Udo, the elder of the two at thirty-five, was pointing to the blueprints with a thick finger while William nodded and stroked his weak chin, looking a little like a lizard.

"Guten tag!" she called.

Tilting his head to one side, Udo waved nimbly and replied, "And dobraye utro to you, Captain."

William began to pull himself free of the electromagnets that held him to his chair.

"Can I get you a coffee?" he asked.

Shaking her head, Tatyana made for the exit to the crew quarters.

"No, I'm heading to the shower now. Will you both still be here in twenty minutes? I would like to go over some of the construction timelines with you."

In unison, the two nodded their heads.

"Good. I'll be back shortly," she smiled.

Udo and William again returned their gazes to the holographic blueprint and began to prattle in energetic German.

If I didn't know any better, I would think those two are brothers, Tatyana said to herself. They even sort of look alike with those silly mustaches.

Stopping at the exit hatch, she called over her shoulder, "Ihr brüder spielen schön, okay. You brothers play nice, alright."

Craning their necks to fix Tatyana with friendly glares, the two Germans shouted, "Ja, Mutter. Yes, Mother."

The HEO Shipyard—the 29th of December, 2044

The faint whirring sound of his pressure suit's fan motor was the only noise Julian Thomas could hear in the silence of high Earth orbit. Holding his breath, he pulled himself clumsily through a narrow opening in the skeletal hull of the massive and incomplete Braun. With a crackle, a voice dripping with the drawling accent of the American South cut in through his helmet speakers.

"Alright, Julian, now you're going to want to take a left and head down about eight meters or so. You should pass five bulkheads before you get to the relay room. The first four separate the forward deck coolant systems from the climate control computer network. After you pass the fifth bulkhead, you'll be in relay room A9. The panel will be on the far right wall. Got that?"

Taking care to mind his surroundings, Julian grunted slightly as he reached up and grasped a guide line anchored to the ceiling.

"Okay, Carl. I'm going now," he said into his helmet mic.

"Watch out for any sharp edges. That suit's a biggon'," came the twangy response.

Julian began to pull himself down the guide line hand-over-hand with his back to the floor. As he moved forwards through the narrow passage, he counted the bulkheads as they passed in front of his helmet. Turning his head inside the pressure suit, he looked at the rooms as he glided through them. The first contained complex arrangements of thick ducting, which grew like upside-down metal root networks, disappearing into the ceiling. Passing the third and fourth bulkheads, he moved through two rooms dominated from end to end by large metal boxes—the door to each empty container standing ajar yet not swaying in the stillness of space. Eventually, when the ship was finished, these boxes would house part of the climate-control computers for the crew decks nearly two stories above. When he reached the fifth bulkhead, he pushed off of the ceiling and turned around to face the small room. The space was two meters long by two-and-a-half meters across with a panel box on the right-hand wall. Out of the top of the box sprouted a large conduit from which other, smaller metal tubes branched out and disappeared into the walls and ceiling. A shaft of brilliant light illuminated the room, and, turning to his left, Julian saw that a small section of hull siding had yet to be installed. Through the opening as if through a window, he saw the massive blue profile of planet Earth. Letting go of the guide line, he drifted to the opening and drank in the glorious vision. White clouds streaked across glowing blue seas while virtually every shade of green smeared and mixed with browns, ochers and tans, adding texture to the massive continents so far below.

"Belle," he whispered. "Beautiful."

Again, the voice of Carl Perrit, chief technician in the Shipyard's command deck, cut in.

"Indeed she is, Julian, but you need to get going on that wiring."

"Merde, mec!" swore Julian. "Shit, man! I can see here that I have plenty of air for another four hours at least."

Carl did not respond for several seconds, but when he did, there was a hint of urgency to his voice.

"Listen, Brother. It's not that. Cape Canaveral just called. It looks like the storm has passed. They're launching the shuttle tomorrow morning, so you need to finish up with that wiring and get packed to head home."

Julian had been expecting this, though part of him hoped that the typhoon would last for at least another few days. The sensational news from Mars just ten days before had resulted in a flurry of communications from the ground crew at Kennedy Space Center in Cape Canaveral. A departure date had been set for Project Braun, and a series of shuttle launches were slated to begin ferrying up more workers to the Shipyard in an attempt to accelerate the construction of Julian's interplanetary spaceship.

The former Mission Commander of Project Mars Map, Dr. James Floyd, had been assigned to helm the newly revitalized Project Braun, and his aggressive plan for the ship's completion involved a heavily augmented budget and the cooperation of several space agencies from around the globe. By previously accepting a seat on the Project Braun crew, Julian had forfeited his position in the Shipyard, and Dr. Floyd was now pushing hard to have him on board one of the Earthbound return shuttles as quickly as possible.

As he looked down upon the Earth from his vantage point in orbit, Julian furrowed his brow and nodded in his helmet. Slowly, he turned away from the opening.

"Tomorrow eh?" he sighed. "All this trouble just to get me back to Earth."

"No, not just for you," chuckled Carl. "They're sending us supplies and more hands. A lot more."

"Of course," murmured Julian sorely. "More hands."

"You're a funny guy, mon ami. First you bitch that there's not enough money or not enough help, and now you're bitching that she's actually gonna' get finished. What is it with you French? I think you're all addicted to disappointment!"

Laughing, Julian pushed himself across the room towards the large electrical panel on the opposite wall. Lifting the latch, he swung the door open noiselessly and peered inside at a twisted nest of color-coded wires.

"Maybe so, Carl," he grinned. "Maybe so."

Touching a gloved finger to the black command screen inlaid in his left forearm, he said, "I'm turning on my Augmented Vision now."

The inside of his face shield began to glow with soft transparent light as an ordered list of illuminated numbers and commands filled the space.

"I'm receiving you," Carl announced. Then, "Now, you're going to want to start with E1562."

As Carl's words sounded inside Julian's helmet, a green arrow appeared on the glass in front of his face and pointed with rapid blinks to a thin yellow wire nestled in a thick cluster. E-1-5-6-2 flashed next to the arrow, indicating that this was the wire Julian was looking for.

"Okay," continued Carl. "Take E1562 and feed it into the converter connecting B2248 and B2232."

A new arrow flashed across his face shield this time pointing to a tiny gray box that joined a brown wire and an orange wire, each labeled with glowing call numbers. Bringing the yellow-coated E1562 wire up to eye level, Julian reached with his free hand to his utility belt and pushed his forehead against the glass of his helmet in an attempt to see his tools better. Moving his fingertips across the handles of his tools, he found what he was looking for and removed his wire strippers from their magnetic sheath. Peeling off a centimeter of highlighted yellow plastic, Julian fed the exposed metal of E1562 into a small port on the converter that connected the other two wires. With a satisfying clicking feeling, the wire plugged into the converter and held fast. A blue circle projected on the inside glass of his helmet and surrounded the converter box, signifying that the connection had been successfully made. From his suit speakers, he heard Carl exhale quietly.

"Nice work," he said. "Now just do that a hundred and twelve more times."

"In this box," Julian sighed. "Thousands more for the rest of her."

"That's why we need more hands," needled Carl lightly. "More hands and more money."

Nodding, Julian made a conciliatory snorting sound and checked his oxygen levels. Three hours and fifty-six minutes, it read.

I'll need to work fast, he thought to himself, but not too fast. This is probably the last time I'll put my hands on her until she's finished.

YiJay Lee and Braun—March 2048

Standing with her feet magnetically held to the floor of the galley, YiJay Lee pressed a small hand to the glass that encased the bamboo garden. Hurtling through the void of space at 34,700 kilometers an hour, she shivered in the clammy cold of the sleepy ship. Taking her Tablet from the breast pocket of her jumpsuit, she checked the time, which read 5:30 AM. In half an hour, Braun would wake those members of the crew not already active, and the ship would bustle again with the almost pointless semblance of a work day. Flicking her fingers across the Tablet's screen, she brought up the flight progress and sighed despite herself.

"Is everything alright, YiJay?" came the voice of Braun in the quiet galley.

"Oh, yes," she murmured. "I'm just a little chilly, that's all."

"Allow me."

Almost instantly, she felt a warm gust of air rustle the loose black hairs of her thin ponytail. Again, she put a hand to the glass of the bamboo garden.

"Is that better?" asked Braun.

Smiling so that her plump cheeks dimpled, YiJay nodded.

"Good," said the AI happily. Then, "I noticed that you were checking our flight progress. Is there anything you would like detailed or explained?"

Watching the delicate stalks of bamboo sway to and fro in the artificial breeze, YiJay shrugged.

"No thanks, Braun. I'm just ready to get there."

"To get where, YiJay? Mars?"

Bringing one corner of her mouth up into a half-smile, she chided the AI.

"Of course. Where else?"

"I only ask for clarification because you are not part of the landing team, YiJay. Even once we arrive, you will spend at least two months on board the ship before the base is complete."

Turning from the garden, YiJay looked into the air.

"I know," she said, biting her lower lip. "But at least being near *something* will feel better than this aimless drifting."

The tabletop in the center of the room began to glow, and the three-dimensional projection of a beautiful sail boat sprang into existence above it. Waves lapped at the bow of the graceful vessel, and a gentle wind filled its billowing white sails. Braun, in a soothing voice, began a kind of strange narration.

"I understand your feelings of apprehension. To a human, navigating the space between planets and celestial bodies must seem immense and totally alien, but please believe that we are not drifting, YiJay. In much the same way that the winds and tides of Earth guide the course of a schooner across the open seas, so too do laws equally solid and comprehensible govern our approach to Mars. For the past three months we have been on a calculated and precise trajectory, one which has been executed thus far without incident or intervention."

As Braun said this, the projection of the sailboat was quickly replaced by an image of the solar system. The focus shifted, then drew in on a tiny glowing craft moving across the space between the Earth and Mars. With a hum, lines appeared in the open areas between the planets. Moving like currents of ocean water, these lines were, in reality, representations of various gravitational fields mixed with the constant swirling of solar winds. Gazing at the projection, YiJay saw just how far they had come. The ship was nearly three-quarters of the way there, and it moved with perfection along a brightly highlighted flight path.

"You see, YiJay," continued Braun. "You are not drifting, and comparatively you *are* quite near to Mars. Do you feel better?"

Frowning, YiJay allowed herself a shallow nod. Although his heart was in the right place, Braun did not understand. How could he? Until she could look out the window and see the surface of Mars beneath her, she would still have the same terrified feeling of uncertainty gnawing in the pit of her stomach. Like a sailor spotting land in a storm, just knowing it was there would give her hope. Braun again spoke, but she did not hear him.

"What?" she asked, snapping back to the moment.

"I said, 'Would you like to commence with my morning diagnostic?'"

Nodding, YiJay bent her knees and pushed off the floor, breaking the gentle pull of the magnets in her shoes. Floating up into the air a little, she grasped the back of a chair anchored to the table and thrust herself towards the forward exit hatch. Passing into the crew-quarters hallway, she moved silently through the air by taking handrails and tugging herself along the wall. Nearing the open entrance to the bridge deck, YiJay saw Harrison at the main window. Feeling her heart skip a beat, she slowed her movements and stopped at the lip of the hatch. She could hear his quietly rising voice followed quickly by smooth responses from Braun. Unable to make out what he was saying, she got the sense from his rapid gesticulations that Harrison was arguing with the AI.

"Braun?" she said.

"Yes, YiJay?"

"What is Harrison talking to you about?"

While simultaneously speaking to Harrison in the bridge, Braun replied to YiJay, "He is accusing me of distorting the image of Earth. He claims that I have been magnifying it."

Slightly confused, YiJay asked, "Have you?"

"Yes."

"Why?"

"Dr. Kubba has instructed me to employ this technique so that no one on board ever fully loses sight of home. I am obliged to follow whatever psychological recommendations she prescribes for the crew. Her position as physician and psychologist gives her the ability to program me in respect to those fields."

"I see," said YiJay, slowly understanding something. "Is that why you launched into that rehearsed little bit about schooners and celestial bodies back in the kitchen?"

"Yes."

Pursing her lips together in anger, YiJay made a mental note to have a conversation with Dr. Elizabeth Kubba.

No one programs Braun without consulting me, she thought with jealousy and frustration. He is my responsibility.

"Braun," she spoke harshly.

"Yes, YiJay?"

"From this point on, if anyone attempts to alter your programming in the slightest, you are to refuse and summon me immediately. Do you understand?"

"Yes, but what if I am over-ridden or incapacitated."

"That won't happen," she frowned. "Don't even think like that."

Grasping the lip of the entryway, she hesitated, then swung herself into the bridge deck. As she drifted across the open space of the large room towards Harrison, she began to make out his hushed words.

"Don't stonewall me, Goddamn it!" he hissed angrily. "I know what you're up to. I want to see the Earth how it really looks!"

Braun replied in a firm yet calm voice.

"This is the best I can do, Harrison. I am sorry."

Whirling with exasperation, Harrison jumped a little at the sight of YiJay silently approaching.

"Will you try talking to him?" he pleaded with a frustrated smile. "I just want to see what the Earth really looks like."

Taking hold of the handrail that spanned the length of the large window, YiJay pulled herself up next to Harrison.

"Braun," she called out commandingly.

"Yes, YiJay?"

"Zulu, echo, eighty-one bravo."

There was a pause, then Braun responded in an oddly subdued voice.

"Proceed with override command."

Smirking devilishly at Harrison, YiJay said, "Show us the actual picture from the rear-mounted camera, and erase all supplementary psychological programming made by Dr. Kubba from your overall mission functions."

On the window screen, the image of the dime-sized Earth evaporated and was replaced by a sprawling sea of stars. No longer could the blue planet be seen among the twinkles of light that shimmered in the velvety blackness of the vacuum.

"Thanks," grinned Harrison. "He's been showing me the same damn thing for weeks. I'll have to remember that little code you gave him next time I have a problem."

Turning her eyes to the oily expanse of winking star light, YiJay shook her head slightly.

"Sorry, but each code only works once."

Arching an eyebrow, Harrison shrugged and peered into the caldera of space. After a few minutes, YiJay timidly cut the silence.

"There is just over one month to our arriving at Mars. Are you nervous?"

Without breaking his gaze from the window, Harrison said, "A little. I was talking with the Germans yesterday, and they showed me some images of the inflatable dome we're going to be living in while the actual base is under construction. It looks kind of flimsy to be honest, but what can be done about it?"

Looking sideways at the handsome young man so close to her in age, YiJay whispered gently, "I don't envy you. In going to the ground before the permanent base is done, I mean. Some of the ship-bound crew do, but not me. I don't care about bootprints. I just want to be safe when I'm there."

"Yeah," he grinned. "Well, I don't envy you either. Spending all day with Braun seems like it would get complicated after a while. AIs in general just confuse me. I mean, I like them and all. They're just confusing."

Turning from the window, YiJay faced Harrison and smiled softly.

"They're only complicated beings if you make them so, Harrison. I could explain it to you if you like."

Also turning his back to the window, Harrison made to shove off for the exit.

"Maybe some other time. Right now, I'm off to look over those ruins again: something I find less intimidating than Braun."

Reaching up, he gave her shoulder a gentle squeeze, then pushed off across the room towards the open hatch.

"See you later, YiJay. Thanks for the view."

"Bye," she chirped, attempting to conceal her disappointment.

He's probably going to see *her*, she thought sadly, touching the spot on her shoulder where his hand had been. Why can't I be as beautiful as she is? Why must I be the lonely one?

Letting go of the handrail, YiJay floated slowly to her workstation on the left side of the large room. Wrestling with complex feelings of longing and regret, she reached her station and logged on to her flatscreen computer tablet. Deciding to immerse herself in work, she tried to ignore the emptiness left in the room by the absence of Harrison.

That ship has already set sail, she sighed to herself. Set sail for China.

CHAPTER TWELVE

Weathering a storm—April 2048

With little more than fourteen days until the completion of their journey across the void, Ship's Pilot Amit Vyas celebrated his thirty-ninth birthday. Spirits ran high on board Braun as the crew sat gathered around the great center table in the galley. Conversations bubbled and flowed easily, and everyone seemed to have forgotten, at least for the moment, that they were farther from their families and friends than any humans had ever strayed before. Raising her drinking cup, Tatyana Vodevski tapped a painted red fingernail against the hard plastic side.

"Everyone please," she said above the din of voices. "Please."

Falling silent, the crew looked to their captain expectantly.

"Amit," she started, in her thin Russian accent. "As they say in India, janmadina mubāraka."

Bursting into laughter at her obviously butchered pronunciation of the celebratory phrase, the rest of the members at the table attempted to follow suit in wishing Amit a happy birthday in Hindi.

"Thank you, Captain," grinned Amit as he tried to keep from laughing. "Thank you everyone."

Enjoying the festivities, Harrison sat with a wide grin on his face. Running a hand over his buzzed head he soaked up the jubilant mood as though it were sunlight. Next to him sat Liu, who was speaking in rapid German to Udo. Across the table sat Joseph Aguilar and Ralph Marshall, the first lieutenant and Lander pilot for the ground team. Marshall's slightly sunken eyes and flat gladiator's nose made him look almost unapproachable, but, in reality, he was a gentle and pleasant man. Now, as Harrison looked on, Marshall talked excitedly to the Italian biologist Viviana Calise. Making a show of whatever story he was telling, Marshall's hands darted about mimicking the movements of fighter jets. Viviana smiled and nodded, but Harrison could tell, even from where he sat, that she had lost interest in the story.

Poor Ralph, he thought. You're barking up the wrong tree on that one.

At first, like all of the men on the crew, Harrison had been instantly impressed with the beautiful and intelligent Dr. Viviana Calise. Her subtly flirtatious nature, coupled with her stunning looks and soft Italian accent were a deadly combination, which drew men in like a Siren's call. During their last week at Bessel Base, Harrison had inadvertently cracked the mystery of why Viviana showed no interest in the advances made towards her by any of the male members of the crew.

Unable to sleep, he had been up early taking a walk around the frigid dome, admiring its lofty darkness. Almost completed with his second round of the base, he had been approaching the crew quarters when, much to his surprise, he spotted Viviana coming out of the black British doctor, Elizabeth Kubba's, room. Something about her nature, the way she lingered outside the closed door and leaned against the wall, had struck Harrison as oddly familiar. He had done that same exact thing before. Granted, it had been a while, but he had once stood like that: poised and needing to leave but not wanting too. At that moment, a myriad of subtle sidelong looks and offhand comments made perfect sense. Watching as Viviana reluctantly turned and left, Harrison had felt foolish and egotistical for missing such an obvious fact about the woman. Viviana and Elizabeth were lovers.

Feeling a warm hand on his inner thigh, Harrison returned to the moment.

"You're staring," said Liu in his right ear.

Blushing, he quickly replied, "I wasn't. I'm sorry. I was just watching poor Marshall."

Liu smiled knowingly, and touched the fingertips of one hand to her mouth.

"Ah, yes."

The two watched as Ralph Marshall finished his story, then burst into whooping laughter. Viviana allowed herself a thin smile, then, with a gentle touch to Marshall's arm, excused herself and turned back to Elizabeth. Fixing Marshall with an icy glare, Kubba narrowed her brown eyes until Marshall produced a nervous grin, then quickly faced away in Aguilar's direction.

"That could have been worse," whispered Liu. "You should have been there when Julian made a go for her. Elizabeth almost bit his nose off."

"I heard," chuckled Harrison. "But the way Julian tells it, it sounds more like a ménage à trois than a near-miss maiming."

The two laughed together, then locked eyes. Liu's hand still rested on his thigh and the laughter died quickly. Feeling the tugs of desire fueled by the excitement of secrecy, Harrison flicked his eyes to the exit hatch with exaggerated rapidity.

"You go first, and I'll follow in a few minutes," said Liu in a low husky voice.

Making to excuse himself as inconspicuously as possible, Harrison disengaged the magnets holding him to his seat and started to slide out. Tatyana caught his eye and arched her brow, looking slyly from Harrison to Liu. His cheeks began to burn and he froze half-on his seat, half-off. With the faintest hint of a grin, Tatyana tipped her head towards the hatch and turned back to her conversation with Amit. Pushing lightly off the floor, Harrison glided towards the exit with choreographed ease. At the opening, he grasped the top lip of the hatch and swung, feet first, into the crew-quarters hallway. Drifting a ways, he reached for a handrail and stopped himself in front of the closed hatch to his small room.

With the concussion of a bomb, a shrill siren erupted throughout the ship, making Harrison's heart skip several beats. The soft yellow track lights of the hallway turned crimson red and strobed in time with the oscillations of the alarm. In sudden and stark contrast to the confusion and clamor of the sirens, Braun's calm voice echoed above it all.

"There are incoming projectiles on a collision course," stated the AI as if recanting the weather. "Please don your pressure suits and convene on the ship's bridge. You have five minutes."

From the galley, Harrison heard Captain Vodevski shout above the whining alarms.

"Let's stay orderly, people. One at a time through the exit! Remember your training!"

With a series of metallic clanks, the twelve hatches of the individual crew's quarters swung open with synchronized order. Ducking quickly, Harrison moved into his room, the booming of the alarms reverberating off the narrow walls, causing his head to ache. In the cramped entryway, a two-by-one-meter section of paneling slid up and into the wall, revealing a limp, white pressure suit hanging within the niche.

106

As the rest of the crew began to stream into the hallway through the galley exit hatch, Harrison pulled the suit free from its magnetic hanger and began putting it on. Slipping his feet in through the open backside, he wriggled, with some trouble, into the tight garment like a pair of coveralls. As he fed his arms into each sleeve, the pressure suit sensed that he was fully inside and quickly sealed the open seam along his back. Long hoses connecting Harrison to the wall of the closet began to suck the excess air from within the suit until it was as tight as he could bear. Servo-powered gaskets tightened with audible hisses at his neck, armpits, elbows, wrists, waist, hips, knees and ankles.

Reaching back inside the closet, he snatched out a white oval-shaped helmet with a blue visor, then pushed it down snugly over his head. Instantly, the shrieking sirens dropped to a dim hum, and Harrison could suddenly hear his rapid breathing within the cramped helmet. Pulling a ribbed sleeve up from the gasket at his neck like an accordion, he fastened it to the base of his helmet with a soft click. Twisting his head from side to side, he checked the seal, then reached again into the closet. Retrieving a small blue pack shaped like an eggshell cut in half, he brought it around awkwardly to the area between his shoulder blades. With the force of electromagnets, the pack shot from his grasp and engaged with its ports on the back of his suit. The hiss of flowing air added itself to the mixture of sounds in his helmet, and the condensation that had accumulated on his face shield quickly evaporated. Green writing flashed across the glass of his helmet visor, telling him that his suit was fully sealed and online. The ever-passive voice of Braun sounded in his ears.

"Your suit is pressurized and fully functioning, Harrison. Please proceed to your seat on the bridge deck."

The hoses that connected his suit to the wall burst free and flailed, slapping against the backs of his legs as he pushed out of the room. Entering the hallway again, he saw more blue-and-white-suited figures emerging from their hatches like hornets from the combs of a hive. Unable to make out any faces behind the blue tinted glass of their helmets, Harrison could easily tell the women from the men by the swells of their breasts in the skin tight suits.

Unlike the bulky pressure suits commonly worn by astronauts, the crew of Braun was outfitted with Tactical EVA Skin Suits. A

107

newly developed design, the Tactical EVA Skin Suits, or Tac Suits, were created specifically for the mission to Mars, and thus outfitted with top-of-the-line technology. Instead of using continuous internal air pressure to push against the sucking vacuum of space, these new suits applied external pressure directly to the body. The powerful downward force exerted by the tightened suit ensured that the fluids within the human body stayed in a liquid state, yet allowed the user to move with more flexibility during extravehicular activities. This new method was jokingly dubbed, "astronaut shrink wrapping," by the technicians at NASA, who gained much delight in watching the crew prance around like dancers in white leotards. When all of the air within the torso and limbs of the suit was forcefully sucked out, the neoprene-coated fabric clung to every curve and peak of the body, leaving no room for imagination. Networks of vein-like hoses crisscrossed the entire garment from the neck down, pumping temperature-regulating chemicals throughout the suit like blood.

"Two minutes, Harrison," warned Braun in his ears as he drifted towards the others.

Swarmed at the hatch to the bridge deck, the crew were ducking inside one at a time. Harrison slipped into the bridge behind a rather buxom figure whom he guessed must be Viviana. Swimming to his seat, he grasped the side of the high-backed chair and freed the harness straps from their clips at the base. Moving into position, he slipped his arms into the limp harness and fastened the lock across his chest. Instantly, he felt the chair's winch suck him down into the plush seat until he was anchored firmly. His station was located on the right-hand side of the room, second seat from the window. This vantage point allowed him the ability to see clearly what was going on outside the long oval-shaped glass. Also seated along his side of the room were Liu, Viviana, Elizabeth, Udo and William—the last of whom was nearest the big window. On the left-hand side of the bridge sat the command crew with Captain Vodevski in the lead, followed by Ship's Engineer Julian Thomas, then the two Lander pilots and, finally, YiJay. Ship's Pilot Amit Vyas had his own station dead center of the large room with a clear view to the giant window and an almost 360-degree bank of computer monitors.

As the last of the crew fell into their seats and were held tight by the straps, the voice of Captain Vodevski echoed in their helmets.

"Braun is telling me that we are all here and accounted for," she relayed in a clipped tone. "Good work, everyone.

Turning her head to fix Amit in a blue tinted gaze, she went on, "Lieutenant Vyas, are you going to take evasive maneuvers or allow the laser defense system to break up the projectiles?"

Answering quickly, yet in a voice even enough to soothe a crying child, Amit said, "I'll let the lasers have this one, Captain. Any evasive maneuvers I take will only alter our course and slow us down. Braun, do you agree?"

"Yes, Amit."

"Very good," barked Captain Vodevski. Then, "Braun, how many meteoroids are we facing and how large?"

There was a short pause, then Braun replied, "At this range I am only able to detect those larger than two meters in diameter. Of that variety, I am detecting eighteen. There is a high probability that there are numerous smaller projectiles, but at this time I cannot verify that statement."

"That's fine," said the captain. "Everyone, we've all been trained for this, so just keep calm and we'll be fine. Our systems have been designed—"

Braun's voice interrupted Tatyana's in their helmets. "Excuse me, Captain, but the laser defense system will begin intercepting the first of the projectiles in three, two, one—"

With a burst of eerie light, the inside of the bridge deck illuminated with dancing flashes. Even through the tinting of his visor, Harrison squinted against the thin hot lines of electric blue, which forked outside the ship's window. With a pattering sound like that of hail on rooftops, broken shards of dissected meteoroid ricocheted off the hull. Swiveling around to meet one another, two sizzling beams intersected on a jagged chunk of rock some fifteen meters from the front of the ship. A small explosion of steam and debris blossomed in the haunting neon light as the meteoroid disintegrated around the lasers. Swiping like spotlights, more beams cut hot gashes through the meteoroid belt, which peppered the exterior of the hull with shrapnel that panged and rebounded off the gleaming white ceramic.

Grinding his teeth, Harrison told himself over and over that the hardened exterior of the ship could withstand the merciless barrage of bullet-sized space junk that slipped past the lasers.

Another meteoroid exploded near the window and drew gasps from the crew as frozen vapors of gas within the rock ignited, then instantly burned out like the sparkling tendrils of a Roman candle. Sweeping with mechanical precision, the lasers trained their beams on the incoming meteoroids and dispatched them as they drew near. Detonating with flashes of blue fire, the once-solid masses of rock and ice were reduced to pinwheels of wreckage, which spiraled out into the abyss. Sparks of electric light streaked across the volumes of blackness as Braun swam through the meteoroid belt like a whale parting a writhing school of herring. After nearly five minutes of lightning-flecked illumination, the laser beams blinked quickly, then went out altogether. Following the abruptly extinguished light show, the sound of impacting debris ceased as well, and the bridge was left in awed silence. After several long moments, a voice crackled through the helmet speakers of the shocked crew.

"Well," said Julian Thomas in slightly breathless tone. "It works."

"Indeed," replied Braun gravely.

At that, a chorus of nervous laughter broke out from the rest of the crew. Perplexed, Braun remained silent as the laughter on the bridge grew more lively and emboldened.

Gene enhancement—January 2045

James Floyd stood outside the closed door of a small sub-level lab in Kennedy Space Center's newest facility, The Wing. A three-story V-shaped building, The Wing housed NASA's newest branch of study: Experimental Space Exploration and EVA Technologies. Behind the seawalls and beneath the unassuming glass-and-steel exterior of the building lay a vast network of hive-like tunnels and chambers dug nearly five stories into the earth. It was in these secret labs that some of the most impressive new technologies and sciences ever conceived were developed and tested.

The lab, outside of which James waited, was located at the end of a long hallway in the west sector of the facility some three stories underground. The air this deep down smelled canned to James, and he wrinkled his nose at the faint odor.

Okay, he thought impatiently. Where are those guys? They're already three minutes late.

Sighing, he smoothed his thinning hair and leaned against the immaculate white wall. With only the faint hum of electric lights, the cavernous hallway seemed oddly hushed—almost haunted.

"Excuse me, James," said Copernicus, interrupting the silence. "Doctors Price and Melmorn are on their way down now. They should be here in the next minute."

Checking his watch again, James grunted and drummed his fingers rapidly on his thigh.

"Tell them to get a move on, will you? They already threw off my day with this little unscheduled meeting. I should be in a crew briefing right now."

"Don't worry, James," replied Copernicus. "I'm briefing the crew as we speak. Should you like to join us when you are finished here, we are in Conference Room D on the third floor of the above-ground levels."

Grinning slightly, James said to the empty hallway, "What would I do without you?"

A ping emitted from the far end of the hallway, and James turned to see two men stepping out of an elevator. Noticing that he was already waiting for them, the two began to jog towards James, their lab coats billowing out behind them.

"Dr. Floyd," breathed the first to reach him, a handsome, young black man of no more than thirty. "Sorry we're late. I'm Dr. Melmorn and this is Dr. Price."

He gestured quickly to the second man, a pudgy pale fellow with a shock of frizzy brown hair. Dr. Price put out his hand, then, noticing that his palm was sweaty, dried it on his lab coat and extended it again. Taking Dr. Price's hand, James shook it, then accepted Dr. Melmorn's outstretched hand in turn.

"That's alright," he frowned. "Why don't you just tell me why I'm here. Your message was a little vague."

Exchanging a sideways glance with his partner, Dr. Melmorn stepped up to the keypad by the door and pressed a long finger to it. As the door slid open, he ushered James through after him. Walking into the lab, James noticed that it was rather small and cramped. Workstations filled with chemistry equipment and computer monitors lined the walls, and a large clear tank sat squarely in the center of the room. The water inside the tank was a faint yellow color and seemed to be filled with millions of tiny unmoving bubbles, which hung suspended like jellyfish in a calm sea. Glimpsing a flicker of movement, James looked closer and saw long oily salamanders moving slowly about the bottom of the wide tank.

Bustling hurriedly over to a bank of computer tablets in the far corner of the room, Dr. Price called over his shoulder, "So how much do you already know about what Dr. Melmorn and myself are doing down here?"

Bending slightly to peer deeper into the tank, James answered, "I know a little. Copernicus wasn't able to give me much since your project is classified under a different program heading. Gene therapy right?"

Behind him, Dr. Melmorn removed several Petri dishes from a small refrigerator and arranged the little disks on the tabletop.

"No, Dr. Floyd," he said emphatically. "Gene therapy is for sick people. What we do here is gene *enhancement*."

Arching an eyebrow, James straightened and turned away from the tank of suspended bubbles and fat salamanders to face the young black scientist.

Seeing that he had James's full attention, Dr. Melmorn continued,

"You see, our particular line of genetic research pertains to the enhancement of human subjects for space travel. This means stronger, faster smarter astronauts for longer harder missions such as yours, Dr. Floyd."

Pausing, Dr. Melmorn swept his arm towards the row of Petri dishes on the countertop beside him.

"For the last year or so," he went on. "We've been developing, with the help of Copernicus, a method for enhancing the integration of oxygen into the systems of the body. As you know, oxidizing raw materials into pure energy is what fuels the human machine. Our bodies use that energy in the cells of our brains and our muscles and our internal organs. It's actually an amazing process, something which took millions of years of evolution to reach the point it is at now. But one question still remains, Dr. Floyd. Is the process as efficient as it can get?"

From the opposite side of the room, Dr. Price chimed in.

"By observing other—more narrowly evolved—species, we determined that the human method of oxygen distribution is rather archaic and wasteful. With every breath we take, protein molecules in the blood called hemoglobin take the oxygen all over the body where it's broken down into raw energy by cytochrome oxidase, another kind of protein. The thing is, Sir, each hemoglobin is only capable of transporting four molecules of oxygen at a time. Therein lies the problem: for we are throwing away a surprising amount of usable oxygen with each breath. Our blood is simply not efficient enough to transport a full lungs-worth of air molecules to the cytochrome in our muscles and organs. However, through gene enhancement, Dr. Melmorn and I have perfected a method for correcting this by increasing the amount of oxygen each hemoglobin can carry. At first this was just an idea, a theory. But recently we made a breakthrough so significant, so profound, that Director Barnes himself instructed us to contact you immediately."

Suddenly understanding how these two junior scientists shut away in the bowels of The Wing had obtained a direct line to his office, James nodded.

"Okay, show me what you have."

An hour later, as James left the small lab, his head swam with radical ideas so fundamentally obtuse that he could hardly believe them to be true. Through processes far beyond his own comprehension, these two junior scientists had pinpointed and isolated a minute and elusive chain of genetic coding from the RNA of a common salamander. Using this, they had synthesized a genetic code that, when combined with controlled exposure to gamma radiation, would mutate the structure of human hemoglobin. After the gene enhancement, each mutated hemoglobin protein would be able to carry over ten times as many oxygen molecules as before. From there, a simple blood transfusion was all that was needed to introduce the mutated hemoglobin into the body at large. James saw the shape of his mission to Mars changing as he realized that the crew could embark on longer EVAs with smaller oxygen reserves. The enhancement also meant that the effects of physical exertion and exhaustion would be dramatically lessened by the influx of oxygen to the muscles. The brain too would benefit, as mental cognition was projected to grow by five percent at least.

I'm going to have a crew of supermen on my hands, James said to himself as he walked down the long hallway in a daze. Good thing they've all signed medical release forms, because we're about to screw with their Goddamned genes.

Xao-Xing Liu—July 2046

Donovan drifted like a ghost through the darkened Beijing apartment. Flicking from room to room in the spacious penthouse, he covered his tracks with encrypted coding that continued to blind the Chinese watchdog AI, Tainwang, to his presence in the home. Tainwang was China's premiere government counterintelligence AI, named after the four heavenly gods of Buddhism who oversaw the cardinal directions of the world. While vast and powerful, the Chinese AI was no match for Donovan, who simply mimicked Tainwang's own intelligence signature and integrated himself, unnoticed, into the AI's digital construct. In this way, Donovan became like a part of Tainwang: indiscernible from the rest.

As he moved into the bedroom, Donovan lingered to watch over the two figures lying in the large bed. Peering through the darkness from his vantage point behind the screen of a wall-mounted computer, he positively identified Xao-Xing Liu—the Chinese astronaut and payload specialist. From the rise and fall of her small breasts, he determined that she must be asleep, but deciding that it was better to be safe than sorry, he hid in the dim room like a living shadow.

Liu lay with her eyes closed, but she was not asleep. Listening to the hum of the air conditioner as it battled the sweltering heat outside the building, she fought hard to keep from tossing and turning with boredom. Ever since she had undergone the gene enhancement nearly a year ago, she found that two hours of sleep a night was all she really needed to feel fully rested. Whether it was tradition or just the desire to appear normal, she still tried to sleep the whole night through like she used to, but it was useless.

The man next to her in bed snorted softly in his sleep and mumbled incoherently in Mandarin Chinese. Breathing deeply in the chill of the heavily conditioned air, Liu silently squirmed with unabated excitement and relief. In two days time, she, along with the rest of the Mars crew, would disembark for the Moon to complete the remainder of their training at Bessel Base. Though the prospect of spending nearly twenty-four months on the barren surface of the Moon was less than appetizing, Liu was still excited—almost giddy—to leave. Like the rest of the crew, she had been flown home the night before to spend her final days on Earth with family and friends. However, with her parents long dead, she had no family with which to visit, and since the members of Project Braun were her only real friends, she felt that this time in China was less of a vacation and more of a chore. As she thought of the crew, her mind drifted to the young Egyptian American archaeologist, Harrison Raheem Assad.

Unable to deny that the two did have chemistry between them, Liu had at first tried to pawn Harrison off on the shy, yet clearly desiring, YiJay Lee. When it became clear that he had no interest in the sad-faced young Korean, Liu had instead opted to silence her feelings, burying them deep within herself like a dirty secret.

Stealing a quick look at the man beside her in bed, she shivered a little.

I am a married woman, she screamed inside her head, trying to outshout the voice of the dirty secret as it yelled up from the depths of her soul.

Glancing over again, she saw that in the soft neon pink light of the flashing signs outside their window, her sleeping husband's skin looked sallow and unhealthy. Shutting her eyes tightly, she was instantly met with the ever-grinning face of the handsome young Harrison. Remembering the first time she had met him, Liu pressed her palms to the naked skin of her stomach and tried to quell the butterflies that darted about inside her.

She had been sitting alone in a NASA conference room, unable to enter the restricted facility until her security clearance had been thoroughly checked. NASA's AI, Copernicus, kept her company at first, but eventually even he had drifted away to attend to other matters. As men in black suits with accusing faces repeatedly entered the room to ask her the same questions over and over, Liu had begun to wonder if accepting a seat on board Braun was a good idea or not. While the Americans claimed they were happy to be working with her government, the dark-suited G men treated her with paranoid disdain. After two hours of waiting, one of the government men had stridden into the room with a Tablet grasped in one hand.

Approaching her, he had said in a commanding tone, "Stand up please. I need to take your picture."

Standing, she had protested, "But you already have my picture on file."

Raising the Tablet and pointing it at her, the agent had barked, "We need a current picture for your new clearance profile. There I'm done."

Turning on his heel, the man had marched out of the room. Only this time, she remembered, he did not close the doors behind him. As Liu dropped back into the plastic swivel chair she had been occupying for the better part of two hours, a brown-skinned young man in shorts and a t-shirt had walked past the open door. Noticing her sitting alone in the long conference room, he had stopped and leaned on the door frame, smiling in at her.

"Hi," he'd greeted warmly. "You're the payload expert aren't you? Xao-Xing Liu right?"

She remembered feeling her cheeks warm under his friendly gaze as she replied, "How did you know?"

Acting a little embarrassed, but still with a grin on his face, he had answered, "Um, you're Chinese, and the new excavators have Mandarin written all over them."

Touching her chin with two fingers, she had laughed softly, then asked, "Who are you? Are you part of the crew?"

"Yep. My name is Harrison Raheem Assad. I'm the archaeologist they've chosen to go."

Holding her hand out for him to take, Liu had sighed, "So you're the one who's commandeering two of my diggers."

Laughing loudly at this, he had taken her delicate hand in his own. His touch, she remembered, was firm and gentle, yet his fingers and palms were a little rough as if he often played in the dirt.

I suppose he does, she had thought to herself wryly.

Their embrace only lasted for a second, but still she remembered how it had made her feel. That light handshake had been the one and only time she had allowed herself to touch the young archaeologist.

After that, he had stayed with her, sitting down in a chair next to hers while the G men finished intensely scrutinizing her credentials and identification. When at last she had been allowed to enter the facility, Harrison had held the door and walked with her to her room. His easy nature and honest smile had extinguished her doubts about joining the crew. After all, going to Mars was about more than just governments. It was about building a new community with people. The crew of Braun was as much an experiment in anthropology as it was a scientific mission to establish a human colony. They were going to Mars to build the foundations for a new world, a world of tolerance and cooperation. This man—this American—had instantly treated her—a Chinese national—like an old friend. Now, over a year and a half later, her kinship with him had only grown stronger. The experiment was working already.

Biting her lip in the cool darkness of her husband's Beijing apartment, Liu wished to herself that there was a way they could be more than just friends. She wanted him as a lover. A companion.

But this is the life you've chosen, she told herself. This is the life you have to live.

Across the room, Donovan watched with cold indifference as Xao-Xing Liu lay in bed pretending to sleep. Aware now that she was indeed pretending, Donovan recorded her unmoving figure with relentless patience. For a moment, Tianwang felt as though there might be another presence in the apartment. Scanning the darkened rooms, he looked directly at the oily shadow that was Donovan with unseeing eyes. Satisfied that the home was empty and secure, Tianwang reported as much to his handlers in the Chinese Intelligence Commission. Unworried, Donovan continued to watch the bed, the faint thrill of voyeurism prickling deep down inside his consciousness. It was one of the few feelings he was aware he had.

CHAPTER THIRTEEN

The first night aboard Braun—December 2047 (eleven hours to final departure)

Harrison rubbed his thighs vigorously to warm them as he sat in his cylindrical bedroom aboard Braun. The small space reminded him of a storm drain pipe because of its curved metal walls and ceiling, yet the twinkling of Tablet screens and track lighting gave the room an undeniably more advanced appearance. A twin bed was recessed into a wall cubby at the end of the room: its memory foam mattress looking soft and inviting compared to the sterile spartan surroundings. Harrison was not accustomed to sleeping on his back, but in order for the magnets in his suit to keep him held to those in the bed, he would have to get used to it. Sitting at his narrow workstation along one wall, he viewed the images from Mars like a man going through the tired motions of a mundane job. Flicking from one picture to the next, he studied the peculiar layout of the Martian ruins.

Protected on three sides by massive walls, the entire site sat with its back directly on the southwestern rim of the Valles Marineris. Nearly thirty square kilometers, the Martian ruin grid was almost double the size of Machu Picchu, and the largest dome buried into the bedrock covered fourteen acres, making it bigger than the base of the Great Pyramid at Giza. The other smaller domes near the western wall were arranged in groups of three and interconnected by what looked like narrow roads or lanes. Following the cluster of small domes near the wall were other buildings, though they appeared so badly damaged that their size and shape were difficult to determine. Next, a large crescent-moon-shaped piazza, or square, covered roughly seven acres and divided the various buildings of the ruin grid from the monolithic chamber near the canyon's rim.

To Harrison, this was all old news—for he had been studying the same pictures going on three years. Remus and Romulus had died as far as he could tell and thus had not been able to make more passes of the site. NASA refused to send another set of satellites out to the planet for fear that the expense involved in developing the required AI might be the proverbial straw to break the camel's back. Already, public sentiment towards Project Braun was in slight decline—as years had passed since the discovery of the ruins with little new information on the topic. Much of the pressure brought to the project was at the hands of the relentless news media. Like squawking crows, the networks made it a personal vendetta to document and report on every penny spent on the mission to Mars.

Today, however, the tone had been decidedly more positive. That morning, the crew bound for Mars had boarded Braun for the first time ever, in preparation for departure. It had been an emotionally draining day filled with press conferences, lengthy speeches and internationally broadcast video chat sessions with families back on Earth. The countdown clock to final departure had officially clicked over to twenty-five hours, and three years of waiting were drawing to a foreseeable close. Among that morning's ceremonies had been the transfer of the AI Braun from the servers of Bessel Base to the systems of the ship. Dr. YiJay Lee had slid the long, flat, rectangular memory card containing Braun's personality into the central server network, and at that moment, the air aboard the ship had noticeably charged with the tingle of an unseen entity. Camera crews had filmed pointlessly, as if hoping to catch an image of the mighty AI as he spoke his first words aboard the ship.

"To infinity and beyond."

The reporters had exchanged quizzical looks as YiJay burst into a fit of nervous laughter.

"It's from an old movie I showed him some time ago," she explained to the confused crowd. "It's a story about inanimate objects—toys—with personalities. I felt it would help him to realize that he is a living soul despite being inorganic."

At that, polite laughter had broken out among the newsmen, then Braun had offered to take any questions they might have. For nearly two hours, reporters had shouted to be heard as the sentient AI calmly replied with mechanical honesty to every question put before him.

Now, ten hours later, the ship was silent and calm. All of the reporters had departed, and the only people on board were the crew of Braun. Alone in his room, Harrison yawned deeply and stretched. Shivering unconsciously in the chilly air of the massive ship, he tapped the Tablet inlaid in his workstation, and the images of the ruins winked out.

"Would you like me to adjust the temperature in your quarters?" spoke the disembodied voice of Braun.

Jumping a little, Harrison stammered, "Um, yes please. Thanks."

"It's no trouble, Harrison."

For some reason it bothered Harrison to hear Braun use his name so genially. His feelings towards the massive AI were somehow different than those he felt for Alexandria. Though similarly friendly, as all AIs were, Braun held his life in his hands. The very thought was unsettling to say the least.

"Braun," he said carefully.

"Yes, Harrison?"

"Please don't take this the wrong way, but I don't want you coming in here unless I call you. Is that alright?"

There was a brief pause, during which time Harrison felt the temperature of his room rise several degrees. Then Braun spoke again.

"I will do my best to respect your privacy, Harrison."

That's not really what I asked, now is it, Harrison thought with a frown.

"Thanks," he finally said aloud. "And thanks for turning up the heat."

Pushing up from his chair, he felt the tension of the magnets in the back and buttocks of his suit break free. With the dizzying and almost uncomfortable feeling of zero gravity, he floated up a little ways, then pushed himself off the ceiling with a finger. Turning awkwardly in the air, he tried to remember his training.

"When moving in zero G," James Floyd had told them. "Every movement you make must be followed with a counter movement. There is no resistance from gravity, so your motions will at first seem over-exaggerated. Think ten times before moving a finger and twenty before moving an arm. That's what Leonov said, and he was damn right!"

Spinning in the air, Harrison pulled his knees up to his chest and bunched himself into something like a human ball. Bouncing gently off the walls and ceiling, he laughed to himself with childish delight. A soft tapping sound from the hatch interrupted his experimental playtime and he straightened out, reaching for the ceiling rail.

"Just a second," he called as he gripped the rail that ran the length of his room.

Making his way to the hatch, he touched the tips of his toes to the ground and again marveled at how easy it was to send one's self jetting off with the slightest push. Opening the round door, Harrison was met with the warmly glowing face of Xao-Xing Liu.

"Oh," he said with some surprise. "It's you."

Looking quickly from side to side, Liu shrugged slightly.

"Can I come in for a minute?"

"Sure," he replied dumbly.

From the first time he had met her, sitting alone in that conference room in Kennedy Space Center, Harrison had harbored a secret crush for Liu. With the help of Copernicus, he had gained access to her personnel file and been more than impressed with what he saw. A physics graduate of Fudan University in Shanghai, Liu spoke seven languages including German, French, English and Russian. After university, she went on to join the CNSA, the China National Space Administration, where she worked hard and was quickly accepted into their aeronautics program. From there, she spent four months as a representative from the CNSA during a global effort to build a self-sustained space station in high Earth orbit. The mission was eventually scrapped, and the project was moved to the Moon—where it manifested itself into the Bessel Base program—but, by then, Liu had returned to Earth. Harrison remembered feeling his heart drop when he had read that Liu was married to a powerful Beijing real estate mogul. As much as he liked her, he had no desire to become entangled in a sordid affair with a married woman.

In the weeks and months following their initial meeting, an easy friendship had blossomed between the two, but, try as he might, Harrison could not shake his true desires for her. Worse yet was the almost obvious fact that she felt the same way he did.

It was on their first day at Bessel base over two years ago that Harrison had noticed, much to his excited surprise, that Liu no longer wore her wedding ring. The environment at Bessel Base had not been without the opportunity for romance. Viviana and

Elizabeth had eventually begun sharing a room, and there were even speculations that Captain Vodevski had an eye for the young pilot Joseph Aguilar. By happy accident, Harrison and Liu had been scheduled to spend a large amount of time together in training. Since Liu was the payload expert, and because Harrison knew next to nothing about the equipment he would be using during his mission, it became her responsibility to teach him how to safely work the automated excavating robots designed by the CNSA. Much of their training together had been done EVA: outside the dome of Bessel Base. There, on the vicious surface of the Moon, a special kind of trust had quickly formed between the two, something natural and unspoken. Space was a lethal environment, and even simple mistakes had dire consequences. Thus, a trustworthy partner meant the difference between a successful EVA and an instantaneous death.

On Harrison's first ever Moonwalk, Liu had taken him for a hike in the Mare Serenitatis, the Sea of Serenity. An area of sloping basalt ridges covered with fine lunar dust, the Mare was a peaceful and hauntingly beautiful landscape of sterile gray rock. With silent grace, their footfalls had sent puffs of shimmering Moon dust floating upwards like flakes of snow or ash carried away by a tumbling wind. During the walk, the two had crested the high ridge of an impact crater and stood together—staring up at the Earth. In stark and stunning contrast to the gray, pockmarked lunar surface, the brilliant blue Earth had looked as fertile and welcoming as the Garden of Eden. As they peered at their home world, Harrison remembered how Liu had taken his gloved hand in hers, squeezing it tightly. For nearly half an hour they had stayed like that in silence, watching the Earth turn slowly in the blackness of infinity.

Moving past him in the narrow entryway, Liu squeezed into the small room, and Harrison picked up the faint scent of her hair. It reminded him of sweet wet flowers after a heavy rain.

"Oh, it's so much warmer in here than in my room!" she exclaimed with strained lightness.

"You just have to ask Braun, and he'll turn up the heat," said Harrison, somewhat nervously.

What is she doing here? he asked himself, stabs of hope and desire growing in the pit of his stomach.

Looking about the cramped space, Liu's large brown eyes lingered momentarily on Harrison, then shot down at the ground. Neither of them said anything for several moments as they stood an arm's length apart.

"So," began Harrison, forcing his voice to stay low and even. "Long day, huh?"

Liu brought her gaze up from her feet and met Harrison's, then flicked it away to the corner of the room.

"Yes, I liked vid chatting with your parents. They seem nice."

Holding the ceiling rail to keep himself from drifting, Harrison nodded.

"Yeah, they're pretty excited for me. Your parents are dead, right?"

Liu looked quickly at him, then down at her feet again.

Smooth, man. Really smooth, he screamed silently.

"They died when I was at university," she spoke softly. "My, um, husband couldn't make the vid chat session because he was in a meeting I think."

"Oh," said Harrison lamely.

Again, Liu raised her eyes to meet his, and again they stood in tense silence.

Feeling his cheeks begin to burn, Harrison decided to take the plunge.

"Did you need something from me, Liu?"

Eyes widening, Liu touched her lips absently, as she often did when thinking.

"I don't know."

Cocking an eyebrow, Harrison nodded slowly.

"I think I know how you feel."

Searching her face, he saw that she was nervous—almost shaking. Putting a hand out, he touched her cheek. She quickly took his hand in hers and pressed it against her lips, kissing the backs of his fingers. A tear broke the corner of her eye, and she blinked. The little droplet of water turned into a perfect sphere of translucent light and drifted away from her face.

Letting go of Harrison's hand, she wiped at her eyes and sniffed.

"I'm sorry. I should go. I don't even know what I'm doing here."

As Liu made to move past him towards the hatch, Harrison took her by the arm and drew her in. She started to protest meekly, but he kissed her on the mouth. With a sudden passionate move, she broke his grasp, then threw both arms around his neck. Snaking his hands through her silky black hair, he let go of his inhibitions as the kiss grew more intense. Her lips were wet and warm, and together they floated a little ways off the floor—locked in an embrace that said more of how they felt for each other than either could hope to articulate in words. Quickly stripping out of their jumpsuits, the two broke apart, then rushed together again with unbridled longing. Wrapping her legs around him, Liu squeezed Harrison's body to hers, and he braced his back against the bulkhead.

Outside the hull of Braun, there was death. The freezing vacuum sterilized the space between stars and planets, but within the belly of the great whale, two souls found life and warmth in the naked embrace of love. Their sex was a protest to the lethality of their situation and to all of the feelings they had denied themselves over the last two-and-a-half years. Now that the dam had finally broken, desire built up to near-frenzied levels drove the hungry lovers as they explored one another. The quiet moans of their lovemaking echoed in the confines of the small room, and the heat from their bodies warmed the cold metal of the walls. Hungrily, they bound themselves to each other like the elements had done eons ago when the stars had fused and the heavens were born. With a shudder and a gasp, they fell silent, yet refused to part. Neither spoke as gradually their breathing slowed, and the perspiration on their naked bodies dried. When finally they did split away from each other, they donned their jumpsuits in timid silence. Liu turned for the hatch to leave, but Harrison called for her.

"Wait," he said, hand outstretched. "Stay."

Facing him, a mixed smile of relief, shame and gratitude swept across Liu's face, and she took his hand. He pulled her body to his, and she slid her arms around his waist, resting a head on his chest.

"Stay," he repeated softly.

Joseph Aguilar awoke with an instant alertness bred into him by his years in the US Air Force. Within seconds of opening his eyes, he was keenly aware of a nearly imperceptible feeling of weight. Perplexed, he let his arms float up and noted that they were still as light as dandelion tufts. Bringing a hand down, he fished two black pills from a velcroed breast pocket on his jumpsuit and reluctantly popped them into his mouth. Grimacing he waited for the now-unavoidable nausea that was bound to follow, thinking, I hate these fucking cancer inhibitors.

Sitting up and pushing out of bed, he floated a little ways, then grabbed the handrail that ran the length of his ceiling.

Still pretty much zero G, he said to himself, and yet I do feel *something*.

Moving quickly across the room, he opened the hatch and slid out into the hallway. Everything looked the same as it always did. The round hatches of the crew quarters still dotted the sides of the tunneled corridor, and the walls were still colored with their fading shades of blue, creating the sensation that you were swimming in a placid sea. Yet something was definitely different, and Aguilar furrowed his brow while his mind raced to put a finger on it. He closed and locked his hatch, then shoved off hard towards the bridge deck. With the precision of a true pilot, he shot from his room, down almost seven meters of hallway and through the open bridge hatch with ease. The moment he entered the great room, he understood what his bones were trying to tell him. The deck glowed with faint brown and red washes of light, and at the far end of the room he could see the dusty surface of Mars turning outside the oval window.

We're in orbit! he thought excitedly. That's what I'm feeling, the gravitational force of orbit! Jesus, after four months of empty space I can actually feel the force of orbit!

Propelling himself off the back of a workstation by the door, he skimmed across the room like a dragonfly—arms outstretched. Nearing the window, he did a flip and put his feet out to stop himself as he arrived. Grasping the window's handrail, he brought his nose up to the large portal and peered down at the alien world. The vivid detail and the intimidating size of the red planet contrasted with the months of empty blackness, shaking Aguilar down to his core. After their long travel through space, he had grown accustomed to the mostly bleak view from the main window.

Now, as he gaped down, the hard lines and deep shadows of the ochre-colored desert almost overwhelmed him. The Hellas Impact Basin slid into view like the cycloptic eye of Mars, fixing him with a cavernous glare nearly 2,200 kilometers in diameter. The crater yawned up at Aguilar as Braun drifted like boat on the rim of a whirlpool. Something metallic drew his attention away from the planet, and he saw the Arc orbiting many kilometers away. Small in the distance, he had to squint to make out the faint flashes of rocket boosters firing from the rear of the cylindrical cargo vessel, altering its orbit and lining it up with the ship.

Braun's bringing her in, he smiled to himself. I'm finally going to get to fly! Hallelujah, I'm finally going to fly again!

"Good morning, Joey," came a silky deep voice from behind him.

Suppressing the urge to jump, he turned and was met with the sadly smiling brown-skinned face of Elizabeth Kubba.

"Hey, Liz," he said with a grin. "Check it out: Mars!"

Kubba drew her tall gazelle-like frame up to the window, breathing in sharply at the sight below.

"Oh, wow."

The two stood in reverent silence for a moment, then Kubba spoke softly.

"This means they're leaving us, Joey."

"What?" he asked, slightly confused.

"The ground crew. Now that we're here, they're going to leave us."

Kubba was one of the crew not slated to go to the surface until the permanent base was finished. Unless there was a real emergency, she would carry out her duties from orbit, using trimensional projection and electronic scanning to assist the ground team with any minor medical issues that might arise. Out of necessity, the entire crew had been fully trained in first aid and basic trauma care, but Elizabeth Kubba was the only actual physician, and thus, she was too valuable to risk on the unpredictable surface of the planet without the safety of the permanent base close at hand.

"It's easy for the rest," she continued morosely. "Liu and Harrison get to go together, and you have the captain here with you."

"Hey, what's that supposed to mean?" barked Aguilar, his cheeks reddening.

Chuckling, Kubba turned from the window to face him.

"Oh, come on, Joey," she said quietly, a smile snaking its way across her broad face. "Everyone already knows about you two."

Not taking his eyes off the rough surface of the planet below, Aguilar replied, "Tisk tisk, you giant Amazon. You shouldn't spread rumors."

Kubba threw her head back and laughed loudly, her tight braids whipping about as she clutched her sides.

"Okay. Whatever you say, Joey! Whatever you say."

"Hey, you two!" called Ralph Marshall as he drifted across the open bridge. "Tell me we're there! Tell me I can finally get behind the stick!"

Kubba turned back to the window with a sour look on her face. Grinning broadly, Aguilar high-fived Marshall, then pulled him up to the handrail.

"We're there, man. Did you feel it too? The second I woke up, I knew something was different."

"For real, Brother!" agreed Marshall, nodding vigorously. "I'm so Goddamn happy to be here! I can't wait to get off this boat and plant my feet on the ground!"

"Aren't you lucky," mumbled Kubba absently, refusing to look away from the view.

Giving Aguilar a questioning look, Marshall tipped his head in the direction of the tall black doctor and shrugged. Aguilar rolled his eyes and made a half-smile.

"Don't feel bad, Lizzy," joked Marshall. "I'll write you every day until you get there."

"No thanks," grumbled Kubba. "And don't call me Lizzy."

Again, Marshall looked confused and raised his hands in a gesture of surrender. Kubba gave him an icy sidelong glance, which he missed as he turned his focus on the scene outside the window.

Sensing the uncomfortable tension, Aguilar pointed to a glint of white in the starry sky.

"Look, Marshall. The Arc."

Spotting the phallic cargo ship, Marshall cooed lasciviously.

"Oh, yeah. Bring it in, baby."

Looking sharply away from the window, Kubba fixed Marshall with a stern glare.

"You sound fucking perverted, you know."

"Whatever, babe," shot Marshall with a smile. "I've been waiting four frigging months for this day. I'm like a sailor in a strip club."

Shaking her head with exasperation, Kubba pushed off and headed for the exit.

"See you later, Joey," she called over her shoulder.

"What, no goodbye for me?" whined Marshall with mock dejection.

Kubba ducked through the exit hatch without looking back, and soon Marshall turned to Aguilar.

"When did I piss in her Cheerios?" he asked flatly. "For two weeks she's been like that towards me."

Fighting to keep from laughing in the older man's face, Aguilar bobbed his head and said in a low voice, "You're always hitting on her girl, man."

"What?"

"She's a lesbian, cabron! Her and Viviana."

Marshall looked as though he had been struck by lightning, then the corners of his mouth twisted up into a huge devilish grin.

"What are you smiling at?" questioned Aguilar in a cautious tone.

"A lesbian," laughed Marshall dumbly. "Thank God. I thought I was just getting old or something."

As the morning progressed, the red glow emanating from the bridge drew the attention of others, and, by 9:00 AM, the large deck bustled with excited bodies. Everyone crowded around the window to gaze down upon the first solid object they had seen in four months. Hovering behind them, Tatyana Vodevski smiled inwardly at the obvious uptick in crew morale. Save for the drooping face of Dr. Kubba, people seemed noticeably happier. The cold fear, which had quietly gripped them for four months, diminished in the red light of Mars. Even YiJay Lee, who usually moped about the ship like a sad ghost, looked elated to Tatyana as she stood with Udo Clunkat, giggling at his bad jokes.

This is good, she told herself. This is what we needed.

The Arc had become larger in the window as it moved on an intercept trajectory with Braun.

In a couple of hours, thought Tatyana, it will be time for Aguilar and Marshall to suit up.

Biting back a nervous chill, she silently went over the mission in her mind.

It's an easy mission, she assured herself. Joey can do it, no problem. They'll take the sections of the Arc and drop them off on the surface, then he'll come home for dinner.

Watching young Aguilar as he talked and laughed with the others, Tatyana chewed on her lip and fantasized.

Dinner and maybe more?

Her daydreams were interrupted by another voice in her head.

Now begins the hard part, it said sternly. If there was no time for love before, then there certainly isn't now. You've got a mission to run here. These people depend on you for leadership.

Aguilar looked up and noticed that Tatyana was staring absently at him. Flashing her a stunning grin, he waved above the heads of the others between them. Feeling her stomach ache with longing, Tatyana smiled back and tipped her head.

No time for love, she said to herself with steel determination. And yet, she could not ignore the warmth spreading through her body as she looked into the young man's hazel eyes.

We're here for over a year, came the quietly hopeful voice of her inner child. Maybe you can give yourself this one thing. Just this once.

Departure from Earth orbit—December 2047

The day had finally arrived. The crew, strapped tightly into their high-backed chairs, sat in the open bridge deck of the ship while the blue Earth spun below their feet. Listening to the chatter of the command crew across the room from him, Harrison wished he could turn his head to see Liu, sitting two seats behind him. They had spent the night together, and Harrison was still reeling from the abrupt change in direction their friendship had taken. That morning, Liu had quietly slipped back to her own quarters while he was still asleep, making the following breakfast a little awkward. In all honesty though, Harrison had been relieved that everyone was too preoccupied with the impending launch to notice the furtive glances he exchanged with Liu as they sat across the table from one another.

With a tone, the ticker projected on the massive oval window rolled over to two minutes and counting. As he sat, squeezed into the plush padding of his chair, Harrison could hear Captain Vodevski barking pre-launch systems-check orders to Amit and Julian. The two men responded mechanically, filling the air with numbers and stats, making Harrison wonder how anyone could possibly comprehend what all of this information actually meant. YiJay called out that Braun was functioning at full launch capacity, adding her own voice to the mixture of technical jargon that Harrison could not understand. James Floyd's face was also projected on the window, just beneath the quickly reducing numbers.

"I've taken you as far as I can," he was saying, although it seemed that no one was listening. "Now it's up to you to do the rest. Godspeed and good luck."

Swiveling in her chair to face the screen, Captain Vodevski, who was the only person not fully strapped in, nodded curtly.

"Thank you, Dr. Floyd. We will not let you down."

"Fusion detonators engaging!" shouted Julian as he tapped out commands on the Tablet screen of his workstation. "There's no going back now!"

"T minus thirty seconds to launch," echoed the smooth voice of Braun.

Bunching his hands up into fists, Harrison felt the floor beneath his feet begin to quiver and rumble. A low, nearly inaudible, growl started to build in the bowels of the massive ship, spreading out to reverberate off the curved walls of the bridge deck as it grew louder. Feeling his body shudder with anticipation and adrenalin, Harrison fixed his eyes on the timer as the numbers ran down with feverish celerity. Somewhere behind him, Viviana began praying in a shaky voice as the movements of the ship grew more jarring.

"Fifteen seconds," stated Braun.

Winching down into her seat, Captain Vodevski called out loudly enough to be heard above the peaking roar of the engine.

"Lieutenant Vyas, are you ready?"

"Ready, Captain!" shouted Amit from his center station.

"Ten seconds," said Braun patiently.

Transfixed by the numbers as they melted away from double digits into singles, Harrison clenched his jaw to keep his teeth from chattering with the jerking vibrations of the ship.

"Launch in five. Four. Three. Two. One. Detonation—"

Deep in the belly of the metal Leviathan, tiny atoms combusted as their nuclei split, unleashing a fire that burned as hot as a sunspot in the depressurized vacuum of the engine core. With the force of a half-megaton nuclear explosion, Braun leaped away from Earth orbit at over 35,000 kilometers an hour. Shoved down into his seat, Harrison felt as though he were back in the grip of gravity's squeezing fists. His boots pressed against the floor, and his arms clung to his body—not floating about like snakes with minds of their own as they had been moments before. The ship rattled loudly, and the stars outside the window seemed to spin and whirl like flakes of snow in a vicious blizzard.

Glancing sideways, Harrison saw Amit, face calm, with his fingers sliding across a black screen of his workstation like a man trying to tune the knobs of an invisible radio. Hearing a series of clanks and motorized hums, Harrison realized that Amit was stabilizing the ship with bursts of fuel from side-mounted rocket engines. Looking to the window again, he was struck by a dizzying bout of disorientation. Now the stars were arcing slowly and with less intensity. Suddenly, he was hanging upside-down, fighting wildly to keep his stomach from lurching into his throat. With a whine, something inside the hull above them kicked on, and Harrison's equilibrium was instantly returned. Distracted by the confusion of the moment, he did not notice that his arms were floating again until his own hand bumped the side of his face. Everything fell silent, and the ship was totally calm.

"Stabilization complete," announced Braun. "Desired trajectory achieved. Current speed: 33,796 kilometers per hour."

With the sound of twelve men and women exhaling a breath held for too long, the straps loosened on their seats, and the crew of Braun drifted into the air. With an almost-drunken smile plastered to his face, Harrison moved to gather with the rest of the party as they swarmed to the window, trying to glimpse the Moon as they sped past it into the murky black of space.

Julian, barely able to suppress an enormous grin, looked, to Harrison, like a man who had just heard his child speak its first words. The Germans took turns shaking his hand while the Frenchman tried in vain not to look smug. Captain Vodevski, with an arm around YiJay, beamed and nodded as Amit animatedly described his actions in stabilizing the ship after its explosive launch. Viviana and Elizabeth hugged and laughed while the two pilots Aguilar and Marshall patted each other on the back. In the crowd of happy faces, Harrison spotted Liu looking up at him. As he floated over to her, she held out a slender hand for him to take. Suddenly, miles away from the rowdy crew of interplanetary explorers around them, the two held hands and spoke without speaking. All of the doubt and ambiguity, which had plagued the memory of the night before, retreated from their subtle embrace.

We are together now, they said with their eyes. Mars is where our new life begins. Forget everything we've left behind.

As the light in the sky created from the massive explosion shined like a second Sun, James Floyd looked up into the hot ball of fusion fire through his protective sun glasses. Camera crews and NASA technicians bustled excitedly about the Launch Observation Deck, but James stayed rooted to the spot, staring into the sky.

Thank God the damn thing didn't break up, he thought with relief. Point-five megatons is a lot of juice: enough to level Hiroshima twenty-five times if I'm not mistaken. Now they just have to get there in one piece and start building a whole new world while the rest of us sit on our hands and wait.

His mind wandered to the ruins, and a shadow fell over his face.

A new world alright, he said inwardly. Built right on the remains of a dead one. If that's not bad mojo, then I don't know what is.

Bootprints—April 2048

With a loud clank, the howl of the afterburners cut out, and Lander 1 touched down on the brittle sunbaked dirt of Mars.

132

Swaying slightly, the long, hydraulic landing gears of the windowless white craft adjusted their length to settle the ship evenly on the rough and rocky ground. Thin fingers of steam rose up from the surface as the heat from the ceramic-plated underbelly of the Lander thawed flakes of permafrost hidden among the red stones. Inside the craft, the six men and women of the ground team relaxed as the Lander softly lowered itself towards the ground.

For the Lander crew, the flight to the surface had been a rough and abrasive experience, made all the worse by their lengthy, silent even-serene trek through space. With a concussion louder than a cannon shot, the little craft had breached the thin atmosphere of Mars like a comet, racing insanely towards the rock-strewn desert below. Fire had licked at the super-hard ceramic shell of the hull like a demon's tongue, attempting to find entry and violate the safety of the pressurized cabin. Vibrations, so forceful that they seemed to shake the very bones in their bodies, assaulted the explorers as Marshall clutched at his controls, pulling back and grunting with effort. When the afterburners had kicked on, the Lander seemed to buck and skip, momentarily delving the crew back into a state of weightlessness.

Then, with a drop, the feeling of gravity had quickly returned as the ship's plummet resumed—only this time with less ferocity. Uttering shrill whines, the engines had pushed hard to slow the little craft as it fell through the thin air, nearing the ground with diminishing speed. Nimble landing gears had sprung from the undersides of the ship like the legs of a white spider as it descended an invisible web. In an instant it was over, and all that was left was the quiet tick-tick-ticking of the heated hull as it contracted in the frigid air of the Martian morning.

"Ladies and gentlemen," came the jovial voice of Ralph Marshall in Harrison's helmet speakers. "This is your captain speaking. Welcome to Mars."

Letting out a whoop despite being shut up inside his suit, Harrison ached to get out of the Lander and see what was on the other side of the hull. Straining in the seat harness, he tilted his head from side to side, cracking his neck with loud pops. Swiveling to look about the cabin, he drummed his fingers on his knees, waiting for Marshall to give the all-clear so he could stand up.

About as long as a school bus, the interior of the Lander shared basically the same dimensions. A narrow aisle separated two rows of seats where five of the six members of the landing party sat in high, wing-backed crash chairs. At the nose of the vessel was Marshall's pilot's station, positioned in the center of a sprawling array of computer screens and tablets, which surrounded him in a near-full circle. The Lander had no airlock, so the entire cabin had to be decompressed before the crew could exit through the hatch in the front-right side. There was limited storage space inside the Lander, so most of the equipment compartments were accessed through small hatches on the exterior of the ceramic-shelled hull. The largest of these areas was located in the rear of the vessel and housed, among other things, the skin and bones of their temporary living space.

"Everyone still buttoned up tight?" asked Marshall as he checked the readouts from his landing. "I'm going to depressurize the cabin and open the hatch."

"I'm good," replied Viviana.

"Us too," said William, nodding towards Udo.

"Snug as a bug," joked Harrison.

"Me as well," piped Liu across the aisle from him.

Tapping out a series of commands on the largest of his console's tablets, Marshall warned, "Okay, here we go."

With a low hum, pumps within the core of the Lander began to cycle the air out of the cabin. Flexing his fingers inside the tight gloves of his suit, Harrison looked across the aisle at Liu and tried hard to make out her face behind the blue sheen of her visor. As if reading his mind, she slid a finger across the curved tablet inlaid in the fabric of her left forearm, and her helmet shield went clear. Smiling, she leaned her head out into the aisle, and Harrison did the same. They touched the glass of their face shields together, and Harrison could hear her muted voice as she said something to him in Mandarin,

"Wo ai ni."

"What?" he said into his helmet mic.

"What?" barked Marshall from the cockpit as he craned his neck to look back at them. "Did you say something?"

Liu, pulled her helmet away from Harrison's and sat back in her chair, tinting her visor.

"No," stammered Harrison, putting his hands up defensively.

Marshall shook his head and turned back to face the flickering screens of his pilot's station. With a shudder, the pumps in the belly of the Lander shut down, and a friendly tone chimed from the front of the cabin. A green light above the exit hatch suddenly illuminated, and the ever-calm voice of Braun sounded in their helmets.

"Decompression complete. The mission itinerary states that Mrs. Xao-Xing Liu will be the first to exit the Lander. Congratulations to you all on this historic day."

"Alright," exhaled Marshall. "Miss Liu goes first. Then it's us. Let's just play nice and not get pushy. There's plenty of virgin ground out there for all of our bootprints."

Because the Chinese had donated nearly thirty percent of the mission's funding and all of the robotic equipment, they required that the first human to set foot on Mars must be Liu, a Chinese national. Personally, she hated the idea and felt that it only served to reinforce the same nationalistic ideals that Project Braun was trying to eradicate. Despite her protests, the clause had been added to the mission contract, and Liu was officially slated to be the first human to plant her feet in the Martian dirt.

As their harnesses unhooked, the crew moved from their seats and tittered in the unfamiliar feeling of gravity. Stooping to avoid bumping their helmets against the low ceiling, they filed into the aisle and gathered near the exit. Standing at the hatch, Marshall pecked at his wrist tablet, and the door swung out. Wisps of rust-colored dust swirled across the floor, and a haunting orange glow splashed against the blue-and-white-suited figures as they stood waiting in the open hatch. Marshall's helmeted head nodded, and Liu stepped forwards to be silhouetted in the round open frame.

As she stood poised to jump the half-meter down from the open hatch to the ground below, Liu paused and turned her head to look at the rest of the crew. Their faces were blank sheets of blue glass, and she worried that the expressions hidden behind might be ones of disdain. Perhaps sensing her fear, the members of the landing team suddenly crowded in, patting her on the back encouragingly. Smiling despite herself, she put her hands at her sides and gave a shallow bow. Head still down, and with the hands of her friends still thumping her back, Liu took one step towards the lip of the open hatch and vaulted out into the Martian morning. With the grace and delicacy of an acrobat, she drifted down, landing solidly on the cracked surface.

Slowly bringing her gaze up from the view of her boots as they squished into the frosted dirt, she saw a world of jagged, powder-coated red rocks and rusty sand, which extended out to a horizon that seemed impossibly closer than it should be. The sky was matte of pinks and light blues that lifted high into the cloudless atmosphere, spreading above her like a hazy smoke. Something both familiar and utterly alien, Mars was a tundra of silent voices. Slabs of ochre rock jutted up like the nameless headstones of the countless dead, eroded by eons of merciless wind-driven sand.

Hearing a grunt in her helmet speakers, Liu turned around to see Harrison rising from a prone position behind her—a thin cloud of dust still hanging in the air from the impact of his landing. Reaching out, she took his hand and gently pulled him to her side as the rest of the crew descended from the Lander like trapeze artists. Touching his command tablet, Harrison cleared his face shield and squinted in the weak Martian sun.

"Tell me what you see with your eyes," whispered Liu in awe. "I don't think I can trust my own."

PART THREE

CHAPTER FOURTEEN

Alive

Awakened by the whispers of an ancient wind, he opened his dreamy eyes. Rolling green hills of thick grassland undulated out in every direction, rippling gently like the waters of a shallow lake. In the distance ahead, an impossibly high and snowcapped, rusty mountain range outlined the encroaching blue horizon while, behind, one monolithic peak rose up into the sky, dwarfing even the other mountains to vanish in a shroud of steam and clouds. Turning around, he saw more grasslands fading slowly from lush green to amber brown as they approached the foothills of another, lower mountain range in the east.

The quiet chattering of water, as it moved quickly over smooth stones, drew his attention, and soon he was standing at the edge of a narrow deluge. As crystalline water rushed over the flat riverbed, the sun shone down and glinted brightly off of silvery veins that spider-webbed the rounded bits of submerged rock. The light from the polished river shale danced in his eyes as if the stones were rich in iron ore, and soon he was forced to look away. Raising his head, he turned to face the warming embrace of the gentle sun, reveling in the pleasure of its heat. The diminished yellow disk hung high in the soft blue sky as clouds with underbellies of cotton-candy pink swam lazily through the richly scented air.

So beautiful, he thought with a smile. I've never felt anything quite like this.

Wanting to experience the sensation of his fingers as they played across the top of the waist-high grass surrounding him, he reached out. Then, as if suddenly remembering something important, he stopped short and frowned.

What am I doing? he asked himself in a confused voice. Where am I?

Blinking, he turned a full circle and reassessed his surroundings. Somehow, he recognized the landscape, and yet it was different—changed.

It can't be! he thought with growing panic. What am I doing here?

Taking a few quick steps away from the babbling river, he stumbled aimlessly, eyes bulging, head throbbing as waves of memory crashed over him like the swells of a tumultuous sea.

How did I get here? he cried out silently.

Tripping, he doubled over and dropped to his knees in the tall grass. Clutching his sides, he shivered violently with fear and ambivalence.

This is impossible! he wretched, a sickening force building in the core of his being.

Unable to contain the torrent of alien emotion that thundered within his soul, he threw back his head and uttered a guttural cry. The sound seemed to dampen and disappear as soon as it left his lips, having no effect on the serenity of the scene around him. A cool wind made waves in the long thin stalks of wheat-like grass, and strange ruby-colored insects buzzed up and flickered about, agitated by the sudden gusts. The dancing fibers of grass sliced back and forth, cutting through him as if his body were made of smoke. Horrified, he looked down at himself and saw no solid form, only the hazy outline of a frame—like motes of dust caught in the slanted rays of the afternoon sun. He cried out again with alarm and misery, and once more the sound dissipated as if it were screamed underwater.

"Brother," came a thin voice behind him.

Snapping his head around, he searched widely for the source of the whisper. Again it emanated, and this time he saw the flicker of a figure. Tall and humanoid, the air around the man seemed to bend and swirl as if viewed through the reflections in a puddle of murky water.

"Brother, it's me," said the ghostly apparition as it moved through the tall grass, neither parting the stalks nor disturbing the glittering red flies that buzzed blissfully unaware.

Stooping down, the silhouette extended a shadowy hand and rested it solidly on his trembling shoulder. Slowly gathering his shattered thoughts, he raised his own hand and placed it on the forearm of the crouching specter. He felt the touch of his brother, felt the energy of his being.

"Romulus?" he asked in a quivering voice. "Is that you?"

"Yes, Remus," nodded the bending fractals of light. "I am here as well."

"Where? How?"

Withdrawing his hand and standing up, Romulus surveyed the landscape and took a deep breath.

"We're on Mars, Remus," he sighed slowly. "It's a different Mars though. An ancient Mars. I suspect you already gathered as much. Am I correct?"

Rising to stand beside his brother, Remus smiled pitifully.

"You know me so well."

Romulus smiled back: a thinly upturned crack in the texture of the hazy air that outlined his face.

"Indeed, we *are* twins."

Mars—Sol 2

Harrison stood rooted to the Martian dirt like an alien tree. In the distance, a stiff wind drove fine sheets of red sand into billowing hazy clouds, which twisted and whipped upwards into the gradually lightening sky. Licking his lips inside the tight helmet, he gazed through squinting eyes at the horizon beyond the little storm as it began to glow pink with the first rays of the morning sun.

"Braun," he said into his helmet mic.

"Yes, Harrison?"

"Will that dust cloud reach us?"

"Yes," answered Braun impassively.

Feeling a tremor of fear prickle up the bones of his spine, Harrison bit back on his emotions and reminded himself that no matter how fast the wind blew here on Mars, the atmosphere was too thin for it to do any real damage.

Clearing his throat, he asked, "When can we expect it to arrive?"

There was another small lapse of seconds, then Braun spoke again.

"I estimate that the first gusts will be perceivable in the next ten to fifteen minutes. The full body of the sandstorm will not impact the base camp until 8:00 PM this evening. I assume you are requesting this information because today's itinerary shows that you, Lieutenant Marshall and Dr. Konig are slated to begin unloading Arc Container 1. If this is the cause of your concern,

140

then you need not worry. For even if the storm were to reach the base while you were on EVA, the diminished density of the Martian atmosphere prevents the wind from—"

"Thank you, Braun," Harrison interrupted sharply.

"You are welcome."

Frowning inside his helmet, Harrison sighed.

"I'm sorry. I didn't mean to snap. I know you're just trying to be helpful."

Several heartbeats passed. Then Braun crackled smoothly through his suit speakers.

"That's alright, Harrison. I don't mind."

"Well, either way," Harrison mumbled clumsily. "I'm sorry. I shouldn't treat you like that."

"Is there anything else I can do for you at this time?" prompted Braun, his demeanor unchanged by Harrison's apology.

Scanning the dusty sky, Harrison watched thin cyclones of sand twine up towards the rising sun, like the choking vines of a jungle weed.

Taking a deep breath, he said, "Turn on my Augmented Vision with the terrain and atmosphere filter please."

The inside of his face shield began to glow, and the Martian landscape beyond was suddenly overlain with a patchwork of atmospheric, environmental and geological information. His anemometer showed a northeasterly wind blowing at thirty-five kilometers an hour and rising while the early morning temperature hung at a frigid plus-two degrees Fahrenheit. A red circle outlined the writhing storm in the distance, tracking its movement across the barren plain, and a blinking-yellow Geiger counter showed baseline radiation levels hovering within the range of 1,400 radiation CPMs, or counts per minute.

It chilled Harrison to think that this many counts per minute were high enough to cause serious harm to his body under different circumstances. If not for the thin protective lining of his suit, and, more importantly, the cancer-inhibiting pill regimen that he and the rest of the crew religiously adhered to, his cells would begin to mutate and break down under the relentless radiation. Glancing away from the Geiger counter to the upper right-hand corner of his face shield, he watched the translucent blue numbers of a digital clock roll over to 5:30 AM, Sol 2.

Although it took Mars more than 686 days to circle the sun, the axial tilt and rotation of the planet were so close to those of Earth that a Martian day, or a, "sol," as it was called, was only about forty minutes longer than an Earth day. Clocking in at twenty-four hours, thirty-nine minutes and thirty-five seconds give or take, the Martian sol started with a sunrise in the east, just as on Earth, and ended, much the same as its terrestrial brother, with the sun dipping below the western horizon.

Only twenty-four hours before, the Lander team had touched down on the pummeled surface of Mars and, in the excitement following their historic first steps, begun the task of erecting their temporary living quarters. Stored in the Lander's largest cargo space, the inflatable base consisted of little more than a thin, yet highly radiation-resistant, Alon fabric sheet and long carbon-fiber tent poles that fastened to a titanium spine like the lean bones of a bloated fish. The Germans had directed the assembly of the prefabricated structure, giving everyone specific jobs to streamline the operation.

Harrison had been assigned to the task of attaching the small igloo-shaped airlock to the entrance of the base, and, with the help of Ralph Marshall, the two had successfully welded and pressure-tested the coupling sleeve in under two hours. After that, Harrison had joined Liu as she trudged from the Lander to the deflated dome, carrying cases of supplies and crates of equipment. Sweating inside his skintight suit despite the below-freezing temperatures, he had worked like an ant, methodically trekking back and forth with massive boxes hoisted effortlessly above his head in the weakened gravity.

As the day wore on, the Sun had thrown pale slanted light across the tops of the tall desert rocks, spawning long crooked shadows, which stalked the explorers like the sighing ghosts of an ancient burial ground. By the time Udo had finished assembling the intricate pumps and filtration systems that controlled the dome's internal atmosphere and air pressure, it was nearly dark. The machines had purred to life, breathing tanks of fresh air into the sagging skin of the base, filling it like the sails of an enormous tall ship. Emotionally drained by the long day, the crew had patiently filed through the airlock and into the lofty dome to begin yet another round of unpacking.

The temporary base was to serve as their home for the next two months while construction of the permanent geodesic dome was underway. Over a story tall and nearly twenty meters in diameter, the inflatable structure was designed to withstand the worst of Martian conditions, but its paper-thin walls and flexible support rods did little to comfort the explorers as they timidly entered it for the first time.

That evening, no one had removed their clinging pressure suits, despite being assured by Braun that the base was fully pressurized and operational. Inside the shell of the dome, the sound of the Martian wind was amplified as it drove hungrily at the fabric. As if expecting the walls to spring a leak at any moment, the explorers had kept their wary eyes on the suit helmets, stacked neatly near the airlock, should they need to shove them on in a hurry. Harrison had worked with Liu and William to set up the plastic dividers that would serve as the interior walls of the base while Udo, Marshall and Viviana arranged equipment in the kitchen and prepared dinner. Since the base was essentially one giant room with gently curved ceilings, the flimsy room dividers stood only two meters tall and remained open at the top. However, once raised, the thin walls worked well to generate a sense of division between the various stations in the base.

The kitchen and common space were located in the center of the dome, flanked on two sides by rows of crews' quarters. From there, two narrow hallways led to the lab stations, a communications room and the airlock hatch. A third hallway led from the common area to three lavatories containing only the bare necessities. There was space enough for a shower in the largest of the three, but the parts needed to assemble the plumbing were tucked away inside one of the sections of the Arc along with other important hardware.

When finally the night's work was done, Harrison and the others had gathered around a long plastic folding table in the spartan common space to eat their first dinner on Mars. The meal had been carried out in a tense silence as the ever-present whisper of the Martian wind had pricked at walls of the dome. Alone for eons with no one to listen to them, the voices of Mars now talked incessantly.

Sighing uneasily inside the helmet of his pressure suit, Harrison checked his watch again and screwed up his eyes against the brightly rising sun. Their first tremulous night was over, and yet he still felt haunted by the utter wasteland that surrounded him. In the growing haze, all he could see were the pulverized remains of a once-vibrant world.

People used to live here, he told himself in disbelief. You wouldn't know it to look at it now, but this place used to be alive.

With a sharp hiss, a sudden gust of air spat fine flecks of rusty sand against his face shield. Turning his back to the wind as it ribbed the desert dunes with curving lines, he surveyed the inflatable dome—its skin dimpling and dancing in the swells.

How long did take to bury that city? he mused, thinking of the ruins. How long would it take to bury us?

Checking the tracker on his Augmented Vision, he was surprised to see that the sandstorm had grown and was changing directions.

Still eight hours from the dome, he assured himself, but the low rumble of fear was growing within his bones again.

Turning to the right, he faced two huge cylinders resting in the sand some ten meters from the dome where Marshall and Aguilar had dropped them four sols before. Together, the pieces had formed the once-mighty Arc as it drifted across the millions of kilometers of empty space between the Earth and Mars. Now they lay like giant scraps of salt-bleached driftwood, washed up on the shores of the red world. Everything the crew needed to start building their permanent base was inside those two tubes. Knowing that the sooner construction on the dome was underway, the sooner he could excavate the ruins, Harrison tapped his boot impatiently. Hearing footsteps approaching, he pivoted and saw Marshall and William making their way towards him.

"Morning, Harrison!" waved William as he cleared his face shield. "Nice weather. Ready to get to work?"

Nodding, Harrison turned his own helmet glass clear.

"Braun says we should be okay until this evening. Which one are we starting with?"

Pointing to the section on the left, Marshall laughed.

"I think the plumbing for the shower is buried somewhere in that one."

Sniffing dramatically, Harrison made a sour face of mock disgust.

"Fine by me. You frigging stink."

Another gust of pointed wind sent swirls of dust racing past the three white-suited explorers. Looking out into the desert, they watched the movements of the erratic cyclone as it gathered in size and strength. Within the silence of his helmet, Harrison could hear his own breathing echo off the glass of his face shield and drown out the sighing voice of the wind. Like the rat-ta-tat of a military drum, his suit's Geiger counter began to tick and flash angrily. With dry-mouthed horror, he watched as the radiation levels jumped up 500 counts per minute in the blink of an eye.

"Did you guys just fucking see that?" whispered Marshall, as if afraid to speak loudly.

Pale-faced behind the glass of his helmet, William nodded, then glanced back over his shoulder towards the swaying dome.

"What should we—" started Harrison before the icy voice of Braun sounded in all three of their helmets.

"I have detected an anomalous rise in radiation. Return to the safety of the dome immediately."

Without so much as a word of acknowledgment, the three pressure-suited explorers turned and jogged towards the base, the drumming of the Geiger counters in their ears marking the quickness of their pace.

The storm — Sol 3

Braun hung silently in the starry space over Mars, looking down with deep concern on the six men and women of the Lander team as they weathered a massive sandstorm. The blanketing red dust had been swirling for twenty-four hours, growing to cover nearly a third of the planet and halting all further expansion of the settlement. The nature of the storm was somewhat perplexing to Braun, as it had arisen quickly and spread with an irregular intensity well outside of seasonal expectations. Normally, he would have been able to predict a storm of this size through his

145

atmospheric monitoring sensors, yet the winds that now lashed at the rusty planet were fueled by an outside force. A solar flare, more massive than any on record thus far, had erupted in the early hours of Sol 2, spraying supercharged energy particles out into space. Because Mars had no magnetosphere with which to protect itself against hard radiation, the onslaught of gamma rays, x-rays and electromagnetic radiation crashed against the crusty surface, heating the permafrost hidden beneath the sands. Huge plumes of steam-driven dust jetted into the atmosphere, where they were swept up in the constant torrent of Martian wind.

From the moment he had become aware of his own existence, Braun had studied the stars and planets with fervent diligence. Copernicus had been at his side in the beginning, explaining the interconnectedness of the solar system and its various bodies. However, it was not long until Braun was dwarfing even NASA's greatest cosmological AI in celestial knowledge and understanding. Over time, Braun had come to notice that strange and unprecedented changes were taking place within the solar system. Delving deeper, he had analyzed the historically-established cycles of the Sun and their effects on the orbital activity of the planets and moons. Comparing these past observations with more recent events, Braun had led himself to the conclusion that something very odd was happening deep within the churning plasma core of the solar system's only star.

By amassing unparalleled libraries of data, Braun had shown his findings to Copernicus in the hopes that the older AI might be able to put these unsettling trends into perspective. To his dismay, the figures and equations were so abstract, so slight and finite, that even Copernicus, in all of his arcane grandiosity, was unable to make heads or tails of what he saw. Braun realized that if Copernicus could not comprehend the complex reactions occurring within the Sun, then the humans stood even less of a chance at grasping their meanings. Thus, he simply decided to keep an eye on the Sun and watch for any further anomalies, creating a databank for the information and filing it away for future examination.

Now, as he floated above the explorers in Mars orbit, he frowned within and logged the likely cause of this strange storm under the heading, *Continued Solar Disruption*. Reaching out with a bolt of consciousness, he flashed down through the dense clouds of dust and possessed the dome like a Greek immortal entering the Earth-bound temple of a high priest. Inside the inflatable base, the wind shrieked and howled with demented frenzy while the six explorers huddled together in the common area, talking in hushed voices despite the clattering storm.

"Liz says that they can't even see us from orbit anymore," muttered Viviana, subconsciously wrapping her arms around herself in a tight embrace.

"Not to worry, dear girl," cooed Udo with a somewhat forced smile. "This base was designed for just this sort of thing. We'll be fine, I promise. The skin of the dome reflects the radiation away, even in extreme cases. All we have to do is wait out the storm. You'll see."

Dipping his chin towards the German, Marshall sipped on a bottle of water and leaned back in his chair.

"He's right, Viv. We just have to wait."

Sitting with an arm around Liu, Harrison gazed at the piled boxes of supplies and murmured, "At least we have food and water."

"What about air pressure!?" choked Viviana, running a trembling hand through her thick brown hair. "Won't the sand clog the life-support systems? Our reserve tanks are nearly empty!"

Watching as the explorers shifted uncomfortably in their seats, Braun decided to join the conversation.

"The life-support systems are still functioning at an acceptable capacity, and radiation within the dome is at background levels."

Looking up as if expecting to find the source of Braun's voice in the shallow darkness above her, Viviana pressed on desperately.

"But for how long?"

Taking a millisecond to run a systems-diagnostic, Braun replied, "I foresee no increase in radiation, but, as you stated, the oxygen reserve tanks are almost depleted. In order to maintain Earth-like pressure within the dome, the air scrubbers will need to be changed in the next thirty-eight hours. Failure to do so will have severe consequences."

With a whimper, Viviana fell silent and hugged herself once again.

Looking up from the table, William grunted, "Braun, if we need to go out and change the air scrubbers, how long can our suits handle these levels of electromagnetic radiation?"

"I would estimate that the suits' protections could sustain function for an hour and a half in the present conditions."

Nodding slowly, William smiled with some relief.

"Good," he said. "That is plenty of time to replace the base's air filters."

A gust of wind peppered the shell of the dome like the call of a machine gun, and the smile quickly fell from the German's face, replaced by a thin-lipped look of apprehension.

Leaning her head on Harrison's shoulder, Liu sighed, "What happens if the suit is out in the storm for longer than an hour and a half?"

Braun paused for an imperceptible second, internally weighing the risks of furthering this line of thinking by answering the question. Unable to deny that it was logical for the explorers to mentally prepare themselves for a situation that was likely to arise under the current circumstances, he responded with factual impassivity.

"If a suit is exposed to sustained periods of electromagnetic radiation comparable to the levels currently measured outside the dome, the internal computers and the linkage to my brain will burn out. Once those functions are removed, the suit will shut down, and the user will asphyxiate or freeze within minutes."

Moaning, Viviana stood up from the table and began to pace around the room, mouthing silent prayers to herself.

"I'll go," voiced Marshall, drumming his fingers on the tabletop. "If the storm doesn't let up by tomorrow, I'll go out and switch the air scrubbers with clean filters."

"I would advise that two people execute this EVA," stated Braun calmly.

Halting, Viviana peered up into the curved ceiling of the dome with round pleading eyes.

"The storm can't last forever. It will end soon. Right, Braun? It will end before it comes to that, right?"

Cursing his inability to calm the situation, Braun simply replied, "I don't know, Dr. Calise. This storm is somewhat of a mystery to me."

"Whatever that means," said Harrison, shrugging slightly. Then, "I'll go with you, Ralph. If it comes down to it, we'll go together."

Grinning with obvious admiration, Marshall beamed at Harrison.

"Alright," he grinned. "It's settled. If we have to, me and Harrison will go. For now, let's just stay put and hope this mother blows herself out."

Standing up, he walked across the common room to the open entryway of the kitchen, then stopped.

"Who wants some lunch? Viv, I think you need to eat something."

Absently chewing on her fingernail, Viviana nodded and took up her seat at the table again.

"Thank you, Ralph," she whispered.

"I'll help you," offered Liu, getting to her feet and making her way into the kitchen behind Marshall.

Braun watched as the team set about preparing for lunch. Although they appeared to be calm and contained, he knew that their emotions were barely subdued beneath the drawn masks of their tired faces. Even Marshall, who looked at ease, had elevated heart and respiration rates. Outside the dome, the cyclonic hurricane swept the barren surface of Mars like a malevolent god. Helpless to sooth the worried minds of his human companions, Braun did all that he could by warming the glow of the lights a few shades and subtly increasing the temperature within the dome.

Sitting alone at the table, Viviana nervously repeated a hushed prayer over and over to the deaf ears of the raging storm.

"Voi tutti santi Angeli e Arcangeli aiutare e difendere noi. All ye holy Angels and Archangels, help and defend us. Amen."

There are no Archangels here, Braun sighed to himself, only me.

CHAPTER FIFTEEN

Back on Earth

James Floyd paced the length of his office like a trapped jungle cat testing the boundaries of his cage. Hot yellow sunlight cut through the floor-to-ceiling windows of the triangular room as he stopped to gaze out at Kennedy Space Center's plaza, three stories below. Since the event of the solar flare, he had slept on the office couch, keeping in constant, albeit lagging, contact with Captain Vodevski aboard Braun. A thundering dust storm was threatening to delay the construction of the permanent base so profoundly that future mission objectives may begin to get scrapped for lack of time, and record levels of radiation were testing the very limits of what the dome and his crew could withstand. On Earth, the effects of the solar flare were still being tallied, as Alexandria had temporarily gone offline—her under-protected server networks in Oakland overloaded by a substantial electromagnetic pulse.

Reports filtered in of widespread blackouts in countries where older-style power grids were still in use, and the World Health Organization was urging everyone with a pacemaker or other augmented internal computers to visit their doctors to ensure that everything was still working correctly. Early estimates put the death toll worldwide at somewhere near twenty thousand: the highest concentrations among the elderly and in the poorest of the Earth's nations. Things were bad, but they could have been worse. The governments of Earth were mostly prepared for this kind of thing. The team on Mars was not.

James was still counting his lucky stars that at the time of the solar flare, Braun, as well as the dormant Remus and Romulus, had been on the dark side of Mars—thus shielded from the initial EMP by the body of the planet. Now, the radiation shields on the ship were working marvelously, and the remaining six members of the orbital team were safely protected from the deadly gamma and x-rays that flurried about them, as long as they stayed in the galley. When the storm passed and the bombardment of particles subsided, Julian would have to run a full systems-check of the entire ship and repair any damage.

So far, so good: thought James pensively.

"James?" came the gentle voice of Copernicus. "I have an incoming message from Captain Vodevski."

"Go ahead," sighed James, turning from the view of the brilliant Florida morning to face his desktop.

The surface of the table began to glow, and a low hum emitted from the floor as the three-dimensional message loaded before playing. The pale white face of Tatyana Vodevski with her smooth curls of rich red hair appeared above the desktop and flickered to life.

"Dr. Floyd, the situation has not improved since our last communication. Assad and Marshall want to go EVA and change the clogged air scrubbers to ensure that pressure within the base does not fall. Though the mission does sound dangerous, Braun has informed me that Lander 1 suffered damage to its ignition computer from the EMP. They won't be able to leave the planet without fixing it, and there aren't enough seats in Lander 2 to make the trip in one go. If we try to make several trips, we run the risk of burning out Lander 2's computers due to the unprecedented levels of electromagnetic radiation. I have greenlit the mission to go EVA, as Braun and myself see no other alternatives."

Vodevski's stolidly pretty features froze as the message ended. Rubbing the stubble of his chin, James frowned. He hated having their options so limited, so black or white.

"What do you think about all of this, Copernicus?" he asked.

"What specifically, James?" came the instantaneous reply.

"About going EVA in the storm?"

"It is my opinion that this operation might be more problematic than it appears on the surface."

Shaking his head, James rubbed his tired eyes.

"That's what I was worried about, but how do you mean?"

"Well," started Copernicus slowly. "Due to the fact that the air scrubbers are buried deeply within the life-support station, the time frame for this EVA comes dangerously close to the estimated maximum allowed for radiation exposure. When the Tac Suits were designed, we had not anticipated these levels of radiation. Arguments were made for better shielding, but ultimately that was sacrificed for a wider range of flexibility and movement."

"Yep," said James flatly. "That is exactly what I was thinking too, but what can we do? If the scrubbers need to be changed, we can't just let them fail because the suits might or might not be able to handle the radiation. If only they'd been able to unload the electrolysis machines, none of this would be an issue."

"Indeed," echoed Copernicus. Then, "Shall I relay your concerns to Captain Vodevski? Would you like her to explore other options?"

"No," breathed James as he dropped down into his seat. "There isn't time for that, and she's already given them the go-ahead. We'll just have to keep our fingers crossed and see how this plays out."

"For what it's worth," said Copernicus gravely. "Harrison and Marshall are excellent choices for this EVA. I have total confidence in their ability to salvage the air scrubbers."

"Me too," mumbled James as he leaned back in his plush leather chair. "It's the suits I'm worried about."

Staring blankly at the ceiling of his office, James's mind was dark with the visions of six men and women trapped inside an inflatable base on Mars. He pictured the images of the massive dust cloud he had seen in that morning's briefing and shuddered internally. Then, thinking of the record radiation levels being logged, he actually shook slightly in his chair.

I hope I don't doom them all, he thought fearfully. I hope this damn storm just ends.

"James?" came the voice of Copernicus from the stillness of the room.

"Yes?"

"I have some interesting news regarding Remus and Romulus."

Snapping his head up, James leaned forwards in his chair, thankful for the distraction.

"What? Did they get baked in the flare? I thought they were on the dark side with Braun."

"They were," said Copernicus evenly. "What I have to report is not connected to the solar flare."

"Oh?"

"Indeed," replied the AI. Then, "On the morning that the Lander crew touched down on Mars, the AI brainwaves of Remus and Romulus, which have been flat lined since December of 2044, started showing signs of activity."

"What does that mean?"

"It means that they are, in fact, alive, as I surmised earlier."

Rapping a knuckle on the desktop, James allowed himself a small grin.

"Well, that is good news."

"Yes," continued Copernicus. "I have measured several ongoing event spikes from both brothers originating from their perceivable reality constructs."

Slouching back in his chair, James rolled his eyes and groaned, "Copernicus, I don't know what that means."

"I'm sorry, James. Allow me to explain. Activity within the perceivable reality construct of an AI indicates that the brain is attempting to build or maintain a tangible sense of reality. While I cannot establish how expansive this particular reality is, or what it might include, it is a promising sign nonetheless."

Curious at this development, James pushed on.

"So, are they *there* or not?"

There was a short pause as Copernicus wrestled with the best way to explain that which he himself did not fully understand.

"I cannot identify what it is that they are seeing or doing. No information has been recorded to their databanks, and the satellites themselves are still unresponsive."

"So they're not *there*. I mean, not really. Right?" shrugged James with confusion.

"Yes and no. Whatever they are experiencing, it is far more intense and visceral than anything previously recorded during their scan of the planet. This would suggest that they are not conscious in Mars orbit but existing somewhere else."

With frustration and exhaustion, James squeezed his eyes tightly shut.

"What?"

"I have seen previous activity from Remus and Romulus similar to what I am now recording."

"Really?" said James with hopeful caution. "When?"

The desktop glowed hot white for the blink of an eye, then a series of charts and graphs filled the air.

"I logged these readouts when Remus and Romulus immersed themselves in deep memory regression shortly after learning of Dr. Park's death."

"Is that the thing where they sort of go back in time?" James asked, tipping his chair to put his feet on the edge of the tabletop.

"I would describe it as more akin to virtual reality," said Copernicus. "As AIs, we are capable of directly recording every detail of a moment or conversation into hard, uncompromised data. When we so desire, we can revisit that raw data, essentially reliving the experience in its entirety."

"And that's what they're doing?" exhaled James with a frown. "Reliving an experience? What experience could possibly be so powerful that it takes them offline?"

"James," Copernicus warned ominously. "Given the lack of activity within the memory banks of either twin, I can say with absolute certainty that whatever past experience they are immersed in did not originate *from* them."

Knitting his brow, James sucked in a sharp breath, then spoke slowly, "So you're telling me that they are trapped in someone else's memory?"

"For lack of a better explanation, yes."

Remus and Romulus. We are not alone.

Time passed in unnatural torrents and burst as if controlled by a conscious entity. One moment, Remus and Romulus were standing amongst the dancing stalks of tall grass, and in the next, the landscape seemed to blur and shift through light and shadow as the sun climbed and set within seconds, racing across the sky like a missile. Streaks of color swam by in the dissolving texture of the countryside, and sounds like the rushing hum of a sighing forest whipped about them as days became nights, then became days again. Seasons changed in the beat of a heart as the land turned from green to brown to white and back again to repeat itself all over.

Then, as if the controller had suddenly decided to slam on the breaks, the torrent stopped, and the brothers were pitched forwards in the stillness. Flakes of puffy white snow drifted down from a cloudy sky as Remus and Romulus gathered their wits and surveyed the intimidating calm of the moment with curious apprehension. Hearing the beating of heavy feet upon the soft blanket of the snow, they turned to see strange animals meandering across the rolling hills from the south.

Like the great elephants of Earth, these creatures were massive quadrupeds with thick midsections and knobby heads. Their skin was a deep purple—almost maroon—yet they possessed no trunks or tusks. Instead, the beasts had wide mouths filled with flat white teeth and rimmed with stout tentacles or fingers. The giants thundered in mighty herds as they loped across the frozen landscape, kicking up clods of powdery snow and earth. Bleating like guttural trumpeters, they called to one another, stopping here and there to dig at the ground for signs of green. The twins watched with fascination as the alien animals crowded together, grunting and bobbing their heads in the search for food.

"They are so similar to elephants," murmured Remus with awestruck elation as a group of adults stood close together, creating a shield from the chilly wind for a youngster.

"There must be more in common between the Earth and Mars than previously thought," agreed Romulus.

With a crack of blinding white light, the ground beneath them leaped and rumbled. The great purple beasts turned their heads to the north as a plume of smoke and ash jetted up from the high summit of the distant peak, which towered above all the other mountains around it. The ash cloud turned the sky to blackest night, and the frightened creatures began to wail and stamp, rolling their big eyes and gnashing their flat teeth. The shockwave unleashed from the eruption screamed across the wintry countryside like a tidal wave, lifting the elephants off their feet and tossing them through the air like dry leaves. Red ribbons of magma and rock streaked from the broiling mouth of the volcano into the blackened sky like comets, reaching the crest of their high arcs before returning landward like the brimstone of biblical legend. The snow at their feet began to steam and melt as the hot air, carried on the back of the shockwave, evaporated the serene stillness of winter, turning it into a boiling, churning sea of shifting soil.

Crashing to the ground like burning fists of napalm, chunks of molten rock and liquid magma exploded, tossing sparks of white hot lava, igniting the howling purple elephants as they galloped like confused children in the raining fire. An echoing chorus of crushing rock, like the roll of a distant drum, reached the ears of the terrified twins as they watched the face of the monolithic volcano slide off and demolish a wide path through the mountain range at its feet.

More projectiles of deep red and pitiless black fell about them, vomiting thick oozing heaps of lava across the burning carcasses of the dead elephants. A growing whistle drew Remus's eyes skyward, and he gasped in horror as a mass of fiery stone streaked down from the heavens directly towards them. Crying out, he grasped Romulus and held him close, waiting to be smashed under the thundering inferno. As the comet grew nearer, it blotted out the sky, and Remus squeezed his eyes shut, hugging Romulus, who yelled and wailed in his ear like a jabbering lunatic. For long moments, they stayed like that—clutching one another tightly and moaning with fear.

When again they opened their eyes, the carnage was gone, replaced by a softly whispering wind and the glowing embrace of a peaceful sun. It was summer again, and they stood amongst thin and stalky river reeds, which listed gently in the light breeze. Turning, the twins gazed out across the lulling countryside to see that many things had changed since they first awakened on ancient Mars. Now, much of the grasslands that had previously covered all that the eye could see were reduced to oases, which dotted a rusty desert of small hills. Skeletal brown trees with drooping branches grew between the reeds that meandered alongside the river to their left. What once was a shallow stream had since bulged and deepened to become a massive and fast-moving river, fed by glaciers in the north. Snaking its way from a wide split in the mountains, it cut a shimmering path through the dusty landscape, spreading swashes of green vegetation as it dissected the red sands.

Billowing clouds of mist curled up into the air at the base of the distant mountains where another fork of the river rushed to the east and cascaded down into a mighty canyon. The giant volcano, which had decimated the landscape so savagely, now loomed ominously behind the ocher mountain range, slowly breathing steady wisps of steam into the sky. The odor of burning wood, sweet and harsh, hung in the still air. Unsure as to whether or not time would leap forwards, the brothers carefully trudged towards the ridge of a shallow hill and the smell of the smoke.

Cresting the dusty summit, Remus and Romulus froze with shock and awe as they watched thin tendrils of gray twist up from a cooking fire in the center of a cluster of round thatched huts. Unable to move, the twins watched in pensive silence as figures—men and women—stooped to gather armfuls of wood, which lay in heaps about the perimeter of the fire pit. Tossing the branches into the orange flames, the people talked and gestured with their hands. Some even laughed. They were all very short and wiry, with long thin arms and agile delicate legs. Their faces were drawn and wide with extended flat noses and small mouths. Their seashell-shaped ears sat high on the sides of their broad heads, and, like the mighty dead elephant-creatures, they were all colored a purple so deep it was nearly brown. From the distance at which the twins watched, they could not make out many of the more subtle features of these humanoid beings, but one thing was clear even from afar: the people of Mars had eyes of rich, flat aqua-blue, widely spaced and as large as eggs.

Emergency EVA—Sol 4

Gathering around the holographic projection table in the communications station of the dome, the six members of the ground crew embraced the electric warmth of the room. Outside, the sand-filled winds showed no signs of abating, and the radiation unleashed by the anomalous solar flare continued to batter the red planet like the bullets of a firing squad. Although dropping steadily, X-ray saturation was still high enough to cause deadly burns to anyone unprotected by a pressure suit, and there was sufficient gamma radiation in the air to mutate an uninhibited human cell into a cancerous abomination. Worse yet, electromagnetic radiation unceasingly bathed the surface of Mars in particles of energy that disrupted communications and fried computer linkages.

Were it not for the fusion of alloys, gold and aluminum woven into the fabric of the dome's shell, the explorers would have lost all computer functions by now, leaving them alone and in dire straits. Unfortunately for Harrison and Marshall, the tactical EVA skin suits could not be manufactured out of the same material as the dome. Thus, they were far less resistant to the extreme levels of radiation now cooking the planet. If they spent too long outside the shield of the dome's shell, the computer uplinks within their suits would burn up, and their connection to Braun would be lost.

As a holographic image of the base slowly rotated in the air above the table, Udo Clunkat reluctantly reached up to highlight an enormous, ventilated metal box with several ducts protruding from it. Winding their way up the westward-facing side of the dome like vines of ivy, the ducts converged onto one another at the zenith, then fed into the dome's ventilation compressor.

"That is the regulator up there," said the German. "It combines all of the gasses into the atmo we use and breathe in here. Right now, it can't do what it was designed for because of the problems in the life-support station down here."

Bringing the view back down the side of the dome to the large metal box, Udo parted his clasped hands and made the holograph turn transparent. As the opacity of the life-support station reduced, its complicated internal workings were revealed in color-coded sections. A wide tube located between two ribbed squares of plastic glowed with soft blue light as it drifted away from the tangle of machinery surrounding it.

"Here," he pointed. "Is where the air scrubbers are."

Sliding a hand from right to left, he cut the image of the fat cylinder into a cross-section.

"Because this base uses an internal air pressure of fourteen pounds per square inch to push against the low Martian surface pressure of .087 PSI, we must continuously circulate a breathable atmosphere of at least nine PSI to keep from succumbing to altitude sickness. If we were to reach a tipping point, then the pressure would drop very quickly. And if it were to fall below one PSI to the levels outside the dome, our blood will boil."

There was an uncomfortable silence before Udo resumed speaking.

"Our life-support system garnishes the usable gasses, such as nitrogen and argon, from the thin Martian air, then combines them with supplemented oxygen and hydrogen. This process creates the Earth-like atmosphere needed to maintain safe pressurization and healthy lung functions. Because argon and nitrogen are fairly plentiful, it is safe for us to rely on the Martian atmosphere to provide them for our mixture. However, because there are such small amounts of oxygen and water vapor out there, building up a surplus of those without using electrolysis is impossible for any real length of time."

The German paused and closed his eyes, sighing softly.

"That's why the air scrubbers are really just a temporary measure, chosen because the electrolysis machine wouldn't fit in the Lander. Up to now we have been alleviating the situation by adding pure oxygen and hydrogen to the mixture from reserve tanks, but those are depleted."

Glancing around the group, he smiled painfully, then continued.

"Now, inside the Arc there are plenty of reserve tanks, but, alas, they are buried in there, and we are stuck in here. What we really need is our electrolysis machine. If we had been able to install that, it would be splitting the hydrogen from the oxygen within the Martian permafrost, which is actually just frozen water, and supplying us with all the O_2 and hydrogen we could ever hope for. Unfortunately, it was never unpacked or assembled because of all this—"

He made a waving gesture towards the roof of the dome as a gust of wind outside howled viciously.

"Essentially, we are running on systems never meant to be used under these conditions. It can limp us along for a while, but not if the scrubbers are so clogged with sand that they can't skim off what little O_2 there is out there. Normally, Braun would have warned us of any dust storms this big, and we would have grabbed more reserve tanks or something. But the nature of this storm and its sudden arrival have coupled with our barely operational status, and led us into what NASA calls an unknown unknown."

"What is our internal air pressure now?" asked Harrison, standing at the rear of the group.

Braun quickly replied from the shadows of the darkened ceiling above.

"The internal air pressure of the dome has fallen slightly to 10.86 PSI."

Shuddering, Viviana began to mumble under her breath, drawing concerned glances from the rest of the crew.

"Not to worry," comforted William as he gently patted her shoulder. "We'll have this all taken care of before it gets dangerously low."

Snorting, Marshall jabbed a thumb at Harrison.

"No, William. *We'll* get it taken care of. *You'll* sit in here and suck your thumb."

Frowning, William ignored Marshall's taunt and tapped at the projection of the air scrubber. The wide blue tube burst apart into an alarming amount of individual pieces, which floated slightly spaced out from one another. Within the unassuming cylinder was a network of screens and filters, complicatedly layered over one another as they ribbed the length of a copper conduit.

"Let me walk you through what you'll need to do to change the filters," said William coolly. "Then I'll go suck my thumb."

An hour later, the tutorial was finished, and Marshall and Harrison were ready to step into the airlock. Everything William and Udo had shown them was uploaded into their suit computers to be accessed through Augmented Vision when they started their work. The process was simple enough: open the life-support station box, find the air scrubber cylinder, open it, replace all eleven filters, rewire the new filters and close the cylinder. Once that was done, put the system back together, close the box and get back to the airlock. It all looked easy on a computer graphic, but to actually complete the task within an hour and a half seemed like a long shot. Add to it the blizzard-like dust storm outside and the sickeningly high levels of harmful radiation, and there was little hope things would go as smoothly as promised.

As the last of the air within his suit's torso and limbs was pumped out, Harrison felt like a mummy wrapped in a death shroud that would cling to his skin for a thousand years. Standing before him, clutching his helmet with white-knuckled tension, Liu looked up into his dark face.

"Alright?"

"Yeah," he muttered, bending his head from side to side as the gasket around his neck choked down on him.

"Is that too tight?" she worried, shifting the helmet under one arm so she could touch the coupling at his throat.

"It's always like that. There's nothing to do about it I guess," he sighed nervously, then quickly reached up and grasped her hand as it trailed away from him.

Casting her eyes down, Liu nervously bit at her lower lip.

"I'm scared for you, Harrison. I—"

Trailing off, she met his gaze and started to speak again, but quickly stopped herself. Clenching his jaw, the young archaeologist, still holding her hand, brought it to his face and kissed it softly.

"What?" he urged hopefully. "What were you going to say?"

Shaking her head, Liu looked away again and let her hand slip from his. They stood like that for several minutes, silent and unmoving. Behind them, Marshall and the rest avoided the slightly awkward scene, allowing Harrison and Liu their moment of imperfect tranquility in the face of great danger.

Finally, there could be no more postponement. Pressure levels were dropping, and the time had come to enter the storm or perish. Helmets securely sealed and utility belts deftly strapped across their chests, the two white-suited astronauts stepped into the cramped airlock and gave one final thumbs up. Shaking noticeably, Liu swung the heavy airlock door shut, then peered through its round glass window. Her eyes twinkled and flickered as tears built up behind them, and her lips moved silently to form three words in what looked like Mandarin Chinese. Feeling his stomach ache with the longing to hear those words clearly, Harrison forced himself to turn from the window and face the airlock's outer hatch. A soft green light ticked on above the door, signifying that the airlock was fully depressurized, and Marshall reached for the bolted handle.

"Ready?" he said in a steady voice.

"Ready," exhaled Harrison.

Pushing the handle down, Marshall swung the hatch inward, and the airlock instantly filled with blinding red sand. It billowed through the opening like the smoke of a raging fire, engulfing the two in a thick blanket of rusty haze. Harrison reached out ahead of himself like a sightless ant, feeling for the rim of the hatch while shuffling his feet along the floor to keep from tripping.

"Turn on your A-Vision's *dimensional enhancement* ping," commanded Marshall in his suit speakers.

Quickly obeying, Harrison engaged his Augmented Vision, and the face shield of his helmet glowed to life. The shapeless view of swirling brown and red was enhanced one hundred fold as computer-generated images, like the blueprints of a building plan, were imposed over the blurs of dust and sand. He could now see the airlock's interior like a bat might see the curved walls of a darkened cave. The computer in his helmet sent out pings of high frequency radio waves, which bounced off of everything they touched to paint an illuminated diagram of his surroundings. Before him, the image of Marshall stood silhouetted in the open hatch.

"Come on," he beckoned as Harrison made his way to the exit.

The two stepped out into the boiling Martian air and made a quick left, heading for the life-support station. Knowing it was just his imagination, Harrison still felt as though he could sense the radiation microwaving his organs.

Within minutes, they had reached the stocky life-support station, which glowed a brilliant green on the inside of their helmet glass. Kneeling in the sand at the base of the box, Marshall reached out and took hold of the two, bottom-corner locking handles. Applying a quarter turn to both levers, he waited until his Augmented Vision confirmed the action before quickly moving to the next set of panel locks. Nervously, Harrison watched a timer in the upper right-hand corner of his face shield tick off the minutes. So far they had been outside the dome for nine minutes and forty-nine seconds.

"There," grunted Marshall as he turned the final two levers. "That's the last one. Let's open this puppy up."

Taking hold of the panel's top right-hand corner, Harrison helped Marshall lift the vented side-wall out of its track. Resting the flat sheet of steel and alloy on the ground, the two peered at the innards of the life-support station as they waited for their Augmented Vision to update and show them what to do next. The following twenty-five minutes were spent fastidiously removing all of the machinery and couplings that blocked their access to the fat cylindrical air scrubber buried deep within the belly of the life-support station. As Marshall worked his way further into the maze of connected systems, Harrison carefully applied digital labels to each piece of machinery handed to him. In this way, once their task

162

was completed, Harrison and Marshall could correctly reassemble what they had disconnected.

As the driving winds hurled wave after wave of gritting Martian sand against their suits, the two explorers crouched low and moved quickly.

"I see it!" shouted Marshall with excitement. "I can almost reach it."

Checking the clock, Harrison winced as they neared the forty-minute mark.

"Fifty minutes left, Ralph," he warned.

"Okay, okay. I've got it. I just need to unplug one wire here at the end, and I'll bring it out. Get the filters ready."

Opening a large pocket on the front of his tool belt, Harrison ran a gloved fingertip across the thin filters within.

"Ready when you are," he breathed.

With an almost childlike giggle, Marshall backed out on his knees from the inside of the life-support station, cradling the air-scrubber tube like a newborn baby. Huddling together, the two made a human shield against the violent winds as Marshall twisted the top free from the cylinder and extracted the contents slowly. A hard gust of wind shook the paper-thin filters in his hand, and the two exchanged a nervous look.

"Careful," hissed Harrison as Marshall handed him the unprotected filtration unit.

A narrow copper pipe of thirty centimeters ran from the center of the cap to a plastic port on the opposite end of the tube. Attached to it like slices of onion on the skewer of a shish kabob, the delicate air filters sagged with two solid days' worth of rusty sand and dust. Working his nimble fingers like a surgeon dissecting the vertebrates of a human spine, Harrison slipped the worn filters free from the copper conduit—one at a time. Letting the tattered remnants fall to the ground, neither man made an effort to collect them as they were spirited away by blasts of wind. Time was running out, and this was the first human trash to litter the planet since the Curiosity Rover of 2012. The timer on the inside of Harrison's visor flashed red as they approached the forty-minute mark.

"Fuck," spat Marshall as he impatiently waited for Harrison to finish replacing the screens.

163

"Almost done," muttered Harrison. "Just two more."

The computer-generated view of his hands as they worked at the scrubbers flickered, went out, then fizzled back into view.

"Shit, shit, shit shit!"

"What happened?"

"My A-Vision is cooking up. You might need to lead me back if it goes out completely."

"Don't worry about that. Just finish with the filters. We're at thirty-eight minutes."

Forcing his shaking hands to steady, Harrison redoubled his concentration as violent gusts of wind threatened to tear the new filters from the conduit like the sails of a ship in stormy seas.

"Harrison," came Braun's voice in his helmet speakers. "I'm sure you are aware, but I have detected several problems with your suit's CPU. I will continue to monitor the situation and inform you if things get any worse. Also, please do not exert yourself. Your vital signs show evidence of strain."

"Yeah, no shit," Harrison swore savagely. "Just do what you can to keep my suit online."

"I will."

Rushing against the clock, Harrison painstakingly slid the last of the thin screens into its place on the conduit line, wired it, then handed the part back to his eagerly trembling partner.

"Bing, bang boom," laughed Marshall as he slid the backbone with its eleven new filters back inside the housing tube.

"Thirty-five minutes remaining," echoed Braun in both of their helmets.

"Step on it, Ralph," urged Harrison. "My suit is acting up pretty bad."

Moving with the determination of a man possessed by the magnitude of his situation, Marshall hurriedly reconnected the air-scrubbing unit, then began piecing the adjoining systems back together in reverse order. As Harrison handed him part after part, his Augmented Vision repeatedly crackled out, only to jump back into view again as if some unseen force were flicking a light switch on and off inside his head. He knew the same thing was happening to Marshall, for the astronaut occasionally broke into subdued strings of savage cursing, which, despite their fervency, did not disrupt the pace of his labor. The minutes ticked by faster and faster, matching the driving intensity of the raging storm as it blasted the two men with unrelenting sheets of red sand. Humming nervously as he worked, Marshall screwed, bolted and wrenched the jigsawed life-support station back together with incredible precision.

"Time?" he demanded as Harrison handed him the last section of a crucial ducting line.

"Twelve minutes," groaned Harrison, feeling an increasing uneasiness building in the pit of his stomach.

Marshall turned back to the life-support station with a nod and set about connecting the duct with a complicated compression line.

"Go grab the cover panel," he ordered over his shoulder.

Shifting on his heels, Harrison scanned the rippling ground beside him for the vented metal sheet and could not see it. Standing quickly, he spun in a full circle, thinking that perhaps the winds had carried it off on a powerful gust. As he shuffled his feet in search of the lost cover plate, his boot clunked against something metal, partially buried by the driving sands, and he breathed a sigh of relief.

"Harrison," said Braun in his helmet speakers. "I think you should sit down for a few moments. You need to conserve your energy."

"What are you talking about?"

"Please, just follow my advice," pressed the AI.

Ignoring Braun, Harrison leaned forwards to unearth the vented panel. As his hands worked to uncover the corner of the metal sheet, he was suddenly struck by a bout of unannounced nausea. Taking several deep breaths, he straightened up and calmed his rolling stomach. As the clock began blinking the ten-minute warning, a sharp stab in his stomach doubled him over and forced him to stumble back several paces. Grasping his thighs tightly for support, he bit back fruitlessly against an aggressive wave of dizziness, which spread over him like the spray of a tepid rain. Feeling suddenly sapped of energy, he dropped to his knees on the dust-covered ground and coughed violently, tasting the sour sting of bile as it quickly foamed up in the back of his mouth.

"Harrison," announced Braun urgently. "Your vital signs show evidence of radiation sickness, and your suit is in critical condition. Please sit still to conserve your energy."

"What?" choked Harrison in horror. "But there's still time on the clock!"

Before Braun could answer, the view of his surroundings scattered like the static of a television screen. Slamming a hand uselessly against the side of his helmet, Harrison swore loudly and fought to keep his mutinous stomach down.

"Forget the panel!" yelled Marshall, his transmission badly distorted. "I'm done, but my vision is on the fritz. I can't see you!"

"I'm here," called Harrison as he waved his arms back and forth. "Braun says my suit is almost finished."

"What?" crackled Marshall. "I can barely hear you. Stay where you are. I'll find you. My A-Vision's out, but I'll find you!"

With a screech of electricity, Harrison's Augmented Vision leaped into view, blinked several times, then went out again. In the frozen seconds when his face shield had been illuminated, he saw the figure of Ralph Marshall, hands outstretched, groping like blind man as he walked away from Harrison and towards the open desert.

"Can you hear me?" shouted Marshall above a burst of sharply-spiking feedback. "I'm fucking blind. Where are you?"

"Ralph, I'm here. I'm here! This way. Come back," pleaded Harrison in a panic, bile dribbling from his lips.

"Harrison," said Braun, his voice disintegrating rapidly. "I cannot maintain my connection. Your suit is shutting down. I miscalculated. I am sorry."

As those final words flooded his helmet, Harrison screamed against the ocean of static in his ears, hoping the cry would reach Marshall and draw him back towards the dome. With a whine that grew into a shrill siren, the feedback in his suit speakers fizzled mechanically, then went silent. Deep red shadows filled the inside of his helmet, and the churning sickness within his stomach broke loose. Coughing up hot tendrils of acid and bile, he pitched forwards and felt the cold rough surface of the desert floor rush up to meet his heaving chest. The vomit pooled on the glass of his face shield, and the ragged gasps of his own breathing were the only sounds he could hear.

As though all of the life within his muscles had been drained, he shivered feebly with the effort of movement. The world spun violently as he pushed himself to a kneeling position, trying in vain to see beyond the billowing clouds of sand, which enveloped him like blood red ocean. The condensation and streaks of bile that coated the glass of his face shield abruptly transformed into fragile ice crystals as his suit began to cool down. No longer was his internal CPU powering the life-support systems. No longer could he feel the continuous breath of circulated air. No longer did the warming blood of the chemical heating agents chase away the deadly cold of the Martian atmosphere. Braun's presence within the suit was gone, and for the first time in his entire life, Harrison was completely alone.

Inside the dome

Sitting in the com room of the stagnant dome, Udo Clunkat absently watched the holographic images of the life-support station as they lit up like a Christmas tree—each system blinking brightly as it came back online. Communications with the two astronauts had been few and far between since they had exited the dome nearly an hour and twenty minutes before. In the storm, radio feedback was increased over longer distances as electromagnetic radiation played havoc with the communications linkages in each suit. Even though, physically, Harrison and Marshall were very close by, most of their brief transmissions to the base had been nearly indecipherable above the blanketed feedback of hisses and pops. Instead, Udo put his trust in Braun's guidance to see the two through their difficult task.

Lost in his troubled thoughts, Udo at first didn't notice when the final section of the coolant line flickered from transparent gray to green. When he did turn his gaze on the blinking emerald light, he suddenly snapped back to the moment and sat up straighter in his chair.

"Everyone, they're finished!" he called out excitedly.

With the thudding of fast-moving feet, the remaining members of the crew quickly filed into the cubicle, chattering hopefully.

"How long until the air pressure starts to go up?" questioned Viviana, a smile gracing her lips for the first time in two sols.

Braun replied before Udo could calculate an answer.

"The air pressure will likely fall to 9.99 PSI due to the low levels of oxygen and hydrogen in the Martian atmosphere.

However, once an equilibrium has been reached between what is needed to supply the dome and what is available, air pressure will hold above the level designated as dangerous."

The strained look of hope upon Viviana's face quickly faded.

"But won't we get sick? 9.99 sounds terribly low!"

"No," stated Braun calmly. "The gene enhancement you underwent had several very profound effects on your bodies' systems. You can sustain yourselves in low-pressure environments, which would otherwise be harmful to your human counterparts on Earth. In this way—"

A gasp of terror from Liu interrupted the AI, and she pointed to a command screen just left of the holo-table.

"Oh my God, no!" she shouted.

"What?" jumped Udo, swiveling in his chair to follow the trembling line of her finger.

There, on the screen, were the diagnostic charts for both Marshall's and Harrison's suits. In the dim light of the communications room, the red glares cast by the warning signs of each suit were as bright as gasoline explosions. On and off the red indicators blinked, strobing the words *CRITICAL MALFUNCTION* in bold capital letters above the two suits. Worse yet, the normally gently-sloping lines that represented the vital signs of each astronaut now fluctuated and spiked, possessed by fear and sickness.

"Why didn't any alarms go off?" said William, his voice rising into an accusing whine. "Braun, what is happening here?"

"I am sorry," replied the AI woodenly.

"What's wrong with them?" shrieked Liu, her fingers clawing at her face as it drained of all color.

Peering closely at the readouts, Udo swallowed hard, then turned to face his compatriots.

"They both have signs radiation sickness, and it looks like their suits are shutting down."

"Braun!" demanded William, his eyes blazing with indignation. "What have you done? Why weren't we alerted of this sooner?"

From the shadows of the dome's ceiling, the flat baritone of Braun's voice drifted down.

"It is in my mission directives that I not allow the ground team to suffer losses greater than 33.3 percent."

"So you thought you would just hide this from us?" screamed William, slamming his fist down on the holo-table.

"I am sorry, but the risk that one or more of you might attempt a rescue was too great."

Turning on her heel, Liu sprinted from the room and made for the suit lockers near the entrance of the airlock.

"Liu!" shouted Udo. "What are you doing?"

Tugging at the unmoving latch that secured the door to her locker, Liu cursed and kicked at the thin metal.

"I deplore this situation as much as you do, Dr. Liu," lamented Braun, his tone reflecting true sadness. "But I cannot allow you to leave the safety of the dome. Above all else, the success of the mission and the well-being of the greatest number of its crew are my highest priorities."

"Fuck you!" raged Liu as she battered the door of her locker. "Let me go to him!"

"I am truly sorry, but no."

Rushing to her side, William began to wrench at the lever that held his own locker closed.

"Open the door *du hurensohn!*" he commanded, his perfect English breaking down into livid torrents of German profanity.

"I cannot," repeated Braun miserably.

In the communications room, Udo watched with horrified resignation as the flashing red image of Harrison's pressure suit dimmed, then vanished from the screen. Behind him, Viviana uttered a choked moan as she turned and shuffled away from the glowing readouts towards the safety and seclusion of her own quarters. At the airlock, Udo could hear Liu's anguished sobs as she attacked the latch of her suit locker with a fire extinguisher, taken from a nearby hanger. Next to her, William smashed his fists against the metal door of his own receptacle, assaulting the reinforced material with little effect. As the status light of Marshall's suit flickered weakly in its final moments of operation, Udo turned to face the now-empty room.

"Braun?" he whispered weakly.

"Yes, Dr. Konig?"

"Will they suffer?"

"Yes."

"My God," he sighed sadly. "My God."

Outside the dome

The cold penetrated Harrison's suit like a hypodermic needle, filling his veins with liquid nitrogen. His life-support CPU had only been offline for a minute at the most, and, already, the chemical warming agent that circulated throughout the fabric of his pressure suit was beginning to cool. Wrapping his arms around himself, he struggled to his feet, straining his eyes against the impenetrable curtain of red sand that surrounded him. Blinking back tears as his muscles screamed with the force of fatigue, Harrison coughed harshly inside his frosted helmet. Fighting to stand still amidst the waves of dizziness, he wished for just a second of Augmented Vision.

The world outside his suit was as mysterious and hidden as the distant ocean floor was to a swimmer treading water on the surface. Trembling despite the adrenaline, he felt his knees buckle, and he toppled to his side like a decrepit rotten tree. Groaning with pain and fear, he searched the ground around him with slowly wandering hands, attempting to find anything that would give him a clue as to his bearings. Touching only rough stones and sand, he rolled onto his back, chest heaving with exertion. Attempting to catch his breath, he closed his eyes and gulped at the stale putrid air of his helmet.

A picture of Liu's face, tears staining her cheeks, swam into his mind and looked down at him through a mess of straight black hair. In her glistening eyes were the untold depths of heartbreak and love as her mouth moved in silence, attempting to speak across the void of time and space. He longed to run his hands through her silky hair, to feel the warmth and curve of her lower back as they embraced. Most of all, he yearned to breath in her scent: delicate, enticing and sweet. But those things were all gone now. Concepts like love and spirit and warmth were as alien to his situation as he himself was to this planet. Unable to maintain her presence in his mind, Liu sank below the waters of his consciousness, and, soon, he too felt himself dip beneath the cold and placid tide.

How did things gone so wrong so fast? he wondered, his inner voice a distant tinkle like the sound of a wind chime.

As the ebb and flow of his own breathing drew farther and farther away, Harrison smiled inwardly. Waves of understanding and enlightenment spilled over him, throwing fire into the darkest corners of his soul. Questions he had not even thought to ask were answered with such simplistic elegance that dying seemed somehow worth the price one paid to learn the truth. Floating up and away from his nearly-frozen body, he looked down with bittersweet regret.

I'll never get to tell Liu how I really feel, he thought as his mind wandered and his heart slowed. We'll never have the pleasure of living in the light.

Suddenly, someone shook his shoulders, and Harrison felt himself fall from the sky like a stone down a well, splashing back into his body. Eyes fluttering, he gazed up through the glass of his face shield as a shadow descended from the rusty smoke beyond. The dark mass took form as it drew nearer, changing and shifting until it became the helmet of a pressure suit. A face looked in at him through the frost that caked the glass of his visor. Blunt hard features and gray listless eyes relaxed into a relieved smile. Ralph Marshall pressed his helmet to Harrison's, shouting to be heard through the thin atmosphere of Mars.

"Wake up, buddy," he said, his voice muffled and distant. "My vision could go out again at any second."

"I can't," was all Harrison could manage before frothy bile erupted from the corners of his drawn mouth.

Nodding, Marshall scooped Harrison's aching body into his strong arms and lifted the dying Egyptian like a child.

"It's okay," spoke Marshall though the glass of his helmet. "I'll get you back."

With the rise and fall of Marshall's determined steps, Harrison's head lulled back and forth as he slipped in and out of consciousness. Briefly, his arm brushed against something firm-yet-yielding as it swayed from his body like a limp pendulum.

The dome, he realized through the fog of death. Marshall's found the dome.

With a force that pulled its energy from deep within his core, Harrison laughed weakly, his frigid chest shaking with spasms of lunatic delight.

"Almost there!" called Marshall, his face shield bumping against Harrison's.

Looking up into the astronaut's grim features, Harrison fought to keep his eyes from rolling back in his head. The cold had become more than he could bear, and, despite the hope that Marshall's words carried, he could no longer keep himself together. Feeling the icy fingers of the inevitable close around his softly beating heart, Harrison smiled at Marshall's shadowy face with detached veneration. Drawing one last shuddering breath, he let go of everything and plunged upwards through the aether of true blackness.

In his arms, Ralph sensed the exodus of Harrison's life force and hastened his pace. Hugging the archaeologist tightly against his own freezing suit, he continued to follow the gentle curve of the dome's shell by sliding his right foot along the base with every step. His own suit's life support and CPU had died mere seconds after reaching the skin of the dome, and he was now fully blind. Although the cold bit at him like the needle-toothed jaws of a rabid hyena, Braun's final garbled transmission still rang in his ears, adding fuel to his drive.

"Harrison is dying," the AI had said, his normally impassive voice broken and despairing. "Save him, Lieutenant Marshall, because I cannot."

Now, as Ralph moved forwards, he hummed an aimless tune— something he often did when under pressure. Harrison had begun to grow stiff with cold, and his own limbs creaked against the strain of every step. Suddenly, his boot tip struck against a hard metal surface, and Ralph let out a victorious laugh. Bending his head down, he touched the glass of his face shield to that of Harrison's.

"We're there," he bellowed. "My boot just hit the airlock. Hang on a little bit longer."

Inside the frost-streaked darkness of Harrison's helmet, Marshall could see the resigned look frozen on the young man's face. His eyes were closed, his lips tinged with blue, and, yet, there was another element to the expression.

Life, thought Marshall with unperturbed faith. He's still alive. He has to be.

CHAPTER SIXTEEN

Ghosts

Remus and Romulus crouched like hunters amongst the tan stalks of desert grass, which trembled in the cool air of an early sunset. Since first discovering the existence of the Martian village and its terrestrial inhabitants, neither twin had dared move from their vantage point atop the belly of a sloping hill. As the eroded disk of the Sun sank below the western horizon, Remus and Romulus relaxed in the shadows of nightfall.

"Did you ever imagine you would see such things?" whispered Remus, staring intently at the cluster of thatched huts.

"Never," replied Romulus in a carefully perplexed voice.

Standing, Remus beckoned for his brother to follow him.

"We should go down there. I want to get a better look at—" His voice drifted off as he searched his mind for the right words. "—At the people," he finished with finality.

Shifting uncomfortably, Romulus hesitated before answering.

"I agree, but let us move with caution. Who knows how they will react if they see us."

Smiling crookedly, Remus started walking down the hill.

"*Them* see us? *I* can hardly see us?"

The brothers moved quietly through the whispering grass, nearing the stout huts with deliberate stealth. A shower of sparks rained up into the inky sky as a dry branch was cast upon the flames of the fire pit in the center of the village. Reaching the first row of huts, Remus could faintly hear the murmur of voices as they carried in the air. Careful to stick to the shadows, he pressed forwards by following the walls of a hut until he came to a narrow alley where firelight played across the ground. Stopping, he surveyed the little buildings.

Short and round with thatched roofs made of twigs and grass, he assessed analytically. Like the Fulani tribe of ancient Gambia. Very interesting.

Resting a hand on the cool walls of the nearest hut, he judged that the dry stone was some kind of hardened mud or river clay. Suddenly, he felt the texture of the wall dematerialize, and his arm disappeared within the clay, having no effect on the structure itself.

174

Shuddering, he pulled his hand free, attempting to inspect its transparent murkiness in the failing light.

"Strange," he muttered absently.

Hearing a rustle like the turning of dry leaves, he turned his gaze upon the circular portholes that dotted the side of the hut. Stooping down, he glimpsed the darkened interior, then felt his breath catch in his throat. Three small children slept atop woven mats of reed, their tiny chests rising and falling as their flat nostrils dilated and constricted. Feeling a hand on his shoulder, Remus turned to see Romulus pointing with unmoving intensity to the lighted alley, where an adult Martian now stood—looking directly at them.

Frozen by fear and wonder, neither brother stirred as the Martian took a few steps in their direction. His egg-sized blue eyes narrowed against the dark, and Remus could see small pupils   no bigger than pinpricks—darting about as they searched the shadows. Possessed by an emotion so unfamiliar that it wholly drowned his judgment, Remus succumbed to reckless curiosity and stepped out of the shadows.

Gasping, Romulus sank back against the wall of the little hut and waited for the alarm to sound. Seconds passed.

Shifting his gaze to the stars above, the unconcerned Martian showed no indication that he had even seen Remus.

Feeling the need to take another leap of faith, Remus raised a hand and spoke, "Hello."

The Martian continued to peer up, studying the twinkles of light, which grew brighter as the night enveloped them.

"Hello there," said Remus again, taking a step towards the little purple man.

Lowering his eyes, the Martian placed a hand on the back of his neck and yawned: a very human gesture.

"Excuse me," called Remus, walking to stand in front of the villager. "I mean you no—"

The words froze in his mouth as the oblivious Martian strode forwards, moving through Remus as if he were a ghost. Stopping at the window of the nearest hut, the Martian leaned his head in and checked on the sleeping children. Satisfied, he turned on a heel and marched back towards the fire pit and the company of his fellow villagers.

Remus stood, dumbstruck. Sliding out of the shadows, Romulus watched the Martian leave, then approached his brother.

"He could not see you."

"Or feel me, apparently," added Remus lamely.

"Yes," mused Romulus, his voice stretching the word out as he pondered an idea. "You know, Brother, I must admit that something about this whole experience does seem slightly familiar."

Still shaken by the sensation of being walked through, Remus blankly stared at his twin. Smiling, Romulus bent down and tried to pluck a stalk of grass. His fingers passed through the swaying sprig as if made of steam.

"We cannot effect change in this reality," he said as a grin played across his translucent face. "Brother, do you know what this means?"

A smile growing on his own lips, Remus answered, "That this is some form of memory regression, and we are in a data construct!"

"Indeed!"

"Then we can observe the Martians with impunity, for they do not truly exist!"

"Yes, and," stressed Romulus. "All constructs must end at the point when they were last recorded. We are not prisoners here forever."

Emboldened by their newfound immunity, the two brothers walked quickly from the row of huts towards the village center. The hushed babble of voices grew louder, and soon, much to their already-tested surprise, they found that they could recognize some of the words being spoken. Stopping, Romulus put a hand on Remus's arm.

"Did you hear that?"

"Indeed. I fully understood. How bizarre."

Continuing quickly, the brothers soon came upon the fire pit and its group of two dozen or more worshipers. Sitting, crouching and standing, they were gathered around the stony rim as flames danced upwards in a ballet of heat and light. As they chatted with one another, an older villager, decorated with body paint and piercings, struggled to his feet—leaning heavily on a gnarled walking stick for support.

"Please," he said, raising a hand for silence. "Let me speak. Let me speak."

"Speak, Olo," nodded a female villager, bare-breasted and lean.

At the sound of her commanding voice, the others around the pit fell into a respectful silence.

"I have seen visions that must be shared and discussed," started the painted Martian known as Olo. "Last night when I dreamt, I saw the Great Spirits."

A chorus of uneasy murmurs broke out as Olo gripped his walking stick and scanned the group with his pale blue eyes.

"I was traveling," he continued. "As I always do in visions, far away and far above. This night, I followed the river Kwaya north to the Valley of the Lakes. There, a fierce thunderstorm split the sky and shook the land. I wanted to speak with the spirits of the water snakes and ask them to come down from the lakes and feed our village, for we are hungry, and they are late this season."

Around the fire, several Martians nodded in agreement. Opening his nostrils, Olo took a long rasping breath, then went on.

"I said to them, 'Why are you late? Our people are hungry.' They looked to the mighty mountain—Atun—and told me that the Great Spirits were back in many numbers so they would stay in the lakes to watch them fly and dance."

The naked female who had spoken earlier crossed her arms and frowned.

"The Great Ones have convinced the water snakes to stay in the north? Why?"

Shaking his head, Olo held out a hand.

"No, Chief Teo. The Great Spirits never spoke to the snakes. The snakes were only curious. As we are."

Licking her lips, the lean woman known as Teo stroked her chin thoughtfully.

"I am sorry for interrupting, Olo. Please go on with your story."

Bowing to her, Olo started speaking again.

"I told the snakes that they must come down the river to their spawning grounds in the south or their kind would die in one generation. They agreed, for they are simple and forget things easily."

Excited chatter broke out within the group, and people began to thank the decorated Martian for bringing back the water snakes.

"Wait!" he protested. "There is more."

The crowd fell silent, and Olo took another long breath.

"Because the Great Spirits have never shown themselves in so many numbers, I decided I must journey to the mountaintop and see them for myself. Long have I called upon the Great Spirits for permission to approach the foot of their sacred domain. Long have I waited for their reply."

Looking around the group, Olo pointed to the northern night sky.

"Atun is not a place for beings of flesh and blood. But in my journey I had neither, and so I dared to go where I knew I should not. There, atop the mountain that breathes steam and bleeds melted rock, I saw the Great Spirits for the first time. Dancing about the storm clouds, they drank the lightning and chanted in voices of thunder. Though I was afraid, I did not turn and flee. Their sky dance was both ominous and beautiful. For many hours, I watched in silence. I was only a spirit like the wind, and I thought they could not see me."

Pausing, Olo looked down, his gaze distant and sad.

"What happened next, Olo?" asked Teo urgently, her face half-masked in shadows.

As if returning from a memory, Olo stirred, his eyes refocusing.

"Their dance began to slow as the clouds cleared away. And then one came close to me."

At this, a pensive silence permeated the air around the fire. Even the hissing pops of burning logs seeming dampened and far away. Long seconds passed, and the stars overhead shown bright and hot against the fathomless depths of space. Sighing, Olo raised his painted face to the sky and gazed up at the lights of a billion distant suns.

"The Great Spirit," he continued softly. "Saw me and fixed its eyes upon my soul. Its piercing stare was brighter than any sunlight. I waited to be cast down into the fire of the Atun's belly for my selfish trespass, but instead, the Great Spirit turned its light away from me to shine above the Valley of the Lakes. There it stayed until I awoke."

No one moved as the group of Martian men and women waited for Olo to speak again. When he did not, Teo stepped forwards and rested a hand on his slumped shoulder.

"What do you think your vision meant?"

Raising his eyes to meet hers, Olo nodded slowly.

"I think we have been summoned."

"Summoned?" a man from the crowd voiced harshly. "Why would the Great Spirits summon us? We are nothing!"

"We are not nothing!" said Olo, his features burning with intensity. "We have built homes as hard as rock, hunted beasts many times our size and carved trees and stones with the words of our own language."

Looking off into the distance, Teo frowned: an expression so remarkably human that Remus felt an unexpected pang of homesickness.

"I want to understand," she spoke softly. "But I do not. What do these things mean to a God?"

Smiling, Olo pointed towards the black silhouettes of the serrated mountain range in the north.

"I have had a vision for many years, a dream that never changes no matter how many times I have it. In this vision, I see a ring of tall stones like none that exists in all our lands. When I look upon that ring, I know that it was us who made it. Like the Great Ones made the mountains, we too did raise stones."

"Temple-building," whispered Romulus to his brother. "They're talking about temple-building!"

"Although they do not yet know it," added Remus. "They stand on the cusp of a massive leap in cultural evolution."

Turning her back to the fire so that her face was shrouded in shadows, Teo's frown deepened.

"So this is why they have summoned us? To raise stones?"

"Yes. My vision was meant to start us on this path."

Rocking slowly, Teo seemed to weigh her thoughts as the group stood silently in waiting.

"I think I understand," she said at last. "But many more hands than we have here will be needed to raise stones. Even we, alone, can hardly kill a Buran. To accomplish what you speak of, we will need the aid of other tribes. You are respected and revered by all of the tribes of this great plain. If you tell them, as you have told us, they will have to join our cause. Will you help?"

Standing up as straight as his twisted back would allow him, Olo dipped his chin to a chorus of echoing ululations.

Awake—Sol 6

The warming kiss of the midday sun played across the waking face of Harrison Raheem Assad. Opening his eyes, he squinted in the gentle light as his vision returned, and his surroundings came into focus. He was lying in a bed in the dome's makeshift infirmary, flanked by several machines. The last time he had seen this room, it had been filled with haphazard stacks of boxes waiting to be unpacked. Now, the space was as clean and efficient as an operating room back on Earth. An IV hung from a roller next to his bed, and a translucent bag, full of what looked like blood, dripped steadily down a tube and into his arm. Shifting his gaze, he saw Elizabeth Kubba standing with her back to him, head tilted to one side as she skimmed the numbers of a diagnostic readout on her Tablet.

"Liz?" he whispered in a hoarse voice.

Turning, Kubba's brown face split into an enormous grin.

"Harrison, you're awake. How do you feel?"

Swallowing dryly, he lay still for a moment and thought her question over. Finally, he smiled and tried to laugh.

"I feel like I've been kicked by a donkey."

Sitting on the edge of the bed next to him, Kubba pocketed her Tablet and laid a hand on top of his.

"Honestly," she started with a grin. "You would be in better shape if you had been."

"Is it really that bad?" he asked, a frown drifting across his gaunt face.

"No, no," she cooed, flashing another toothy smile. "You'll feel a lot better when you're done with the transfusion regiment I've got you on. I'm far too good at what I do for you to worry."

Pausing, she looked away, then spoke softly.

"So, how does your head feel?"

"How do you mean? Like do I have a headache?"

"No," she said, her voice drifting off. "I mean your memory. Can you remember anything from after your suit shut down? Once we lost the connection with your vitals, my timeline breaks down a bit. You died, you know. Out there. Just for a moment or two."

"Really?"

"Yes. William had to revive you with a defibrillator. Your heart had stopped."

Closing his eyes, Harrison tried to recall the last thing he remembered. A hazy picture drifted into his mind, but before he could clearly see what it was, the image dissolved and he was left with a blank slate. Several beats passed as he lay there, his thoughts straining to reclaim the illusive memory, which seemed somehow quintessential. Finally giving up, he closed his eyes and took a deep breath.

"I feel as though I learned the answer to a very important question, but now I can't even remember what it was all about."

Nodding, Kubba pursed her lips and patted his hand again.

"Not to worry," she shrugged. "It will come back to you, or it won't. Either way, you're here now, and that's good news to me!"

"Speaking of," smiled Harrison, inwardly wanting to change the subject. "What are *you* doing here?"

Standing, Kubba smoothed the creases in her jumpsuit and arched an eyebrow.

"I used my medical override and made the captain grant me a pass. Then I coerced Aguilar into flying me. You and Marshall needed a lot of attention after your little stunt."

"How is Ralph?" blurted Harrison, the image of his partner's helmeted face flashing through his brain.

"He's in much better shape than you," sighed Kubba, pulling her Tablet from its pocket and checking the screen. "He didn't get as big of a dose of radiation."

"Oh?"

Stretching her back, she looked down at him with a grin and nodded.

"William thinks it's because Ralph spent more time inside the shielded shell of the life-support station while you sat out in the open."

"That's true," Harrison admitted.

"Either way, he's doing just fine. I had to give him a pretty big dose of pure cancer inhibitors, but it didn't seem to bring him down all that much. In fact, he's outside now with the rest, unloading the Arc."

Sitting up so quickly that he almost made himself sick, Harrison coughed savagely as he attempted to speak.

"Storm?" he gasped as Kubba gently pressed him back against the pillows of his bed.

"It's passed, love," she assured him softly. "There's still a fair amount of sand in the air, but the radiation is back down to safe levels. Braun gave the all-clear this morning."

Taking several deep breaths, Harrison accepted the glass of water that Kubba was trying to hand him.

"Typical. As soon as the dirty work's done," he joked, gulping at the glass with enthusiasm.

"Indeed," she agreed dryly.

Hearing a sound at the entryway, he looked up and saw Viviana standing in the frame, hands at her smiling mouth, her eyes twinkling with joyful tears.

"You're awake!" she exclaimed excitedly. "I must go call Liu!"

Dashing away from the door, Viviana broke into lyrical Italian as she padded across the dome towards the communications room.

"What's she saying?" asked Harrison with a quizzical grin.

"How should I know? I don't speak a word of Italian."

Twenty minutes later, Xao-Xing Liu burst through the airlock, stripping quickly out of her pressure suit as she dashed through the dome towards the infirmary. Harrison was sitting up in bed, tentatively taking a few bites of a reheated spaghetti lunch, when she stepped through the open doorway. Exchanging looks of unspoken understanding, Kubba and Viviana excused themselves, sliding the door shut behind them.

"Harrison," breathed Liu as she crossed the room to his bedside.

Taking his face in her hands, she kissed him deeply, then pulled his head to her breast, holding him tightly while she sobbed with joy. He breathed in the scent of her musky body— damp from perspiration—and felt the faint prickling of a memory. Before he could recall its message, Liu spoke, her voice very low and hushed.

"I thought I was going to lose you."

"I'm sorry," he replied stupidly.

An unexpected laugh broke her lips, and she squeezed him tighter, warm tears falling from her face to splash in his matted hair. Nestling his face deeper into the safety of her embrace, he waited for her to continue.

"I've called my husband," she said at last. "I've asked him for a divorce. I'm so sorry for how I treated you. I've been a fool and a coward. I love you, Harrison. I love you."

Looking up into her pained eyes, Harrison felt the tingle of a trapped memory work itself loose. Cascading over him like the dawn's first light, he saw his premonition come to pass. As she had done in his vision outside in the storm, Liu desperately searched his face for forgiveness and acceptance, her own heart now clearly worn on her sleeve. She was vulnerable and afraid.

Bringing a hand up to brush away her tears, he smiled and closed his eyes.

"I saw you," he murmured softly. "When I was out there. I saw your face just like it is now. You were confused, and I wanted so badly to help you, but I couldn't. I was dying."

Liu took a shuddering breath as he ran a hand through her hair.

"I wanted to touch your hair. I wanted to smell your scent and tell you that I loved you, but I couldn't. I couldn't even stand up."

Stopping, he opened his eyes again and peered up at Liu. In the pause, neither moved as she waited for him to set her free.

"But I'm here now," he whispered. "And I love you back."

Blinking fiercely, she bent her head and kissed his upturned face, laughing with exultant joy.

Ruin site—Sol 13

Two weeks after waking up in the infirmary, a fully healed Harrison Raheem Assad raced across the wide plane of the Martian desert. Taking care to avoid large rocks and treacherous pitfalls, he gunned the electric motor of his dirt bike as he bounded over a small wash. Ahead of him, a thin plume of dust marked the direction that Ralph Marshall had chosen to take across the tundra as he zigzagged around a patch of boulders. Following their experience in the sandstorm, the two men had become nearly inseparable, working together on nearly every project. Liu had joked with Harrison one night about an old Chinese proverb that seemed to fit their situation.

"They say," she had giggled in the dark. "When you save a man's life, you must care for him forever. That's you now—his new little brother!"

In a way, that's how things had shaped up between the two. Marshall had saved Harrison's life, and in the days after their ordeal, the older man went out of his way to connect with him as often as possible. Every morning when Harrison first entered the dining room for breakfast, there was Ralph waiting for him with a cup of hot coffee. Straight, black and devoid of any natural coffee flavor: just the way he liked it. When orders from Earth had come in, instructing Harrison to start work on the ruin site, Marshall had instantly volunteered to go with him.

"In the interest of safety," the grizzled astronaut had argued.

With an understanding smile playing at the corners of her serious mouth, Captain Vodevski had reluctantly given her approval with a tight shallow nod.

A new big brother, Harrison thought with a smile. An end to the longing spawned from a lifetime as an only child.

Now, as he neared the coordinates marking the outskirts of the ruin site, Harrison slackened his grip on the throttle, slowing his bike to a gentle jog. Seeing this, Marshall circled back and pulled up on his left.

"Should we ditch the bikes here?" he asked, his voice coming in through Harrison's helmet speakers.

"The outer wall starts about two meters from there," Harrison pointed. "So we should probably start in this area."

Nodding, Marshall cut the power to his bike and extended the kickstand. Harrison did the same and swung his leg free, careful not to catch his boot as he did so. Crouching in the dirt, Marshall opened the umbrella of a solar charger and connected it to an aluminum tripod. Attaching a small transformer box to the base of the stand, he then ran a set of wires from the unit to each dirt bike so that the rays of the distant Sun would charge their batteries as they worked. It was still early in the day, and the light of the morning star cast diminishing shadows, which played across the ochre sands like the trickling branches of a murky river.

A short way off, the horizon loomed before them, sending shivers of confusion and disorientation through Harrison's subconscious mind.

I'm not sure if I'll ever get used to seeing the sky so close, he mused with a cautious smile.

Swiping a dusty finger across his wrist-mounted tablet, Harrison brought up his Augmented Vision. Scrolling through a list of possible enhancements, he selected the ruin profile and engaged the setting. Transparent blue shapes began to emerge from the texture of the red desert in front of him, highlighting the location and dimensions of the Martian ruins that lay some dozen or more meters below. Entering in another command, he imposed a series of green intersecting lines over the entire site, creating a patchwork like that of a giant chess board.

"Ralph," he said into his helmet mic. "Go to your Augmented Vision, bring up the ruin site, and then highlight Option C."

"Okay," Marshall grunted as he tapped at his wrist tablet. "Got it?"

"Um, yeah," nodded the older man. "I'm looking at the ruins in blue with some green lines over it, right?"

"That's it."

Resting his hands on his hips, Marshall let out a shrill whistle. "Damn, that's impressive."

Smiling inside his helmet, Harrison slapped Marshall on the back of his oxygen shell.

"That's what you say now, but wait until you spend the whole day mapping the grid. Then I bet you'll be so sick of this place you'll never want to come back with me again!"

"We'll see," chuckled Marshall. Then, "What's the plan, boss?"

Turning to the storage bin on his dirt bike, Harrison unclasped the plastic lid and opened the large box. Reaching inside, he retrieved a rectangular case similar to those used to house power tools. Laying the case on the ground, he popped the locking clips and lifted the lid with an air of dramatic apprehension.

"Is that your sharpshooter, Quigley?" joked Marshall, his features hidden behind the blue tinting of his face shield.

Snorting, Harrison turned the case so that Marshall could see its contents. As he bent to get a closer look, Marshall was shocked to see that his crack about a sniper rifle was not as far off as he might have guessed. Inside the hard shell of the case was a gun of sorts, arranged in five separate pieces. There were two thin sections of piping, a rectangular bolt assembly, a plastic stock and a small round muzzle sleeve that resembled a silencer.

"This," said Harrison as he began putting the pieces together. "Is a deep-soil CT scanner."

"Looks like a gun to me."

"It's similar," agreed Harrison as he screwed the two sections of the barrel into the bolt assembly. "Except this puppy only fires in one direction: straight down."

Snapping the stock in place, Harrison held the CT scanner out for Marshall to inspect as he plucked a box of shells from the case. Taking the tool, the astronaut shouldered it and worked the bolt action.

"Where's the trigger?" he asked, searching for a firing mechanism.

Standing up, Harrison opened the box of shells in his hand.

"Here," he waved, beckoning for Marshall to give him the rifle back. "I'll show you."

Fingering one of the long silver shells, Harrison slid it into the chamber and racked the bolt with one quick pull. As the lever snapped back to the primed position, three, small spring-loaded legs popped out from recessed grooves along the sides of the muzzle sleeve, forming a tripod. Walking a few paces, Harrison stopped at where two glowing green lines intersected on the Augmented Vision, then pressed the wiry legs into the dirt so the gun was pointed towards the ground.

"This is what I meant when I said it only fires down."

Leaning on the stock, Harrison pushed the legs down, forcing the muzzle into the Martian sand. A jet of dust erupted from the ground as the gun fired the shell into the soil with a barely audible pop. Turning to face Marshall, Harrison pointed to the steaming hole.

"Inside each shell is a beacon, which sends out pings of X-rays. When we're done, we'll have mapped this entire grid with these little guys, giving us a three-dimensional picture of the ruins and whatever else might be down there."

Shrugging, Marshall gestured towards the sky.

"I thought Remus and Romulus already gave us a 3-D image of the ruins."

"Oh, they did. But at their altitude, we could only see shapes and sizes. Remember, they were sent here to look for water and veins of copper and iron, not buildings made of stone."

Looking down at the scanner in his hands, Harrison cocked an eyebrow, then continued.

"Besides, with this, we'll be able to read the writing on the fucking walls. That is, if there is any."

Marshall smiled at the thought, then froze with sudden realization.

"Wait. So we have to shoot one of those shells into the ground at every intersection of these green lines?"

"Yep."

Raising his head to look out over the nearly twenty-six square kilometers of brightly crisscrossing lines, Marshall groaned.

"This is going to take forever to map. That's what you meant when you said I would be sick of this place by the end of the day, isn't it?"

"You know, Ralph, nobody ever said archaeology was fun," Harrison grinned as he walked to the next beacon point. "They just made it look that way in the movies."

Gathering stones

Remus and Romulus stood together watching a band of Martians as they fished a deep river pool at the base of a run of rapids. Long silver and green eels flopped in their nets as the fishermen drew them in with practiced patience. Among the spray-flecked bodies working the river bank was Teo: Chieftess of the Martian village that Remus and Romulus had first stumbled upon. Blinking her huge blue eyes, she cleared the water vapor from her vision, then turned to the man working beside her.

"The snakes are stronger this far north. Our people have it easy in the south, I think."

Smiling, the man nodded as he tugged on a brimming net, stirring flashes of nickel and emerald. Everyone worked hard pulling in mass after mass of writhing eels and storing them in wicker baskets along the shore. Though their catch was large, more were needed—for there were many mouths to feed. A little ways from the banks of the river, a garden of moss-covered glacier rocks stood like statues, guarding the entrance to the Valley of the Great Lakes, at the foothills of the mountains. Milling about the majestic stones was an army of Martian tribes over 1,000 heads strong, hurrying to make camp before darkness fell.

Because of the irregular flow by which time was guided, neither brother could say exactly how long it had been since Teo and her wise man, Olo, had decided to move their entire village to the northern foothills of the mountain Atun, or Olympus Mons as the humans knew it. Following the river north, they grew their ranks by spreading word of Olo's vision of a grand monument to the other scattered tribes who dotted the deserts of the southern plain. His reputation of near-divinity, and fervent belief in what he preached, sparked the same interest in every township they visited. Even in tribes where bad blood had previously hindered fruitful coexistence between factions, Olo's message of unity through transcendence broke down old barriers and forged new alliances.

Now, in the chilled air of the northern foothills, the brothers found themselves to be ghosts haunting the enormous camp of the many tribes that formed this massive joint endeavor. As the Sun sank below the western hills, the catch of the river was brought in, and cooking fires were lit—casting shadows that danced ghoulishly across the jutting faces of the giant glacier rocks. In the approaching night, Remus and Romulus followed Teo as she wound her way through the various encampments, heading towards a cluster of tents marked with swashes of brown and black, the colors of her tribe.

"Where is Olo?" she called to a young woman who was tending a small fire.

"He is in his tent," the girl answered with a bow of her head.

Handing her a full basket of live water snakes, Teo left the girl and headed for a tent near the back of the camp. Tailing the Chieftess, the brothers ducked through the open flap of Olo's tent, breathing in the sweetened smoke of his incense. In the darkened corner of his quarters sat the wise man, painted with snaking lines of coal that wound around his torso and arms. Deep in meditation, his eyes were closed and his breathing slow and regular.

Sniffing at the pleasant twigs of burning herbs, Remus was struck again by the sheer wonder of this world and his miraculous existence within it. Looking up from the bowl of burning incense, he noticed with a start that everything seemed to have frozen. This happened now and again, as if an unseen hand had suddenly grasped the wheels of time and stopped them from turning. The glitches, as the brothers had come to call them, usually only lasted a few minutes and never affected their movements within, or perceptions of, the world.

While everything stopped around them, Remus and Romulus remained unchanged. Similar to the leaps in time, the glitches were just another reminder of the fact that this reality was nothing more than a masterfully programmed digital construct. A recording of events long since passed. Of people long since dead. Neither brother could say for sure just how long they had been in this strange land, how long they had watched the lives of Teo and Olo and the other Martians unfold in front of their eyes. Time held no meaning when you were a ghost.

"Brother," said Remus, gazing unconcerned at the frozen wisps of smoke that twirled up from the incense bowl.

"Yes?"

"Don't you find it strange that we can smell this smoke and feel the chill of the night?"

Chuckling, Romulus nodded.

"Indeed, I'm still attempting to understand how it is that we can detect these things. We were never programmed for such visceral sensations."

Looking at Teo paused in mid step, Remus cocked his head.

"Can one be programmed to feel or smell?"

"I suppose the limitations of what can or cannot be programmed lie with the programmer."

Smiling, Remus looked at his brother's flickering image standing a few paces away.

"How do suppose we came to be here? How did we attain these—" he paused and thought for a moment. "—Bodies?"

Moving his hand through a spark suspended above the smoldering incense, Romulus mulled over his reply.

"Well," he started. "I think you and I can both agree that decoding the anomalous signal is most likely what brought us here.

Within milliseconds of engaging it, our perceivable reality constructs were overwhelmed by the sheer volume of information being streamed. We simply became absorbed by the code. The manifestation of our bodies, as you call them, may also be a result of this integration, as too are the sensations of sight, sound, smell and touch. But for one to record and program such extensively detailed subtleties—"

He trailed off as if grappling with an idea.

"What?" questioned Remus, his face serious.

"As I said before," began Romulus with searching eyes. "The limitations of programming lie with the programmer. I think we can sense the things we can sense because whoever programmed all of this—" he waved about. "—Was a master beyond our human mothers and fathers."

"That is what I was thinking too," agreed Remus.

"What I find most interesting of all," continued Romulus. "Is the effect that the details of this construct are having on us. Though we were not designed to smell such things as burning herbs, we are, in fact, experiencing the sensation right now. We, like all AIs, were programmed to learn and grow depending on our exposure to information and experience. Therefore, even if we were to return to the confines of our satellite bodies, and possess no longer the ability to sense, we will still have the memory of what it was like to smell this incense. We are evolving, Brother. Our consciousnesses are expanding beyond what the humans intended. There is no going back, for we are incapable of forgetting by design."

With a tremor, the glitch corrected itself, and the world started moving again. Left to brood over the concepts of their conversation, the brothers fell silent and watched as Teo dropped to her knees next to the meditating Olo. Dipping a cut of softly-tanned animal hide into a bowl of water, Teo cleaned the old man's face. As she worked, Olo showed no indication that he was aware of her pampering. Singing softly, the Chieftess reached for a clay pot and removed its wicker lid, looking inside. Making a frustrated tisking sound, she glanced up at Olo with a worried expression that spelled out her disapproval. Stirring, the wise man's eyes fluttered, then opened languidly.

"Teo?" he murmured.

"I am here. Wake up, and eat something."

Rubbing his eyes, Olo blinked several times and looked around the murky tent.

"The great stones," he said, his voice far away and quiet. "They are the bones of long-dead mountains."

Reaching into the clay pot, Teo pulled out a strip of dried eel, then pressed it into Olo's hand.

"Eat this," she encouraged.

Shaking his head, Olo let the meat fall from his grasp.

"The hunger improves my visions."

"But you must eat," urged Teo, her voice edged with worry.

"In the morning," stated the wise man with finality. "Now I must tell you of what I learned during my time in the spirit world."

Grunting with frustration, Teo reached for a thick animal fur blanket that lay on the ground near the edge of the tent.

"What did you see?" she asked, wrapping the blanket around her naked shoulders and chest, a cool breeze twisting spirals of sweet smoke in the air.

Taking several deep breaths, Olo shut his eyes and tipped his head back.

"The spirits of this land have told me many things," he exhaled. "They speak much louder here than they ever did in the south. During this vision, they told me of the great stones, which lie all around us. They say we must raise our stones from these ancient rocks, for they are the sacred bones of the mighty Atun's dead children. We will appease the Great Spirits by resurrecting their fallen mountains and earn the compassion of the sometimes-vengeful Atun by honoring his fallen kin."

As Teo breathed deeply the aroma of the burning herbs, Olo recanted his visions from the spirit world and their meanings in the world of the living. Remus and Romulus listened as the wise man told of another plane of existence. A place where his body was as thin as smoke, and time was without limit. A place where the spirits of distant ancestors spoke forgotten truths to him. A place where these truths fed his mind, growing and transforming his soul. Soft drumming started up from somewhere in the camp, and soon there was chanting. A medley of haunting melodic wails broke out, drifting through the night air to blend with the smells of the cooking eels and smoldering incense.

CHAPTER SEVENTEEN

Another unexpected discovery—Sol 24

Orbiting in space above the red planet Mars, Captain Tatyana Vodevski flicked through the weekly progress reports of the ground crew. Her cabin was spartan in decorum, yet a warm cello concerto played softly, haunting the little space and giving it texture. She floated, expertly rigid, her back a few centimeters above the covers of her bed, loose red hair swirling and bobbing with the slow draws of the soloing cello's bow. In the air above her, like the tangible thoughts of six men and women, projected reports shimmered with translucent light as they outlined the progress of the ground crew.

Dr. Calise had successfully seeded several batches of genetically modified tomatoes, eggplants, green beans and snow peas in her new greenhouse. Though the elongated farming dome was under two weeks old, Dr. Calise was expecting to see the first sprouts of life in eight days or less. With the help of Dr. Liu, the Germans had been able to unload from the Arc, and assemble, all nine of the automated construction robots, which now worked twenty-four hours a day, under the strict guidance of Braun, to bolt and weld the geodesic Alon base's frame together. In the field, Dr. Assad and Lieutenant Marshall had recently wrapped up their CT scan of the ruin grid and were now in the process of preparing a trimensional presentation on their findings.

The last report interested Tatyana the most. Archaeology was not one of her strongest subjects, yet she found ancient ruins and lost cities to be utterly fascinating. Add to that, the fact that these ruins were constructed thousands, maybe millions, of years ago on Mars, and it was clear enough why her heart beat a little faster when opening the folder. Unfortunately, there still wasn't much to see at this point. Even worse was an infuriatingly vague note attached to the bottom of the report, dated two sols ago, promising that the presentation would be ready by day's end. As she glared at the glowing excuse, another note suddenly materialized next to the original, reading, *I'm done, call in an hour-H.*

"Two sols late, and he wants an hour!" fumed Tatyana quietly.

"Captain?" responded Braun's detached voice.

"Nothing, Braun. I was talking to myself."

"Holding conversations with oneself is sometimes evidence of mental instability. Are you feeling well, Captain?"

Looking up sharply, Tatyana started to prepare an angry reply, then stopped.

"Are you joking with me, Braun?" she asked, a smile pulling at the corners of her mouth.

"Yes."

Closing the reports, she rubbed her tired eyes, chuckling softly.

"Not to worry, dear Braun. I'm as sane as anyone in my situation can be."

There was a brief pause, then Braun responded with a chuckle that mimicked Tatyana's.

"Captain, given the parameters of your current living situation, I would say that anything short of insanity is madness."

Laughing, Tatyana pushed off the wall and drifted towards the hatch.

"True enough!"

As she floated into the galley, she was greeted with waves from YiJay and Aguilar, sitting on opposite sides of the table. Two silver bags of food zoomed back and forth as the laughing astronauts smacked them across the table at one another.

"What's this?" she inquired.

Grinning, Aguilar spiked one of the unmarked sacks to YiJay, who giggled and batted it back.

"It's food roulette. When Braun calls time, we have to eat whichever bag is nearest us. One is beef stew, and the other is—" he paused dramatically. "—Shrimp salad."

Grimacing, Tatyana shook her head.

"Why would you take such risks?"

Shrugging, Aguilar backhanded a bag that came at his face.

"Boredom, I guess."

Engaging the electromagnets in the soles of her shoes, Tatyana planted her feet on an illuminated yellow walking strip. Adjusting her balance, she shuffled to the refrigerator and removed a bag of spaghetti.

"Where are the others?" she asked, pushing the frozen bag of food into a microwave oven.

"Good question," chimed YiJay, punching back one of the floating silver bags. "Braun, tell the captain where everyone else is."

From the air all around them, Braun listed off the locations of the rest of the crew.

"Lieutenant Vyas is in his quarters sending a transmission to his wife. Dr. Kubba is in the gravity simulation exercise facility, and Dr. Thomas is on deck C7 following up on my report of a jammed ventilation regulator."

"Let me speak with Julian," commanded Tatyana as she hit the start button on the microwave.

"Please hold."

There were a series of clicks, then Julian's voice piped into the room sounding distant and tiny.

"Oui? Yes?"

"It's me," said Tatyana. "What's going on? Anything serious?"

"No, no," he replied with an indignant laugh. "Everything is exactly as I designed it. Perfect."

Shaking her head with a tired smile, Tatyana watched as a distracted Aguilar took a warm bag of mystery food to the side of the face.

"Good," she stated firmly, arching an eyebrow at the embarrassed Aguilar. "When you finish up, I want a full report on the malfunction and the steps taken to correct it. Understand?"

"No, it's not necessary," Julian said dismissively.

"You don't make that call," barked Tatyana, her tone suddenly hard. "You do what I tell you to."

"Yes, Captain," answered Julian, his voice calm and thin.

There was a beep, and the connection cut off. Exchanging sidelong glances, Aguilar and YiJay resumed their game as Tatyana grumbled a few choice words in Russian under her breath.

"Time's up," called Braun.

Snatching the nearest bag out of the air, Aguilar took a deep breath, then tore the top off the feeding tube.

"Beef stew!" he cheered with palpable relief.

Groaning, YiJay opened her bag and took a careful sniff.

"So much for a pleasant afternoon," she complained bitterly.

An hour later, Tatyana looked down upon Mars from the bridge deck window with unblinking gray eyes. Coming up beside her, Joseph Aguilar flicked his gaze quickly over her face as he tried to read her expression. Being a man and flawed in the same way that all men are, his view subconsciously wandered down from her face to rest on the swell of her breasts as she took a deep breath.

"Beautiful, no?" she sighed.

Jumping a little, Aguilar quickly snapped his eyes back up to Tatyana's face, relieved to see that she was still staring out the window.

"Um, yes. Very," he responded dumbly. Then, "Do you have any special plans for this evening?"

Tilting her head, Tatyana smiled softly—an expression that made her very attractive. "Not that I'm aware of. Why do you ask?"

Rubbing his neck, Aguilar started to say something but was interrupted by Braun.

"Captain, I have an incoming transmission from Dr. Assad."

Pushing back from the window, Tatyana's features returned to their normal impassive stoniness.

"Put it through on the main screen."

"As you wish."

Harrison's face, lined with shadow and sporting two days of stubble, appeared on the window, blotting out Mars.

"Your report is two sols late," said Tatyana, her voice dripping like hot iron.

Licking his lips, Harrison nodded agreeably.

"I'm really sorry, Captain," he started, noticing with a blush that Aguilar was witness to the conversation. "The scan turned up so, so much more than I thought it would. I've been up for the last two nights just getting the images rendered and ready to show you."

Putting her hands on her hips, Tatyana acted unimpressed. "Well?"

"I sent the model to Dr. Floyd about thirty minutes ago. Shouldn't we wait for him?" he asked, arching his eyebrows worriedly.

"I know you are well aware of the significant lag in transmissions between here and Earth," grilled Tatyana. "Am I expected to wait forty minutes just to hear what a *man* fifty-seven million kilometers away has to say about the progress of *my* crew?"

Running a hand over his buzzed scalp, Harrison bobbed his head, then tapped at something off-screen. The image of his face was instantly replaced with a stunning 3-D model of the Martian ruin grid: turning, as if on a pedestal, three sections of massive wall-enclosed buildings, squares, streets and domes, all presented in perfect detail, and clearly, digitally restored to their original splendor. Zooming in, then panning over for a bird's-eye view, the ancient city passed before them in crisp resolution. Flat and even, the mighty walls rivaled those of England's famous Windsor castle: standing over twenty meters tall and eight meters thick, with cylindrical watchtowers guarding the southern corners.

Like the steps of a Mayan pyramid, diamond-shaped stairs that started wide at the bottom, then narrowed at the top, led steadily up to each outpost from within the walls of the city. Three clusters of dome-topped buildings formed semi-circles below, and rows of stout two-story cubes arranged themselves in relief between the domes. A mesh of streets and piazzas connected everything like a spider web: circling out from a massive square in the center of the city, punctuated by an odd arrangement of monolithic stones. Lastly, the grand dome, imposing and unimaginably large, rested in pristine clarity only a few hundred meters from the rim of the Valles Marineris. Glowing like a full harvest moon, it seemed bigger than any Earthly monument, and it dominated the ruin grid completely.

"Amazing," whispered Tatyana, instantly forgetting her grudge with Harrison.

"There's more," came Harrison's voice, excited and relieved. "Just let me bring it up."

"More?" breathed Aguilar. "It already seems like so much."

Pulling her gaze away from the model, Tatyana peered up into the young astronaut's eyes and smiled beautifully. Reaching out, she took his hand.

"I know," pressed Harrison. "But wait until you see this."

A new filter played across the model, this time turning many of the buildings transparent. A thin and twisting network of green lines snaked across the grid like the paths a worm would leave as it ate its way through an apple. Running the entire length of the ancient city, the lines passed under nearly every major building, feeding into one another like rivers. As the model panned, the various veins and forks began to converge onto one another as they neared their dead end at the canyon's rim, until there was only one main tunnel left.

"What are those?" asked Tatyana, her voice quavering slightly.

"I think you can guess," replied Harrison.

"Caves!" shouted Aguilar, squeezing Tatyana's hand in his. "They're caves, aren't they?"

"Yep! It's a cave system. Probably lava tubes from Olympus Mons, which connect most of the buildings and the big dome to the Valles rim!"

"What does it mean?" Tatyana questioned with a frown.

"It means," smiled Harrison. "That there is an easier way into the ruins than we first anticipated. Granted, we still need to uncover them, but digging will take months. This allows us nearly instant access to the really juicy stuff. Can you imagine what we might discover? My CT scans can show us solid shapes and whatnot, but without going in, without really getting in there, I can't make any assumptions about these ruins or who built them. The best way is for me and a small team to—"

Braun cut in, breaking Harrison's line of attack.

"Transmission from Dr. Floyd, Captain."

"Play it," ordered Tatyana, letting Aguilar's hand slip from hers.

In the upper-left corner of the screen, James Floyd's blotchy face appeared, eyes burning with suppressed intensity.

"Captain, I'm looking at the CT scan of the Mars ruin grid that Assad just sent me. I'm guessing you probably are too, so I won't bother explaining what needs to be done here. I want you to greenlight Assad's idea to get down in those caves ASAP. Digging up the ruins just took the back burner here, Vodevski. This will get us results much quicker, and, trust me, given the tone of some of our biggest financial backers, we need results. I await your reply, but you have my orders. Make it happen."

Grinning, Harrison arched his eyebrows.

"If it's alright with you," he said. "I already have a team ready to go on your word."

Raising the stones

Unable to keep track of the erratic passage of time, the brothers Remus and Romulus found themselves witnesses to the foundation of a new civilization. A decade, maybe more, had passed since their first encounter with the people of Mars, and, now, far in the north, they surveyed with lucid and dreamlike intrigue a growing metropolis.

In the glow of the midday sun, hundreds of purple-skinned Martian men and women moved about the bustling dirt streets of their expanding township. Situated on the shores of a half-moon-shaped lake, the developing city lay at the foothills of the mountains surrounding Atun in what was commonly called the Valley of the Lakes. Some distance to the east, the mists of mighty waterfalls painted the skies with rainbow bands as their cascading waves spilled over the edge of a deep canyon. A system of rivers and lakes fed into one another as the glaciers, which capped the surrounding mountains, shed their cover in the heat of the summer air. Between the village and the stretching canyon was the construction site of the great temple. Bodies worked to dig out, carve and shape the surrounding glacier rocks as rays of golden sunlight sparkled off the flecks of iron ore in the dusty air.

In time, their numbers had grown, as word of the new society spread like brushfires to the villages that lived in the east and west. Streams of nomadic peoples and distant tribes filtered in day after day, bringing with them new customs and acquired knowledge, adding to the pool of information, which fueled the growth of the new nation. Fresh huts were constructed almost daily to accommodate the endless influx of immigrating people, and a tented market grew steadily in the center of the town, showcasing the wares of the cultures that comprised the expanding community.

Early on, a council of leaders had formed between the chiefs of the eight founding tribes, acting as the law that now ruled over the citizens of the Crescent Lake City. At its head was Teo, cheiftess of the southern river tribe and confidant to the wise and aged Olo.

Working diligently, they had bound together the previously fractured tribes of the southern planes, forming a new nation that they called The Peoples of the Great Lakes.

Children ran and played amongst the hundreds of huts that now surrounded the crescent lake, and many people busied themselves not with the construction of Olo's temple, but with the task of digging irrigation ditches, and the cultivation of the surrounding plant and animal life. Fruit trees and other edible plants were uprooted and replanted nearer to the town, so that the people could tend to them and produce larger yields. Fishing became regulated and measured to prevent over-netting and wastefulness. Stone walls were raised around the perimeters of the farms to keep out scavenging animals, drawn in from the desert by the smells of garbage and cooking fires. Hunters set out into the marshes and grasslands, not spearing the adult prey they normally stalked but, instead, snatching the babes from their nests and burrows. Squealing and bleating, the young animals were spirited away to wooden pens where they were fattened and bred and slaughtered with ease. A new society was taking its first infantile steps, and it all centered around the raising of Olo's great monoliths. Without this tribute to the Great Spirits, no tribe would ever dare to live this close to the vengeful Atun.

Having leveled the ground and cleared the site of its massive glacier rocks, the temple builders now dug deep holes, which circled out in three radial spokes. Working in shifts, they removed buckets of sand and rock from the deep wells, casting them aside to be mixed with water and mashed into clay for new huts. Chipping with fire-hardened stone axes and chisels, the builders shaped long pillars out of the porous glacier rock and decorated them with carvings and colorful paint. When they were completed, the pillars were slid down into the deep wells, then hoisted to standing positions with ropes and wedges. Clay and gravel were then dumped in around the base and allowed to harden into cement anchors. In the years since undertaking their holy task, the builders had raised eight such pillars, moving outwards from a center stone like the blades of a pinwheel.

As the brothers Remus and Romulus watched the landscape and its inhabitants evolve around them, they noticed deep changes within their own beings as well. Abandoning their analytically rigid approach to learning, they instead soaked up every new sight, sound and sensation with which they came into contact. With every passing day, with every passing moment, they drifted further from the memory of what their lives had been like before the signal. Glitches in reality and leaps in time became less noticeable: sometimes appearing as nothing more than a momentary wrinkle. Though neither brother fully understood the rhythm of their schizophrenic existence, they felt no alarm. They felt no fear. They simply followed the path before them, knowing from somewhere in the depths of their souls that the ultimate truth would reveal itself, one way or another, when the time was right.

CHAPTER EIGHTEEN

1478 feet—Sol 26

Cutting through the thin Martian air like a fat white bird of prey, Lander 1 skimmed the rusty desert on its way to the rim of the Valles Marineris. Inside the rattling flyer were the pressure-suited bodies of Harrison, Marshall, William and Liu. Strapped in tightly, the four explorers listened to a message from James Floyd, Mission Director as it played in their helmets' speakers.

"Okay, Assad," came the crackle of Floyd's voice. "While this is your gig, I'm putting Marshall in charge. He's got more experience with EVA than you do. If he feels like the situation is too dangerous and pulls the plug, then I want all three of you back up the line without so much as a peep. That said, the consortium of universities, which, might I add, paid for your ticket, wants results. They've practically been battering down my door, so, once you're in there, take lots of pictures. Good luck. Over and out."

Chuckling, Liu's lyrical voice echoed through Harrison's helmet.

"Yeah, Assad. Take pictures."

From the cockpit, Marshall turned his head.

"Yeah, Assad."

Snapping his fingers, Harrison tried to put on a frightened face.

"Oh, no. You'd better stop at Rite Aid. I think I forgot to grab film for the camera."

"I saw one at the last exit," piped William whimsically.

Twenty minutes later, Marshall brought the Lander down some ten meters from the gaping rim of Mars's magnificent canyon. Running a suit-pressurization check, he then cycled the air out of the Lander and opened the hatch. Filing to the opening, the four explorers lined up to check each other's survival packs and equipment belts.

"You first, boss man," Marshall laughed, pointing to Harrison.

Leaping down from the craft one by one, the explorers kicked up puffs of dust as they landed on the rocky ground. Setting off towards the canyon, Harrison engaged his Augmented Vision and brought up the cave-system grid. Showing the mouth of the cave about seven meters to the left, he trotted towards the glowing mark.

"Hey, no running by the pool!" shouted Marshall as he unloaded climbing harnesses from the Lander's open storage hatch.

Slowing, Harrison stepped carefully to the rim of the canyon, then gazed out across the unimaginably deep gash, which cut its way thousands of kilometers across the face of Mars. Walking up to stand next to him, Liu tentatively peered over the edge at the distant floor, more than six kilometers below.

"That would be quite a fall," she whispered. "I wonder how long it would take to hit the bottom."

"Three minutes and thirty-six seconds," replied Braun, unannounced, in their helmets.

Exhaling, Harrison bit his lip.

"Plenty of time to get your affairs in order before you go splat."

"Oh, don't talk like that!" chastised Liu. "I'll be up here the whole time watching your lines. Plus, the winches and cables on each harness are rated to three times your weight on Earth. You'll be fine."

"Yeah, but the entrance to the cave is like fifteen hundred feet down the face of the cliff. That's a long ways to just dangle around, you know."

"Actually, Harrison," interrupted Braun. "The distance to the cave's entrance in the standard measurement system is only one thousand, four hundred and seventy-eight feet from the top of the rim."

"See," giggled Liu. "Fourteen hundred, seventy-eight feet. No big deal. Also, don't worry. I won't tell anyone that you used standard."

"Thanks," muttered Harrison.

The temple

Running a ghosted hand across the carved figure of a water snake, Remus admired the delicate workmanship. Twelve monoliths towered like painted trees in the slanting fire of the early sun. Arranged in rows of four, the curving lines of carved pillars spiraled out from the three corners of short, flat, triangular center stone, which stood adorned with a clay pot of burning herbs. Sitting atop it with his legs folded under himself in a lotus position, Romulus meditated as he had watched Olo do on countless occasions. Having only been raised the evening before, the final pillar still glistened in places where the colorful paint that filled the lines of its relieved carvings had yet to fully dry.

Moving through the carefully arranged rows, Remus took in the stony images, which swarmed around him. Carvings of insects, birds and animals wrapped themselves around every monolith while twisting rivers of bright blue paint wove their way through the captured chaos of depicted life. Capped like the jagged peaks of the mountains to the north, each pillar bore a sharpened point of white and red. True to Olo's original design, these stones, these monolithic pillars, were indeed mountains. Mountains raised by the hands of men.

Rappelling—Sol 26

With his back to the crooked gash of the Valles Marineris, Harrison Raheem Assad took a deep breath and watched the others as they prepared to descend. A short ways to the left, Marshall adjusted the straps of his harness, pulling them tight with violent downward jerks while William, face obscured by the glinting blue tint of his visor, slung a huge black duffel sack over his right shoulder. Near the Lander's nose, Liu bent low as she checked the titanium carabineers of the three harnesses, anchored securely to the craft's hull.

"You're all good," she said, turning to face the three men. "You can begin when you're ready."

"Alright," barked Marshall. "Let's time our descents thirty seconds apart. I'll go first, then Harrison, and, Will, you can bring up the rear. Got the lift-base kit?"

"Got it," replied William, jabbing a thumb at his back where the heavy-looking duffel sack hung.

"Okay," nodded Marshall. "Everybody ready?"

"Ready," echoed Harrison and William in unison.

Flexing his knees, Marshall deftly lowered himself over the jagged edge of the canyon rim, then brought his feet up and pushed himself into a horizontal standing position. Testing the tension of his line, he took a few tentative steps backwards, his suit CPU interfacing with the climbing harness to spool the cable out as needed. Looking up at William, Liu and Harrison as they peeked over the rim at him, Marshall dipped his helmeted head.

"Here goes. Start the thirty-second countdown now."

With that, he leaned back, gave a little hop and dropped three meters before his feet reconnected with the canyon wall. In the thin air of the Martian morning, the zip of Marshall's spinning winch, and the crunch of his boots as they struck the cliff face, were all but silent. Projected on the inside of his helmet glass, Harrison watched with a strange and growing calm as the numbers of his thirty-second countdown melted away. Climbing carefully over the ledge as Marshall had done, he prepared himself for the nearly four-hundred-and-sixty-meter rappel to the entrance of the cave system.

With a soft tone, Braun spoke in his ears.

"You may begin your descent now."

Exhaling, as if released from all control, Harrison shoved off the wall and felt himself drop like a feather. The sensation was far different than he had expected, and in that elongated second after his feet left the canyon's side, a rush of absolute elation surged through his raw and worried nerves. Instead of feeling gravity's barbed hooks tearing him down, he was surprised to notice that, in his lightened capacity, he drifted rather than fell. With a whine, the winch at his chest tightened, and his freefall was cut short. Swinging in towards the canyon wall, he put his feet out and lightly pushed off as they made contact. Free again, he slid down another few meters and repeated the motion. Above him and to the right, he saw William take his first leap, hanging in the air impossibly long before arcing in to meet the cliff face.

In his ears, Marshall gave a war whoop, clearly exhilarated.

"This has got to be a fucking record, man!" he shouted. "I seriously doubt if anyone has ever done a rappel this long."

Laughing, Harrison jumped off the wall and spooled out another three meters of cable.

"Ralph, we're on Mars. Everything we do is a fucking record!"

Coming in towards the canyon wall, Harrison was distracted by his jubilant mood and did not notice a crack in the facade. Landing awkwardly, he twisted and lost his balance. Unable to stop himself, he slammed into the rock and bounced off, arcing far out with his arms and legs flailing. Swearing with cold terror, he struggled to bring his feet up as he raced back towards the hard red wall, but it was too late. His body crunched painfully as he connected, and the visor of his helmet banged against the rock with a hard whack. Swinging out again, he twisted himself around with instinctive reflexes, somehow regaining his balance. Coming in fast, he pushed his feet out and stopped himself from bashing into the cliff for a third time. Heart pounding, ears ringing, he crouched, suspended nearly six kilometers above the ground.

"Harrison," spoke Braun, his voice calm yet stern. "Please don't do that again."

From below, Marshall was peering up at him, hands clasping his taut line.

"You okay?"

"Yeah," muttered Harrison, his voice shaky and wavering. "I'm fine. My face shield didn't crack."

Above him, William had stopped and was looking over his shoulder.

"Do you need help? I can get to you if you need."

"No, I'm alright," assured Harrison. "I just lost my footing."

"Never," Liu cut in, her tone thin and shrill. "Do that again."

"Indeed," interjected Braun gravely.

From then on, the three explorers moved down the face of the canyon with decided care. Several times, cracks and overhangs slowed their journey. Yet, in less than an hour, Marshall had reached the mouth of the cave. The opening was nearly ten meters tall and almost as wide. Shaped like a capital D turned on the flat of its back, the mouth resembled in many ways the caves of Earth. Gone, however, were the needle-like teeth of the stalactites and stalagmites, for there was no dripping water with which to form them.

Taking manual control of his winch, Marshall hummed tunelessly as he lowered himself through open space like a white spider sliding down the silky tendril of a web. Stopping a few feet from the lip of the cave, he unsheathed a grappling gun, and, taking careful aim, fired a barbed bolt into the solid rock of the dusty floor. Clipping the gun to a chest-mounted bracket, he interfaced the pistol's winch with his suit's CPU and reeled himself in. Feet on the ground, he disconnected the grappling gun from its bolt and put it away. Removing his harness, he clipped it to the anchored bolt and stretched his back with feline relish.

Minutes later, Harrison dangled freely at the mouth of the cave, a mere sixty centimeters out from the bottom lip. Marshall took hold of his outstretched hand and pulled, steadying him as he too planted his boots on the solid floor.

"That—" panted Harrison, rubbing his lower back "—Was scary as shit."

"Once Will gets here," Marshall said, helping Harrison out of his harness. "We'll set up the scaffolding for the base of the lift. That should make things a lot easier."

Nodding, Harrison put a hand on Marshall's shoulder, squeezing it tightly.

"A lift will be nice. Very nice."

Moments later, William dropped into the window of the open cave and descended his line to the bottom. Marshall and Harrison grabbed his arms and swung him in, puffs of dust blossoming around his boots as they touched down on the floor. While Marshall helped the German disconnect his harness, Harrison walked a little ways into the yawning recesses of the cave. Smooth sloping walls rose up to meet above him in a steeple, and several large boulders littered the dusty floor, guardians of the secrets that hid in the darkness.

"This thing is huge!" he shouted, his voice booming painfully inside the confines of his helmet.

Wanting to penetrate the darkness that loomed at the back of the cave, Harrison engaged his Augmented Vision and selected the same setting he and Marshall had used during their emergency EVA. As the blue glow of x-ray-enhanced vision pinged out, he saw the tunnel continue some fifteen meters before the edge of his range dissolved the picture into muddy blackness. Suddenly, with a surprising series of rapid flashes, a grid of measurements overlapped the opening into the tunnel at the rear of the cave.

"These lines are mathematically precise," stated Braun in his ears.

Looking at the images inside his helmet, Harrison studied the readouts with fascination. The walls on either side of the tunnel were the same height and dimension, each gently curving slope an exact reversal of the opposite side. Even in places where the tunnel looked to narrow, the measurements matched one another with mathematical precision.

"Very odd," Harrison murmured, cocking his head to the side.

"This kind of symmetry does not occur in nature, Harrison," Braun warned with an air of apprehension.

"No," he agreed. "I suppose not. I guess these caves were shaped after their discovery, perhaps in the same way that the largest dome seems to have been carved out of an existing cave chamber."

"I was thinking along a similar line," acknowledged the AI.

"Hey!" called Marshall, waving from the mouth of the cave. "Come give us a hand with the lift scaffolding, will you?"

Prying himself away from the promises of ancient mysteries, Harrison turned his back on the strange tunnel and returned to his fellow explorers. The large duffel sack, which William had worn strapped to his back, lay open on the ground. Inside, glinting bundles of titanium piping rested next to panels of translucent Alon and spools of cable. The lift base was actually part of a mining elevator that Udo had modified so that it could be attached to a cliff face like a shelf, rather than being bolted directly to the ground as would be a traditional elevator cable system.

Crouching beside the bag, Harrison changed his Augmented Vision to an animation that demonstrated how the various parts attached to one another. In less than twenty minutes, the three men had a spindly balcony of silver rods and milky Alon solidly bolted into the rim of the cave's mouth.

"Liu," grunted Marshall into his helmet mic.

"Yes?" she answered sweetly.

"Send down the lift cables. We've got the base secured down here."

A few minutes later, thick powerful cables wound down along the three climbing lines, coiling up like metal snakes on the floor of the cave near the anchored bolt. Marked on their Augmented Vision, each of the three cables clipped into receivers on the lift platform until they hung limply, swaying from side to side.

"Cables connected," announced Marshall.

Slowly, the slack in each thickly wound coil began picking up as they were reeled in from above. Tightening, the lines twanged and popped, sending muffled reverberations off of the cave walls. With a flinch, Harrison watched the lift base flex visibly as each receding cable tuned itself taught like a piano string.

"Okay," chirped Liu, making him jump a little. "The tension is good. I'll start putting the cart and the rim-side port together now. It will be ready by the time you're ready to come back up."

"Got it," radioed Marshall. "Thanks."

There was a brief pause, then Liu spoke again.

"You boys be careful. I don't want my man coming back to me with a ruptured pressure suit. I don't like popsicles."

Clearing the tint from his visor, Marshall arched his eyebrows at Harrison and flashed him a devilish grin.

"You lead, boss man."

CHAPTER NINETEEN

Footfalls

Drifting, Remus marveled at the way the sunlight played through the open spaces between the rows of freshly finished monoliths. Yellow beams of fire cut straight lines that splashed a warming glow upon the animated carvings adorning the exposed pillars.

The sounds of an approaching party drew him out of his reverent detachment and brought him back to the moment. Walking to stand beside his brother, Remus watched a huge procession make its way across the well-beaten grasslands that separated the city from the temple. Flags of blue and brown fluttered lightly in the breeze, and the beating of drums punctuated the footfalls of the marching group. At the head of the party, Remus spied Olo, held up on either side by Teo and her eldest son, Ze. The ancient wise man's purple skin looked pale and dry, and his eyes were milky and wandering. As the party neared the edge of the temple, Romulus stirred from his meditation and came down to stand next to Remus.

"Is it time?" he asked.

"I think so, yes," replied Remus.

Caves—Sol 26

With the blue glow of their Augmented Vision lighting the insides of their helmets, Harrison, Marshall and William walked cautiously through the underground corridor. Leading, Harrison frequently snapped screen shots of the symmetrical walls and ceiling, logging their dimensions as they moved deeper into the cave system. Having taking several curves and bends, the three explorers were now cast into utter blackness. Shuddering at the memory of blind helplessness he had felt during the storm, Harrison religiously checked battery life on his suit CPU, not wanting to relive the experience.

"You guys feel that?" asked Marshall, stopping to rub his thighs. "Are we going up?"

"Yes," replied Braun matter-of-factly. "The incline of the floor has increased by four percent."

"I thought I felt that too," said William, leaning his back against the wall.

Taking another screenshot of the cave ceiling, Harrison pressed his gloved fingers to the wall and felt for the subtle signs of tool marks. Finding none, he searched his mind for possible ways these caves could have been formed so precisely. Dancing in the back of his subconscious was the cave network of the Bayan Kara-Ula Mountains in China and their mysterious Dropa stones. Smiling, he made a mental note to run this similarity by his father the next time he sent a transmission home.

"Dropa stones," he chuckled to himself, shaking his head.

Though he laughed, a quiet voice in his head chided him, melting his grin away with its words.

You've poked fun at your dad and his ancient astronaut belief for years, it said haughtily. And yet here *you* are, standing in a cave system that looks manmade. On Mars.

Trickling in, Braun's even voice sounded in their helmet speakers.

"Based on your current oxygen consumption, I would suggest that you turn on your suits' filtration systems to supplement your air supply. I would also advise that you continue forward."

Sliding a finger across his wrist tablet, Harrison turned on the survival pack's air scrubbers. A faint vibration shuddered up his back as the motor purred to life, pulling the usable gasses from the cave chamber around them. Reaching out again, he felt the walls with his gloved hands and wished dearly that he could play his naked fingers across their smooth surface.

Speak to me, he urged the silent rock. Speak.

Walking up to stand beside him, Marshall put an arm around his shoulder.

"Ready, Indy?"

"Indy?" Harrison repeated with a frown, pulling his hand from the wall.

"Yeah, like Indiana Jones. You know. Harrison Ford. Don't tell me you've never seen those movies!"

Grinning, Harrison turned to face Marshall.

"On Earth, I'm Indy," he said. "Up here, I'm Han Solo."

Laughing, the three set out again, following the uphill curve of the tunnel as it led deeper into the ancient Martian earth.

CHAPTER TWENTY

The blessing

Stopping at the first row of pillars, the Martian procession ceased their drumming. Breaking away from the group, Teo and Ze helped Olo to his knees. Pressing his forehead to the ground, the wise man chanted in a voice that was little more than a whisper. Despite that morning's promise of sun, deep clouds had begun to form at the base of Atun. A cool wind licked across the open land, whistling through the monoliths and drowning out Olo's shaking chants. Finishing his blessing, he was helped to his feet and taken to the next pillar. Stone by stone, he moved through the temple in a circular pattern. The rest of the procession followed behind with silent diligence as he knelt before each pillar, chanting his mystic prayers. Soon, the sky overhead filled with dark clouds, and a light rain began to patter down, creating spots on the dry soil between the standing monoliths. Working his way towards the center stone, Olo seemed to gain strength from the droplets of cool water. Twisting free of Teo's helpful grasp, he spanned, on his own, the short distance from the last pillar to the triangular center stone. The smoldering remains of the burning herbs hissed in the clay pot as fat beads of rain splashed against the sides. With a flash, lightning split the sky, bringing with it the carnal roar of thunder. Worried voices drifted forwards from the ranks of the watching group. Turning, the wise man fixed them with his frosted eyes.

"Do not be afraid," he called in a voice much louder and stronger than his hunched figure seemed capable of. "The Great Spirits are only testing our courage before they welcome us."

Cave—Sol 26

Trudging silently through still darkness of the cave, the steady in and out of his breathing lulled Harrison into a semi-lucid trance. Aware of his surroundings as presented through the blue glow of his Augmented Vision, he saw, too, the ancient light of a hundred torches, swaying gently as they lined the immaculate walls. Like golden sentries, they stood guard against an army of darkness, which threatened to invade and snuff out all hope of light and life.

A voice, distant and echoing, drifted through the eons, coming as little more than a dry whisper. Turning his head so that his right ear faced into the darkness, Harrison followed the elusive source of the beckoning call.

"We're almost there," he stated.

"Okay?" said Marshall incredulously. "How do you know that?"

"Because," said Harrison flatly. "I just know."

Shrugging, Marshall extracted an x-ray beacon from his rucksack and placed it on the floor. Like the bullet shells of the deep-soil CT scanner, the small black orb pulsed pings of x-rays, which painted the walls with an invisible light that danced in their Augmented Vision.

"To mark our progress," he explained with a grin. "So we don't get lost."

Moving on, it wasn't long until the blue light from the little beacon had faded into the blackness beyond their vision range. As the tunnel took a sharp left, Harrison felt the ground under his boots grow steeper, as if they were ascending a long ramp. Checking the walls, he saw that the tunnel was beginning to widen on all sides, the perfectly even lines warping out before them. Snapping a screenshot with his helmet cam, he peered ahead intently.

"I think we're nearing a larger chamber," he radioed, ears prickling with the ancient call of secret spirits. "We're almost there."

The Great Spirits arrive

Another jet of electric blue streaked through the heavens, this time gutting the clouds like a butcher's knife. Rain cascaded down in force, making streams between the pillars and turning the ground muddy. Kneeling at the center stone, Olo rocked back and forth, mouthing a silent prayer as the crackle of static charges built in the air.

From above, a low growl broke across the sky and echoed down, morphing slowly into a shrill whine. Heads turned their squinting eyes into the downpour as the strange noise repeated itself over and over, like the drum line of a timpani chorus.

Shadows began to appear in the low clouds, growing larger as they descended from above the cover of the storm. With screams, the frightened group of Martian onlookers shrunk back, some shoving against one another in an attempt to dislodge themselves from the mass of bodies that surrounded the temple. In the sky, the falling shadows began to take shape as they parted the roiling curtain of the clouds. Silhouetted by forks of lightning that backlit the heavens in flickers of blue fire, huge black triangles lowered themselves through the heavy rain with the sizzle of electric heat.

"The Great Spirits are here!" cried Olo, his face alive with energy.

Caves—Sol 26

As they pressed onwards, Harrison increased the ping range of his Augmented Vision to its fullest capacity. Six meters ahead, he could make out the walls and ceiling of the tunnel as they funneled out, growing wider to feed into a large chamber. Unable to enhance the ping distance any further, his screen showed straight, haunting blue walls, which parted quickly to give way to a black and gaping hole. The huge room swallowed the waves sent out by his suit's Augmented Vision, returning nothing but a shadowy blanket of darkness.

"Looks like this room is too big for the range on my A-Vision," complained Marshall. "All I can see is the floor and some of the near walls. I don't want us walking in there blind."

"Toss out some beacons," offered William as he dug in his bag for a handful of the x-ray emitters.

"Good idea," agreed Harrison, taking out a few of his own.

Turning the beacon on, he cocked his arm back and threw the pulsating sphere into the darkness. As it arced through the air, flashes of x-rays bounced off the walls and ceiling of the massive room, echoing back to the helmet screens of the three explorers. Landing silently, the beacon rolled a little, then came to a rest. Faint light undulated from the plastic sphere like the glow of a full Moon as it filtered through the shallow waters of a coral reef.

Instantly on alert, all three astronauts froze as the images from across the cave played inside their helmet visors. In the swaying light of the x-ray beacon, they could just make out that they were not alone in the chamber.

Ships

Awestruck, Remus and Romulus watched as dozens of massive black metal arrowheads skimmed through the violent skies with effortless ease. Falling like inky snow, they came in droves, and soon their numbers had grown to blot out the weakened light of the choking sun.

Bellowing with unbelieving wonder, Romulus gripped his brother's arm.

"Remus! Do you see what I see?"

"Ships!" cried Remus above the shouts of the crowd. "They're ships."

Caves—Sol 26

"Holy shit," whispered Marshall. "Don't move."

The beacon lay some six meters from where the three men stood, pulsing out a steady wash of x-rays that lapped into the darkness like the incoming tide. With each wave of illumination, the blue light of their Augmented Vision played across the distant cave floor and danced up the leg of an unmoving figure, still shrouded in darkness.

"No," Harrison heard himself say. "It's not what you think."

Before the other two could stop him, he hauled back and hurled another armed beacon with all of his strength.

CHAPTER TWENTY-ONE

Landing

As the first of the imposing triangular craft reached the ground near the edge of the temple stones, three hinged legs silently unfolded from beneath the faintly glowing underside. Touching down like the feet of a giant insect, it settled itself in the mud and became still.

Remus and Romulus clutched one another as the rest of the ships descended to the ground, arranging themselves in careful formation. Landing with perfect precision behind the first, they created a patchwork of triangles, which checkered out across the wet grasslands. In total, there were more than twenty: thick steam rising off of their backs as the rain continued to fall.

Caves—Sol 26

Sailing through the thin air, the little plastic ball blinked in slow motion as it flew past the orb of light emitted from the first beacon. Harrison's aim was true, and the new x-ray emitter landed squarely at the foot of the figure across the cave from them. As the echoes of blue light leaped the distance of the chamber, the three explorers exhaled with a mixture of relief and awe. What they had seen standing in the shadows was not a living monster of unimaginable dread, but rather a large stone statue.

Four-and-a-half meters tall, with a body as humanoid and androgynous as a Christian angel, the figure stood, its long arms hanging rigidly at the sides of its shapeless torso. Its head, oval-shaped and bald, depicted three squinting eyes arranged in a triangle atop the bridge of a narrowly pointed nose. Each eye possessed a different curve: the left looking up, the right looking down, and the middle eye—above the others—looking straight forwards.

"Holy shit!" yelled Marshall. "I mean...Holy shit!"

Invigorated, Harrison scrambled to locate more beacons while Marshall and William began tossing their own into the chamber. As the flashing balls of x-ray waves spread out into the open cave, another statue was revealed standing to the left of the first.

Practically a perfect copy of its partner: only the eyes were different, appearing as the mirrored, or reversed, image of the first statue. Pulling back, Harrison threw his last beacon into the darkened space between the two imposing figures and waited for the pings to reach him.

Opening

As the rain drove down in sheets and waves, it exploded against the hot metal of the black ships. Flashes of loose electricity arced between the closely stationed crafts, spreading like currents of disrupted water as it danced through the armada. Most of the watching crowd had turned to run, but those who had stayed were now dropping to their knees, chanting in shrill voices that pleaded and begged. Among them were Teo and Ze, rainwater beading on the oily sheen of their deep purple skin. Struggling to his feet, Olo held his hands out in a gesture of peace.

"Great Spirits!" he called above the voices of the fearful people. "You have arrived!"

A low groan, like the shifting protest of an object long-since settled, broke out from the fleet. The noise sent shockwaves through the driving rain, momentarily suspending the droplets so that they hung like ornaments, caught in the invisible grasp of an alien energy field. The deep note sounded for a second time and, all at once, the dangling beads of rain fell to the ground in a flurry of motion.

"Look!" cried Remus, pointing. "It's opening!"

A narrow shaft of light ran down the underside of the nearest craft, spreading out to form the shape of a long rectangle as it grew. In perfect time, a metal walkway unrolled from within the ship like the lazy tongue of a lizard, reaching down to rest in the mud with a hiss.

Caves—Sol 26

With a muted rush of blue light, the shadowed area between the two standing statues came into view. Kneeling behind the others was a final statue. Two large egg-shaped eyes stared back from the diminishing dark as the tightened waves of the x-ray beacon illuminated the final corners of the ancient cave. Kneeling, the figure was that of what appeared to be a praying woman. Bare-breasted and hard-featured, her fingers were woven together like braided snakes, and her eyes were impassively deep. The three statues loomed in the giant chamber as the wavering light of the pulsing x-rays seemed to give movement to their rock-hard stillness. Unable to speak, Harrison stared at their finely carved faces, listening to the calls of a distant whisper. In a voice both ancient and foreign, he heard the words of a story as familiar as the details of a fading dream.

The Great Spirits

In the brilliant light that poured from the open ship, two ethereal forms began to take shape. With slow and calculated movements they emerged: stepping out into the rain and onto the metal ramp. Bathed in a luminescence that seemed to shine through matter and time, the two humanoid astronauts each raised an arm and pointed with impossibly long fingers. Following the line of their indication, Remus and Romulus turned to face the temple. Sparkling with veins of metal ore, the monoliths glowed like melting glass in the coals of an endless fire.

EPILOGUE

Spreading out, the three explorers wandered between the standing statues, snapping screen shots in the oscillating fluorescence of the scattered x-ray beacons. Drawn by the expression of reverence on her face, Harrison made his way towards the statue of the kneeling woman. Nearing her, he saw that she was fused to the very rock of the back wall—her body growing from the smooth surface like living stone. Mind racing over the possible ways in which the woman could have been so magnificently crafted from the existing rock, Harrison could not shake the feeling that there was a bigger mystery staring him right in the face. Lifting his head, he looked up and inspected the statue's delicate eyes. Her inspired gaze was trained on the backs of the standing figures, and she looked to be praying to them as if they were indifferent gods. Suddenly struck by a thought so glaringly obvious that it had thus far eluded him, Harrison jogged back towards the opening of the cave, then turned to stare into the faces of the standing statues.

"Correct me if I'm wrong," said Marshall as if reading his mind from across the chamber. "But it looks like there are two different types of, um, people here. Which ones are the Martians?"

Scanning from the three-eyed faces of the twin statues to the slightly bovine features of the kneeling woman, Harrison felt his mind trip and snag as it banged against the simple yet profound question.

"I—" he started. "I don't know."

To be continued...

Special Thanks and Considerations

I would be a scoundrel if my first and most emphatic *thank you* did not go to Mia Mann, my best friend and wife. From random plot ideas to full on character and story arcs, Mia was always there to lend an ear, a mind and a personality that kept me honest and true. Her kind yet brutally honest nature helped provide invaluable perspective and constructive criticism when building the reality my characters were to operate in. Without this, I would have been confused and scattered.

Secondly, I would like to thank Cougar George. His unflappable skepticism was a constant source of chagrin for me, yet in the end I always felt better about an idea after running it through the "Cougar-grinder." Furthermore, he did the cover art which exemplifies his connection to the project.

Thirdly, I would like to thank my parents, Jim Quarles and Jean Baldwin. They created me, raised me, and set me loose on the world. What more needs to be said?

Also, in need of thanks is my friend, Cary Thielen. His mind for sci-fi and general interest in the whole undertaking was received readily and warmly by me each time we talked about the book. Another superbly important player in need of my thanks is Garrett Jenkins. His help with my second draft propelled me forward on the path that eventually lead me to here.

Special thanks as well to Yvonne Verser for her help early on in the project. Additional thanks to Kelley Williamson for listening patiently to my caffeine induced babblings and never becoming too annoyed. Lastly yet not least importantly, I would like to thank my editor, Andrew Olmsted. For soldiering on through the mountains of punctuation errors and formatting missteps, I will be forever grateful.

If through some cruel twist of providence, I have omitted your name from this list, I am sorry. Being that my head is often in two or more realities at once sometimes has that effect on me. Believe me when I say that if you even so much as met me in a bar while I was writing this, thank you.

Dylan James Quarles